D0837860

"A MASTERPIECE; AN ENDURING WORK."

—*Detroit Free Press*

"AN ASTONISHMENT . . . a kind of epic poem, a recapitulation of the rhythms of female consciousness . . . I KNOW OF NOTHING LIKE IT."
—*The New York Times*

"A semi-mystical, militant feminist novel . . . a visceral experience, replete with tastes, sounds, odors, sharp pains and warm caresses."
—*Washington Post*

"E.M. Broner's first book, *Her Mothers*, established her as a tough, witty writer in the forefront of feminist fiction. In *A Weave of Women*, she leads us through her consciousness as through a Fellini epic."
—*Ms.* magazine

"CHALLENGING, PROVOCATIVE, OFTEN MOVING READING that at times seems fable, at times parable, at times a look at a surrealistic world. Her imagination and probing are fresh, shocking, revealing."

—*Publishers Weekly*

"AN ENGROSSING, IMAGINATIVE BOOK."
—*Boston Globe*

THE BELL JAR by Sylvia Plath
CANCER WARD by Alexander Solzhenitsyn
THE CONFESSIONS OF NAT TURNER by William Styron
DARKNESS VISIBLE by William Golding
DELTA OF VENUS Erotica by Anaïs Nin
THE END OF THE ROAD by John Barth
THE FIRST CIRCLE by Alexander I. Solzhenitsyn
THE FLOATING OPERA by John Barth
GILES GOAT-BOY by John Barth
GOODBYE, COLUMBUS by Philip Roth
THE LONG MARCH by William Styron
THE MEMOIRS OF A SURVIVOR by Doris Lessing
THE MIDDLE GROUND by Margaret Drabble
MY LIFE AS A MAN by Philip Roth
NIGHT OF THE AUROCHS by Dalton Trumbo
ONE DAY IN THE LIFE OF IVAN DENISOVICH
    by Alexander Solzhenitsyn
SET THIS HOUSE ON FIRE by William Styron
THE SNOW LEOPARD by Peter Matthiessen
SOMETIMES A GREAT NOTION by Ken Kesey
THE STONE ANGEL by Margaret Laurence
THE SUMMER BEFORE THE DARK by Doris Lessing
V. by Thomas Pynchon
VISION QUEST by Terry Davis
A WEAVE OF WOMEN by E. M. Broner
WHEN SHE WAS GOOD by Philip Roth

# A WEAVE OF WOMEN

## E. M. Broner

BANTAM BOOKS
TORONTO · NEW YORK · LONDON · SYDNEY

To Women of the Sword
and Sharpened Tongue

A WEAVE OF WOMEN

*A Bantam Book/published by arrangement with
CBS Educational & Professional Publishing*

PRINTING HISTORY
*Holt, Rinehart and Winston edition published May 1978*

*These chapters have appeared in slightly altered form: "The
Bird and the Thieves," Epoch 22, no. 2 (Winter 1973);
"Habibi," Florida Quarterly 6, no. 1 (Spring 1974); "Joan on
Meron," Story Quarterly 1, no. 1 (1975).
Acknowledgements:
MacDowell Colony, Spring 1977;
Marian Wood and Helen Merrill, prickly and smooth,
fighters, editor, agent;
Union Graduate School, Yellow Springs, Ohio,
in partial fulfillment of the Ph.D.*

*Bantam edition/February 1982*

*Cover painting by Henri Matisse, "Dance I."*

A Weave of Women

ISBN 0-553-14727-7

*Published simultaneously in the United States and Canada*

PRINTED IN THE UNITED STATES OF AMERICA

0 9 8 7 6 5 4 3 2 1

## the women

*Israelis*
Terry, Director, Home for Jewish Wayward Girls
Simha, mystic
Hepzibah, religious from Haifa
Dahlia, singer from Beer Sheva
Mickey (Mihal), divorcing woman from Haifa
Vered, social worker from Tel Aviv
Rina and Shula, wayward girls

*British*
Antoinette, Shakespearean from London
Joan, journalist and playwright from Manchester

*German*
Gerda, the scientist

*Americans*
Gloria, the convert from California
Tova, the curly-haired actress
Deedee, the Irish-American
Robin, a wayward girl

*Children*
Hava, daughter of Simha
Rahel, daughter of Hepzibah

*and the men they encounter*

# 1
# The Birth

They embrace and face Jordan. They are turned golden in the evening light, like the stone. There are several of them. The weeping one will not turn to salt. In fact, she drinks her tears. She is a full-bellied sabra and her fruit is sucking away inside.

The women breathe with Simha. Heavy labor has not started yet. They sit in the doorway of their stone house in the Old City. They move inside and breathe with Simha into the stones.

Simha groans. They echo. Simha loses her water. The Dead Sea. The River Jordan. The Nile. They wait for the baby to float on a basket from Simha's reeds.

They have notified two midwives. It is a mistake. The doctors have refused home delivery. A nurse warned them against it.

Deedee leans against the stones and tells of a friend who bore a son on Christmas Eve under the Christmas tree.

"Was it planned?"

"No. It was an accident."

"Which?"

"Both the pregnancy and the birth."

"What happened to the baby?"

"He was put into the Dirty Baby Ward at the hospital because he was covered with pine needles."

The midwives arrive. One is a Jews for Jesus girl, dressed modestly in kerchief, long skirt, covered arms. She knows her Old and New Testaments but not her Biology. The other is a Swede who is into health. She worked as a volunteer at a border kibbutz and volunteered herself to a kibbutz member. She arrives nursing her new baby. The Swede is intent on smearing ointment onto her sore nipples. The other midwife is reading Leviticus in variant texts.

Simha exclaims. She is in pain. The women are joyous. Pain quickens the moment to birth. Pain quickens the excitation.

They see the cervix. It is purple, a reddish purple.

The midwives look disturbed.

"Hot water?" asks the social worker.

They don't think so.

Simha is sitting on a stool. The women put a soft blanket between Simha's knees.

One midwife tries to hear the baby's heartbeat. She cannot. The Swede listens and hears the regular beat. The midwives do not know how many fingers Simha is dilated.

Simha shouts at them from her stool. They leave.

The social worker goes to a house with a phone and, from there, she telephones accomplished women. She phones Martin Buber's granddaughter, Golda Meir's cousin, Ben Gurion's niece. She phones women in the parliament, the law courts, at the university.

Gradually the experts gather. They surround Simha, crouched on her stool. They have books of instructions in several languages.

Antoinette is in the room, a Shakespearean from London. Joan is there, a playwright, a Britisher, but from Manchester. A scientist arrives, originally from Germany. Dahlia is there, a singer from Beer Sheva. Tova has been there all along, the curly-haired actress from New York. Hepzibah jitneys down from Haifa wearing her padded scarf against the wrath of the Father-Lord. Mickey arrives in the midst of her divorce. Gloria, the redhead, has been there for the fun. She came over from California for the fun. Another social worker arrives from Tel Aviv, serious Polish Vered.

Simha has left her stool for the mattress on the floor. Her labor has stopped and she dozes. Why is the baby so bad? It will do nothing on time or within reason. It will cry and the mother will never know why. Simha, matted hair, parched lips, is having nightmares.

The scientist says this is not her field of expertise but nothing seems wrong, the head down, labor proceeding.

Hepzibah barely refrains from covering Simha's full, long hair with a kerchief. Simha is not married and, therefore, does not need a head covering, but perhaps the rules are different when it comes to unwed mothers.

Deedee is both intense and amused. The Jews are something else! She is Irish and prefers her own, and then the Greeks and then the Jews. But Israel is warm and she has women friends here who will neither let her starve nor weep.

They are up all night on this night of vigil. The women brew tea. The redhead, Gloria, knows a special way to make Turkish coffee that she learned from an Arab cab driver. He added cardamom seed. She talks on about the cab ride. All of her tales wander, often with cab drivers, jitney drivers, young students from the university who cannot resist her and follow her across the wadi near campus.

The women drink the thick coffee. They are not sleepy. It becomes chilly and they put naphtha into the heater. They open the door a moment. The bad odor escapes, the blue flames light and the early morning air is warmed.

The Shakespearean has a crisp accent and a bustling manner.

"Did someone call the father?" she asks.

Gloria from California did.

At dawn the father runs into the little stone house. He has hitchhiked from his kibbutz. Gloria's message was delivered to the dining room and shouted from table to table. Ah! He is on his shift in the cow shed. His brother takes over and his mother gives him a basket of freshly baked bread from the kibbutz oven, also her own jam and a plant from her garden.

The kibbutz, accepting paternity, sends wishes of easy birth and warm blankets to receive the son.

A daughter is born.

By the time of the birth the father does not care what comes from Simha's cave, what small, furtive animal that is gnawing at her and making her scream. When the animal slides out, it has soft hair on its head and soft fur on its body. It is a daughter-puppy.

The women prepare the mother.

Mickey, in the midst of her divorce and of her hatred, combs Simha's hair. She braids it. She brushes it out again and puts it up. She lets it hang down Simha's back.

Antoinette gathers flowers from the valley of the Old City.

"There's rosemary, that's for remembrance.... And there is pansies, that's for thought. There's fennel for you, and columbines ... daisy ... violets...."

"That's morbid," says Joan. "Ophelia of all things!"

Antoinette does not deign to reply. What does a Manchester person know of repartee, of the deft thrust? She wraps herself in London imperial dignity.

Gloria stares at the father of the child. He fell asleep wearily. He interests her, the natural man who eats hungrily without good or bad manners, sleeps easily, loves shyly. Gloria looks at his kibbutz stomach stretching the buttons of his cotton shirt. His hand is curled. She touches it and it jerks.

Hepzibah takes out her Daily Prayer Book. Terry, the social worker, readies a manifesto. Gerda, the scientist born in Germany, looks at this new marvel of science.

Dahlia from Beer Sheva goes out to exercise her face and chest. The total person sings, not just the vocal cords. She returns red-cheeked and lively-eyed. She sings to Simha of happiness, of bodies, of seas of the moon, of inner caverns that hold tropical fish, of waters that flood and the fish swims clear. The fish has no gills and now must sing instead of gulping.

Tova, the actress, strokes and smoothes the baby daughter. No one will spank her, croons Tova. Life is not a slap on the behind.

The women stroke the animal, pet it behind its ears, pet its scaly legs, its stretching turtle neck, its lumpy head.

Tova brings the stage property—an Indian bedspread with monkeys and fruit-bearing trees. Simha is sat up on the chattering monkey and the lush tree. A garland is twined for her hair.

Gloria tries again to awaken the kibbutznik. He opens his eyes, looks into Gloria's goyishe pale blue and smiles. He has forgotten Simha, who was his happiness. He has forgotten the new daughter. He looks at Gloria's incandescent hair, her straight nose, her American long legs.

The women watch him silently. The kibbutznik feels a crick in his neck. He is a father. He must speak up at kibbutz meetings, in public, and ask for her maintenance. He is the lover of Simha, and she is a head taller than he. She has wide hips, pendulous breasts, large brown eyes, thick hair. He sighs. Never will he feel that canopy of red above him, those blue eyes sunlit upon his arrival. He belongs to furry animals and hairy, big women.

They surround the mattress and chant:

"Welcome to the new mother. Welcome to the new daughter."

Simha is happy but sloppy. She grabs at her breasts, which are beginning to fill and hurt. She cannot close her legs. The womb is sore. But she looks young again. That old woman who went into childbirth is rejuvenated.

Their home is a busy one and across the narrow street is a busier one. That is the Home for Wayward Girls, actually the Home for Jewish Wayward Girls. They are wayward because they ran away. Or because they stand along the roadside near the universities, secular or religious, crying out in the holy tongue, "Come and fuck me!"

Committees have met on these girls. Terry has sat on such a committee as Director of the Home. It is the committee decision that the girls are prostitutes because they are psychologically disturbed.

"No," says Terry, "economically disturbed."

She brings out charts on inflation, lack of education, illiteracy.

"What is left for these girls to do?" asks Terry.

"No one tells them to," says the committee.

But they, the girls, know it's what they have to do. And, afterward, their mothers scratch at their eyes. Their fathers whip them. The daughters have failed the religion and the socialist state.

The girls leave both religion and socialism. They wear pointy bras, beehive hairdos or they straighten and blow-dry Arabic-Jewish-African hair. They wear high-heeled chunky shoes and miniskirts when no one is mini anymore, not the Israeli policewomen or the women in the army, who have lengthened skirts to mid-knee.

Rina arrives for the ceremony, Rina from development town, court and prison. Rina wears a long skirt. She wears eyeliner along her almond eyes. She covers her pointy breasts with a shawl. Her parents threw her out because she was lazy in the house. Her lovers threw her out because she was fearful in bed.

Shula is invited, Shula the Westerner, the Pole. She is blonde and buxom. She spits on her parents. She does not honor their days in the land. She spits on her teachers. She does not follow the command to honor the teacher above all. She spits on the police. She spits on all uniforms: traffic, civil guard, nurses, beauty parlor.

"Who taught you to spit, Shula?"

"My grandmother. She spat on me when she saw me and said, 'An ugliness. May the Evil Eye leave her on this earth. May she only be seen as ugly and undesirable so that we never lose her.' And so I am—ugly and undesirable."

The ceremony begins.

Simha wears a wraparound skirt to cover either taut or flabby belly. The kibbutznik is present, bearing another basket from his kibbutz, sensible girls' clothing of strong kibbutz material.

He stares at both of the women, his daughter and his love. And he feels jealous. His daughter fits on the mother's hip, on her breast. There is no need for a father as there was no need for a husband, and he has traveled by bus a winding route for four hours to arrive in Jerusalem.

"Find a girl in the kibbutz," advises the kibbutz psychologist. "Forget her. She takes advantage of you."

Ah, she did! She did! His first love. She took advantage of him and deflowered him.

Gloria is there wearing a low-cut dress. She has found sun during this chilly weather, and her freckles reach into her cleavage.

The kibbutznik stares into the basket he is carrying.

Tova from New York is there. She has an Arab lover. He is too shy to attend, but he sends a song.

Mother, I would leap from the mountain for you.
Mother, I will never forget you.

Shh. It is Simha's prayer.

"I come into your house, O Mother God. You inclined your ear toward me, and I will whisper into it all the days of my life.

"The cords of life and death encompassed me. From the hollow of the grave, from the cave of the mouth of birth I called. I knew happiness and anguish. You delivered my soul from death into birth, my eyes from tears, my feet from falling. I shall walk before You in the land of the living."

The baby is poking at her own eyes. She grimaces. A thin cry.

Hepzibah says, "Let her become a comfort to Simha in her old age."

Hepzibah puts down her prayer book and kisses Simha.

"She may need it," murmurs Hepzibah.

Terry says, "Let there be peace. Grant this daughter of her people peace."

Ah, they do not know what will befall or that there will be no room for the daughter or for her people.

The kibbutznik says: "May she serve however she wishes, in the chicken house, the barn, the rose garden, the cotton field, the kitchen, the guesthouse. May she be a member of the community of people."

Simha knows why she chose him to be the father.

This is a story of the birth of Simha's daughter, of the births of other daughters, of the piercing of the women of these two houses. It is a story of women who are born in or arrive in the land, of some who stay and of many who leave.

It is a story of women who are ceremonious and correct with each other, who celebrate sermons and hermans, birth rites, death rites, sacrificial rites, exodus rites and exorcism rites.

It is the story of sanity and madness in the house of women.

# 2
# Ceremonies in Dirty Old Men

To Terry there is a sorrow. Her District Supervisor and the Director of Religious Affairs, under whose jurisdiction social work programs fall, wish to remove her from directorship of the Home for Jewish Wayward Girls. Why? Because she lives across the street with an unwed mother, a living bad example to her clients. Already, Rina visits the social worker's house and Shula brings flowers.

Terry's friends in the Union of Social Workers rally to her cause and elect her their representative on the Council of Street Workers.

"Street workers?" asks Deedee, giggling.

"Street workers," says Terry.

Terry does not tell jokes.

To Terry there is a new happiness. She is in love with an old man, she who will have nothing to do with young men anymore for they hurt you with words and with or withholding love. They hurt you with the palm of the hand. They hurt you by not being ready for you. They needle you. They are dull and bore you. They hurt you by shouting and by quiet.

What do old men do for you, springy old men? Their eyes light up, their back straightens. They are courtly. They pay your bills. They make sure you have the blankets around you in bed. They have learned many things with and without teeth. They gum you; they suck you like thick-skinned fruit. Their knees poke and make bruises on you, but their voices are soft, their hearts are light. Terry sleeps sweetly in the arms of an old man.

She washes the old man's hair. He is grateful for her fingers in his scalp. She dries his hair vigorously, shaking his head. He is a bit dizzy.

She showers with him, soaping him until he becomes old all over—hoary-haired, soapy white, and she spreads his age and pulls on his age. She rinses him and dries him limb by limb by half-limb. Even the limbs of eyes, the limbs of ears.

Everything is a gift to an old man—a breast against his chest, a nipple meeting the eye of a penis, a pap in the mouth.

Sometimes Terry rides a cockhorse, a fine lady upon a white horse. Sometimes Terry goes back to the roots of things, genealogy, gerontology, origins, and the old man tells her his branches, limbs, twigs. His tongue becomes leafy.

Terry needs the old man. Simha's baby cries at night. Simha becomes tired and cries at night. The experts float in and out. The nonexperts stay.

Gloria is there constantly talking to Simha, talking to the baby, to Terry, to visitors. She serves nothing but Turkish coffee until the people in the house develop loose bowels.

Tova and Gloria quarrel. Tova wants theater, not conversation, movement and not discussion. Tova brings plants into the house. Tova squeegees down the terrazzo floor. Tova sponges Simha and the baby.

And, in the bedroom, Terry attends the old man.

The old man is like the worm used by Solomon the Great to split the hardest stone, to construct his Temple. The worm of the old man is sung to, blown, played upon, wiggled.


Outside of the bedroom door the girls tell stories. Gloria begins. Although Tova is the actress, red-haired Gloria is the most dramatic. Gloria tells kibbutz old-men jokes.

"They grab you in the potatoes."

"In the potatoes?"

"They grab you in the orchard."

Dahlia, the lusty singer from Beer Sheva, spent alternative military service at a kibbutz when it was her time to serve in the army.

"They grab you in the cold storage room," says Dahlia.

Her hair is auburn. Her eyes are green. Her breasts are small and widely spaced. Her hands milk the air.

"One old man sneaked in when I went to get cucumbers, and he closed the door. He was willing to give me his cucumber. Outside they heard muffled yells and opened the door. We were running round and round inside the cold storage room, shoving carts this way and that. I was frozen and the old man hot."

The girls begin to laugh. The old man in the bedroom is distracted. Are they laughing at him? He is careful not to creak the bed. But it doesn't creak. The mattress is on the floor.

Simha tells a kibbutz tale from her lover's kibbutz.

"An old man in a Habonim kibbutz became a widower at the age of ninety-one or ninety-two. He took to sleeping with younger women, in their eighties."

"Eighties!"

Simha talks while smiling. Terry in the bedroom embraces the old man and listens to her friends' laughter. She does not feel excluded or judged. It is a feather quilt around her. It is pillows. Terry begins to laugh. A feather is in her nose. The old man feels spurts of Terry's breath, her stomach going in and out with him in her. He cackles.

"What happened to the old man, for God's sake?" screams Terry from the bedroom.

Silence.

Shrieks.

Simha calls. "He chased all the women in his kibbutz. He had them and moved on to a neighboring kibbutz of a different movement."

"A deviationist!" shouts Terry.

"He was a moderate socialist but the members of the next kibbutz are old Stalinists."

"Watch out for an intermarriage!"

"There he finds a love, a gorgeous eighty-seven-year-old."

"Experienced."

"Mature."

"Settled."

"Knows her way around."

The old man pulls out of Terry.

Simha continues. "One night the eighty-seven's husband comes in upon them. They fight! A terrible fight. The neighbors send for the members of the moderate socialist kibbutz."

Terry calls, "You see what permissiveness, ideological permissiveness leads to?"

"The socialists come rushing in to separate the oldsters. Too late. The fight ends up in the hospital."

Terry appears wrapped in a sheet. She closes the door on the old man. The women point and wipe their eyes. Simha holds both a pillow and her baby to her breast. Everyone hurts.

"They asked him to retire," says Simha, "from a little store he managed. It was the final blow. So he said to my kibbutznik, 'You know what day today is, the third day of the week? The third day of next week I will die. It is time for me to join my wife!'"

"Finally," says Gloria.

"Did he?" asks Deedee.

"Exactly when he said," says Simha.

Mickey hates men. She hates her divorcing husband. She hates her divorcing in-laws. She hates the rabbinical court which delays and delays the divorce, which humiliates her and orders her to buy her way out of the marriage.

Mickey tells a mean dirty-old-man kibbutz story.

"My parents sent me to the kibbutz for summer holiday," says Mickey, "when I was twelve or thirteen. I had these kibbutz parents, a wife about sixty, her husband in his seventies. My memory isn't so good about their age because you know how older people look to a young girl. The old man had a face dried from fifty years of working in the sun on that kibbutz. It was leathery. It had freckles of age. Every day when I went for milk and cookies the old man would say, 'Daughter, kiss me.' I didn't want to. One day his wife went to the hot springs in the Negev to get a cure for arthritis. I came by for milk and cookies because they bawled me out if I didn't. There he was. He grabbed me and kept kissing and hugging me and wouldn't let go. I ran out of their apartment. Afterward they wrote to my parents accusing me of stealing cigarettes, coin and candy from their dresser drawers."

The women become depressed. After much laughing is hiccuping and depression.

Simha remembers that the landlady wants them to

move. Terry is chilled and goes in for jeans and a T-shirt. She remembers that the municipality wants to close down Wayward and imprison the girls. Mickey remembers another court date.

Tova remembers that there is no experimental theater in Israel. Gloria remembers that no man has wandered with her on the new road to Haifa or down the old road past Ein Hod and the Arab village of Faradise.

Deedee remembers, as she does always, the men who hurt her in America, Ireland, Crete, and, just recently, in Jerusalem.

Rina and Shula come in from next door. The women are sitting, their hands tucked under their legs, to protect them from the cold floor.

"Oh!" says Rina. "What is happening here?"

"I know," says Shula. "It is about our house. They will be kicking us out of it, back onto the street."

Shula spits and wipes the spittle into the floor.


At this time the old man emerges from the bedroom. He is neatly dressed. His pants are creased, his shirt starched, cuffs stiff with neat cuff links. He has a rich brown silk tie, brown socks, shoes of the softest leather. His face is flushed. His lips appear almost rouged. The women stare. He is wearing a yarmulke.

He cannot tip his yarmulke at them but he nods.

"Shlomo Sassoon, ladies," he says.

He is carrying a sample case of material.

"Do you like these, ladies?" he asks.

No one speaks. Terry stands in the doorway, the setting sun silhouetting her short, black hair. Shlomo Sassoon spreads his materials.

"He came to the door to sell them," says Terry.

"They are the finest in Kashmir," says Shlomo.

Silks, paisley, swirls of colors. The material lifts and

billows, balloons in the slightest breeze. As Shlomo talks the remnants breathe.

"I'll give you a good price," says Shlomo.

Gloria sidles over. Tova wraps a remnant around her head. She is a voodoo priestess. Simha wraps material around her hips. It is a sarong.

"I've seen better cloth," says divorcing Mickey.

"Oh, not I!" says Dahlia from Beer Sheva.

Shlomo Sassoon drapes material across the wide chest of Dahlia. Dahlia lets out a note, a tremolo and the material blows away.

"Listen to his story," says Terry.

Shlomo Sassoon sits on the floor with the women and with his cloth. He is in the Yoga position.

"I am from Kashmir," says Sassoon. "I had a whole factory. My wife never lifted a finger. I spent my time in the factory, in the shul, and practicing Yoga."

"There's a shul in Kashmir?"

"A House of Gathering?"

"A synagogue?"

"A Yoga synagogue?"

"I am a learned practitioner of Yoga and Halakah."

"Halakah?" asks Deedee.

She stares at this Jewish Kashmiri. There *is* an international conspiracy.

"The orders of God, the righteous way."

"Why did you leave Kashmir, the shul and Yoga?"

"Because of the Indian invasion, when I lost my factory, my wife lost her servants, my shul its scrolls, my land its freedom."

"You came here with nothing?"

"No, with a great deal, some bolts of material and three strands of the spirit of Judaism."

Deedee yawns. "Braids."

"I know," says Simha, "for I have those strands intertwined within me."

A religious man does not hear a woman. He may only feel her presence.

"I have my *nefesh*," says Shlomo, "my proper soul."

*"My* nefesh," says Simha, "hovers over the dust of my body, and when I die it will hover between life and death like a white butterfly."

Shlomo snorts. "Secondly, I have my *rouah*, the wind and spirit of my soul."

*"My* rouah," says Simha, "will enter the Garden of Eden dressed for Sabbath and will dance on all Sabbaths and on the Festival of the New Moon."

"Thirdly," says Shlomo, "I have my supersoul, my *neshama*."

*"My neshama—"* shouts Simha.

"This I cannot allow!" says the old man. "A woman has no supersoul."

Terry suddenly tires of her lover and notices his leathery face, the wrinkles and age spots.

"Because of my neshama, my supersoul," says Shlomo, his hands hooked under his armpits, "all lights are lit on festivals."

*"Because of my supersoul,"* says Simha, *"the stars and the moon light up."*

The women applaud.

Dahlia wearies and lies on the stone floor.

"Because I practice Yoga and Halakah," says Shlomo, "I am also a seer."

Simha is quiet.

Shlomo stares at Dahlia.

"You are suffering," he addresses her. "You are bruised by men."

"Who isn't?" asks Gloria.

Dahlia startles. On her leg, under her long skirt, is a swollen bruise. A young man with whom she went boating hit her with the paddle when she refused to succumb to his advances.

"You are quarreling with your family," says Shlomo. "More precisely, your mother is your daughter."

Dahlia begins to weep. Her mother must be constantly comforted, spoon-fed when she loses appetite, lullabied to sleep.

"Your spirit is disturbed and your passions too great for the men of this small land."

Dahlia is always enflamed.

"Watch my ears," says Sassoon.

His ears turn bright red.

"I am taking your passion from you so you can find calm."

A breeze cools Dahlia's body.

"I will put my hands on your shoulders. My strength will enter you."

There are muscles in Dahlia's arms. Her wrists feel as if they can wring out sheets or squeeze the breath out of dangerous boatmen.

"Tell your mother she can no longer be your daughter. Tell angry men that you are stronger than they."

Dahlia's hands are still, untrembling, now quiet at her side.

"I bless these daughters of The Land," says Sassoon.

He does a courtly strut, kissing hands and foreheads. He stops at Terry.

"For you, Terry, my supersoul is lit. For you I soar to heaven."

The women applaud again. It is even.

Shlomo does not gift them with his remnants. They are, after all, his livelihood. He gathers them up into his case, peeling them from Dahlia's breasts, from Tova's curly head, from Simha and Gloria.

The room darkens. No one has turned on the lights.

The old man's walk is thin, bony, insectlike. He hops. His shoulder blades are the beginning of angel's wings. His fingers elongate. His hair is incandescent. He flaps and rises into the air to fly suddenly out of the opened window.

"Whose soul will turn on the lights in the room?" asks Gloria.

For this is the Old City and all that is holy and foolish, pure and malevolent happens here.

The wayward girls cross the narrow path to their house. Terry's womb is sore. She showers alone and sleeps, gratefully, alone. There has been too much company in the house and in all one's orifices.

Simha's baby cries. It will soon be time for her hymenotomy.

# 3
# Ceremonies on the Throne of Miriam

It is during the second orange harvest that Simha's baby has her hymenotomy. The air smells of orange blossoms. The clementines are sweet, the grapefruits not tart. Cucumbers are light green and long. Radishes are large and mild. Nothing growing in this season is bitter.

Simha has not taken her baby from her breast these eight days. If she does for an hour or two, she worries about what else she should be doing.

The wayward girls, Rina and Shula, wander in, washing

their faces, arms and hands carefully before they sponge Simha or handle the baby.

Mickey attends them between appointments at the rabbinical house. She burps the baby and says, *Momzera*, little illegitimate girl.

Vered, the Polish social worker from Tel Aviv, comes with warnings. She tells Terry about the statistics dealing with bastards. There is no longer the old, benign kibbutz attitude about marriage or the lack of it. This is a conservative time. The baby will suffer.

Vered's clients these days are the Russians, the dwindling number of them who still want to settle in The Land. Vered wants the Israelis to provide a good example. Simha, lying indolently, her robe always open, her breasts leaking, does not provide such an example.

Nor later will Vered.

The women gather for the ceremony.

They giggle nervously.

"What should it be called?"

"Hymenectomy."

"No. That sounds like an appendectomy."

"It sounds like you're getting rid of your Uncle Hymen."

They wait for Gerda. They enclose the house, covering the windows with cloth, placing lace on the chosen chair. Tova has brought lace that she uses in the theater, old, torn, delicate lace she found in the suk in Old Jaffa. Tova drapes it. Simha sits in lace, the baby on her lap. Deedee, the oldest of many sisters and brothers, has made a christening dress for this baby.

"Christening?"

Deedee sighs. Jews and etymology. Jews and sensitivity. Here in the land of her God, also, they are still fighting any mention of His name. "B.C." they call "Before the Common Era." "Christendom" they don't mention at all. December 25 falls into whatever Jewish month it falls into—Tevet or Shevet the twenty-fifth. No one is named Christine or Christopher. No one buys Christian Brothers wine. They tease her about New Year's Eve. It's either Christ's circumcision or they call it Sylvester, and no one gives a party but a few lonesome Americans. The flora is not called Christmas fern, Christmas rose, Christmas berry. There is no Christ's thorn that she can find. Christmas trees they call a German invention. . . .

"It's such a beautiful dress," says Simha. "We're proud in it."

Deedee relaxes and Gloria tenses. Too much attention on Deedee.

Gerda enters.

"Name the baby."

They tell her the name of the baby.

"Hava, mother of everything living."

*Hava* translates into Eve, they explain to Gloria, a recent convert. Gloria tells them about her conversion and about the young Reform rabbi laying her on the floor of his study.

"Is this part of the conversion?" she asked him.

The girls don't want to hear Gloria.

"Name the mother," says Gerda.

Simha is the mother.

Simha says, "Here am I acting upon the command that is not yet written that the daughter of eight days shall be pierced."

Simha rises and hands the baby to the godmother, her roommate Terry. Simha walks with difficulty to her bed. Terry sits in the draped chair.

"This is the Throne of Miriam the Prophetess," says Gerda. "May she be remembered for greatness."

Gerda lifts Hava from Terry's arms.

"This is a daughter of Eve."

"What do you mean?"

"We trace our descent from Eve."

Rina and Shula are whispering. They object to the baby being called "a daughter of Eve."

"They use that name for us," says Shula. "It is another name for whore."

"But the son of Adam means human being," says Tova.

"So it is," say the girls.

Terry says her part.

"This baby is descended from Eve. This baby is descended from Sara. Sara's name is princess, the origin of 'Israel.' From her will come tribes and ceremonies."

Tova lifts Hava.

"This child Hava, may she one day be great."

Hepzibah cannot bring herself to say unfamiliar prayers. They are difficult, as well, for Antoinette, a traditionalist.

The women of the room bless the fruit of the vine. They bless the fruit from Simha's womb.

Simha begins to cry from her bed. Terry's arms are shaking. The wayward girls dry Simha's tears and avert their eyes from the ceremony.

Gerda hesitates.

"Do you want it?"

"Yes," says Simha sobbing.

"Yes," says Terry trembling.

"No, no." say Rina and Shula. "She should be a virgin at her wedding."

"I stop here," says Gerda and refuses to continue.

"Explain it to us, Gerda," says Dahlia from Beer Sheva. "No one ever explains to us so how can we choose?"

Gerda lectures easily at the university, over the phone, at the homes of friends.

She diagrams. Two views. A lovely mouth. It is surrounded by lips, the labia majora and the labia minora.

*"Menorah?"* ask the wayward girls. "Lamp?"

It is like an opening, parted lips, with a kind of jagged tooth, with the jagged bits of membrane.

Gerda makes another diagram. The tiny hymen.

"Just a poke with a pick, with something sharp," says Gerda, "that will pierce it. The hymen is so tiny in a baby."

A third diagram. The entrance, the tissue that blocks it, the vaginal wall, the cervix.

"It is usually broken," says Gerda, "by the time young girls see doctors, either by accident or through intent."

"Do it, Gerda," says Simha.

"I did not invent this ceremony," says Gerda. "You did. I'm the scientist. You're the mystic. I will not proceed alone without agreement."

"What is it called, Gerda?"

"It has no name. It has not been done before."

"Name it."

"Hymenotomy."

"Sounds like lobotomy," says Gloria.

"Why hymenotomy?"

"*Tomy*," says Gerda, "a cutting of a tissue."

Antoinette becomes alert.

"Actually," says Antoinette in her crisp London accent, "it is from the root *tem,* to cut."

"What are you using?" ask the women of Gerda.

"Any sharp cutting instrument will do," says Gerda. "I have one here."

"Will it bleed?"

"Not really."

"Will it hurt?"

"Scarcely at all."

"And," says Antoinette to Hepzibah, who is also trying not to participate, "*tome* is a cutting from a larger roll of paper, one book in a work of several volumes."

Gerda says, "There is the thin membrane that separates the outside from the inside of the vagina. It is a vestigial structure."

"Cut it," says Terry, against all vestigial structures, social, physical.

Antoinette's voice rises. *"Dichotomy, anatomy."*

Gerda is swift. The hymeneal membrane is pierced. She has poked easily through the hymeneal ring.

Hava is startled and wails. Simha gives Hava her nipple, first dabbing wine on it.

There is a loud sigh from the group.

Tova says, "Now you are one of us."

Terry, the godmother, says, "May all orifices be opened."

Dahlia says, "May she not be delivered intact to her bridegroom or judged by her hymen but by the energies of her life."

The baby drinks and lets go of the nipple to cry. Hepzibah frowns. The wayward girls are shocked. There is so much to shock wayward girls, much they encounter that others do not—physical violence, rape, but this devirginizing of an eight-day-old is the most shocking of all.

"Who will love her?" they whisper to each other, "once they find out?"

Deedee awakens. She fills a large silver cup with sacramental wine.

"May she never suffer again from piercing," says Deedee, "of the body or of the heart."

The lace at the window stirs. It is old Shlomo Sassoon. They shoo him away.

There is a knock at the door. It is the father. He is too early. Would he mind waiting? Gloria brings him a cup of her Turkish coffee. The bitter brew will cool him, will rest him from his hard journey.

"Did you ask his permission?" asks Vered from Tel Aviv.

Simha says, "I told him I wanted to do it, but I did not ask his permission."

"Did he want to do it?" asks Vered.

"No," says Simha.

"Then you did it without his permission."

"I do not have to ask his permission."

"It's being done to his baby," says Vered.

"It's being done to a girl child," says Simha, "and he knows nothing of that."

"Of what?" ask the wayward girls.

"Of the ways that women must open themselves."

Shula sulks. She opens herself. She is a wishbone, sometimes bending her legs around small, bony men, sometimes around large, fat men. One day she will crack in half with no wishes ever granted her.

Dahlia sings in her throaty voice: "I will open my lips with song and my bones declare, Blessed is she that cometh in the name of the Shehena, the womanly God."

They seat themselves on chairs, pillows, an Arab rug and around Simha's bed.

Dahlia sings of women's chairs: the birthing stool, the throne of Miriam, the chair of the longing woman at the window, of the cooking woman at the table, of chariots of war and chariots of angels ascending.

The song ends shrilly. The women worry. Does little Hava so soon have to think of war?

"We are always at war," says Dahlia, "in our land and in our lives."

Deedee is bored. These Jewish friends never cease from whining and dining. The Irish talk, lovely, lively chatter, but this endless talmudic tract, spiritual gossip, this daily poop of prayer. Who is she, Deedee, to such commentary and ceremony?

Tova says, "It is not only Simha's baby who has been pierced. We should each tell of the piercing."

You first, Tova.

"I was pierced," says Tova, "by the angry glance of my enemy."

"Arab lover!" says Mickey. "But what's the difference? Your friends become your enemies too. I stayed a virgin and I will always regret it—that I was pierced by the bastard, my husband. I saved it for the man who threw it away."

"Threw what away?" asks Rina.

"Threw me away, stupid," says Mickey. "What are *they* doing here?" she asks about the girls from across the way. "Isn't it their bedtime?"

The girls huddle together.

"He had me," Mickey says, "and told me, 'What do I need you for? You're not a virgin anymore, you're common and any man can have you.'"

"He was not a son of Adam," says Hepzibah, reaching for Mickey's shaking hands. "He wasn't human."

Deedee relaxes with her friends. They take a long time getting there but, eventually, they do.

"My boss pierced me," says Deedee. "Small, fat boss. I, his secretary, towered over him. Only when I was at my desk and he standing next to me each morning was he taller than I. On my nineteenth birthday he took me for drinks to the bar in our building. Sitting next to him in the booth I could see down on the top of his head where his pink scalp shone through the thinning hair. He bought me a cocktail, one, two, a few. He helped me to his car to take me home. We ended up at the park. Not dark yet. Dusk. People walking around us. What did he care? He parked near the fountain. The water was turned off because it was getting cold and the pipes would freeze. Not his. He had his heater on. I was dozing. 'Want to see who's bigger,' he said, 'you or me?' I bled on his car seat, which he didn't appreciate. He took me home. 'It's my period, ma,' I said and ran upstairs. My ma followed me. When she saw me sobbing, she knew it wasn't and slapped me down into the bed. 'You're of no use to anybody, including yourself,' said my ma. In those days I, only nineteen, was supporting my ma and all the kids, for my dad had left us years before."

Deedee's head is on Tova's shoulder. Terry holds Deedee's hand.

"Hava," says Deedee, "let your piercing be among friends. Let it be ceremonious and correct. Let it be supervised. Let it be done openly, not in anger, not in cars. Ah, Hava," weeps Deedee, "how I envy you."

Gloria says, "The guy who pierced my ears pierced my hymen. On his jewelry shop window was a sign, FREE. EARS PIERCED FREE. I went in. 'I've pierced women all over the world,' said the jeweler. 'Is it free?' I asked. 'You doubt it?' said the jeweler. 'I could be arrested for false advertising.' I said, 'I'm afraid. I'm afraid of pain.' He said, 'I'll be gentle. You won't feel a thing. Only choose an earring and I'll pierce you with it.' 'What are those numbers on the earrings?' 'Nothing. My bookkeeping,' he says. I chose pearls with the number forty. He smiled, seated me in the Piercing Chair and pierced me with the pearls. 'That's forty dollars,' he said, 'for the earrings.' Of course I didn't have it. 'Ask your mother.' 'I don't have one.' 'Ask your father.' 'He'd beat you first and me afterward.' He said, 'Only one way I'll get my money's worth.' "

Gerda, the scientist, says, "I pierced myself. 'Why make a fuss?' I asked myself. 'If I ever marry do I need blood on a sheet? Do the neighbors have to be called in? I went through my Ph.D. to be judged this way?' I had no boyfriend, no one really interested in me, but I could not wait. One must control one's destiny. I am my own bridegroom."

Antoinette has not married. She is shy about not marrying and about having a hymen and about the stories the women have told.

"It is there," says Antoinette softly, "like tonsils or appendix. It never really gave me any trouble. It's there, a part of me, like a scab or a scar, a lock or protection. Let it be there. I like politeness, someone knocking, announcing. All doors and windows need not be open."

Antoinette sits self-consciously. She double-crosses her legs.

Hepzibah does not speak. She refastens her scarf more securely. Hepzibah always smiles. She refers to her husband and to her male sons as her "soldiers," and to her daughter as "one day the mother of soldiers." Yet she is with these women and full of love for them. But she cannot speak of what is under the scarf, the blouse, the skirt, the stockings, between the legs.

Vered says, "I was lucky. A fifty-two-year-old man did it, skillfully, carefully. No young man could have been so kind to me."

They listen.

"And even now," says Vered, who is twenty-nine, "I can be with no man younger than fifty."

Some have not spoken yet—the wayward girls, Dahlia, Joan from Manchester, Terry or Simha.

It is getting dark.

"Ach! Where's my daughter's father?" asks Simha.

Gloria opens the door. The kibbutznik has gone. The Turkish coffee cup is on its side. There is a thick residue of the coffee on the step.

"I'm such a shit!" says Simha.

Abruptly she smiles. "I always was. I lived in an isolated part of town—Jerusalem—where no houses had been built. We lived together, Jews and Arabs. I played with everything in The Land, stones in the wadi, the insides of caves, snakes, insects. I played with the Arab shepherds and their goats. I lay with them in the grass and we had each other, watching the goats."

Hepzibah sighs. Why does she come here after all? This is irrelevant to her. She rises and leaves silently. The women do not always notice when she goes but long for her afterward. Her hand in theirs is dry and steady.

"And you, Dahlia?" asks Simha.

"I pierced myself with a high note," says Dahlia.

That is good enough. The women applaud.

Terry said, "I lived in New York. I worked there but hated it. I had a scholarship offer to one of the schools in the state system to work on my M.S.W. and I accepted. But to leave the city a virgin, to be pierced in Schenectady or Binghamton. What would the choices be? A midget or someone with stumps or a Paul Bunyan who would cripple me? The week before the school semester began I quit my job and spent the day looking for my piercer. I found him easily, a fellow from the lunch counter where I ate, the fastest waiter, smooth, everything in one motion, athletic, younger than I. I waited until his shift was over and asked him to accompany me home. I said I was afraid to walk alone in the dark. But he was street smart. He never held my hand or looked at me; he just accompanied me up the stairs to my room and closed the door himself. I was right—everything in one motion, elegant, smooth. I never regretted it and did not eat at the counter again."

Joan, the playwright, said, "I was pierced on the Mediterranean. I was starting a new life and had to start with a new body. He was a tourist from some northern country, one of those that invaded England. I let him invade me on deck, under the bright moon."

The wayward girls are shocked. They would not dream of speaking about such a private matter.

The women cut cheese, eat it with fresh white bread and slices of mild radish. They cut sweet cucumbers, tomatoes and green peppers into small pieces for a kibbutz salad. They drink wine and say the blessing afterward.

"As it shall be written, may the mother be gladdened with the fruit of her body and the father rejoice in his offspring. May they live to rear her, may her friends learn to help her, may the law accept her and wisdom guide her."

Gerda says, "Terry, all the guests present and the mother Simha have observed this hymenotomy. Let us rejoice that we have performed this deed of piety."

The women make a tent around the baby.

Terry says, "Let us send forth the tidings that a daughter of the blood has joined us."

Simha is weary. She and the baby have both bled into the chair, Simha through her stitches, the baby through its tiny wound. Tova's lace is stained, torn, lying awry. The ceremony has ended.

Rina and Shula decide not to tell the girls of Wayward what they have witnessed. It might get Terry into more trouble. The young girls return to their house wondering and silently crying.

No one welcomed them at birth. Rina's mother said:

"I had hoped for a daughter that looked like an angel, and you, dark one, came along. I had hoped for a son, and a daughter was sent. I had hoped for a good baby, a crier lay. I had hoped for an eater, a fusser was in my arms. Why did God punish me? I had hoped for a circumcision, instead there was blood on her diaper. I screamed for the nurse. She laughed. 'Well, you have a girl for sure,' she said."

The women are dozing. Gloria stays over another night. She has some data for Deedee.

"In Japan," says Gloria, "you can have an operation and have a hymen sewed in. They stick in goatskin for one hundred thirty-seven dollars and no one ever knows. When it tears, you bleed."

"Gross," says Deedee.

They sleep and dream.

They are all virgins again.

# 4
# Street Workers and Streetwalkers

Vered tells the women in the stone house four dreams she has had since sleeping with her beloved.

In the first dream the lover meets her in the lobby of the Jerusalem Hilton. She is crouched in a corner awaiting him. He picks her up like a suitcase and carries her to the elevator.

In the second dream Vered falls in love with her lover's wife.

In the third dream Vered takes her sharp chicken knife and slits her lover's throat. Then she uses her pluckers to remove his body hairs.

In the fourth dream Vered spoon-feeds her lover's wife baby food. The wife makes Vered taste everything Vered feeds her. Vered hates the mashed carrots and prefers Hawaiian Delight. At the end of the meal Vered wipes the wife's face with a bib. The wife extends her dirty fingers for Vered to lick off.

Then Vered tells Terry and Simha the actualities, not the dreams, while Simha's baby noisily suckles.

To protect the identity of her lover, a member of Parliament, they go to the drive-in, the only drive-in movie in the land. An "adult" film is playing, which will accompany their lovemaking. But the ticket-seller recognizes the lover. At the refreshment counter, a former schoolmate from Poland recognizes Vered. When they nervously decide to leave, a policeman stops them for speeding on the road to Tel Aviv. Her love shows his Knesset membership card. The policeman, an Arab, winks suggestively and lets them off without a fine.

"Do you know what happens now?" asks Vered.

Simha and Terry do not, and they are not sure they care. They are tired of Vered's love tales and of the fifty-year-olds in her life. No variety.

"I give presents," says Vered, "to his wife. I give her flowers every Shabbat. Guess what kind? Roses, the small orange roses."

Terry sighs. Vered's name means "rose." She is giving herself to the fifty-year-old and to his wife. And he will take and they will take.

"How do you expect to keep him, Vered?" asks Simha.

"I tell him tales," says Vered. "I weave a spell. I accompany him everywhere with words. I tell my lover that he is going home, but that I am going with him. He lies down and I indent his bed at night, sometimes next to him, sometimes between them, while his wife sleeps near the fresh flowers I've sent. I tell him I will visit him at the Parliament, in the Members' Dining Hall. I am under the table, tickling the space between his socks and pants, pulling up his pant legs and licking his calf, opening his zipper. His party leaders speak to him and he responds vaguely. When he travels on business for the party, with the gas subsidized by them, I am next to him. He drives with one hand. The other is inside my blouse."

Terry and Simha look at Vered's breasts, encased in an old-fashioned, pointy bra. The breasts are squeezed tightly together, no natural cleavage, no falling away of swinging orbs. There is a straight line that shows through Vered's blouse, more like a behind than cleavage.

"Make me less passionate," sobs Vered.


## A COOLING-OFF CEREMONY FOR IMPASSIONED WOMEN

Simha and Terry give Vered water to drink, cold water from their large clay pitcher that is kept in shade. Vered's face is less flushed. They pour droplets on her wrist. They leak water down the tight cleavage and ask her to unhook her bra. They give her a striped Arab robe to wear and ask her to remove her girdle. They give her slippers and ask her to withdraw her feet from the high-heeled shoes she wears to work, on dates, even on visits to the women.

They take turns fanning her. They speak not of the *hamsene*, the fifty hot winds that blow in from the desert, but of winters outside of The Land. They speak and throw buckets of water on the terrazzo floor. The water steams and spreads. The floor is cool underfoot. They speak of yogurt and radishes and chives. They speak of ice cream. They speak of cold people. They speak of calm Gentiles. Vered's creases and crevices are free of perspiration. Vered's eyes are clear. Her forehead is dry.

They are ready to begin the March.


The Home for Jewish Wayward Girls has displeased everyone. It has displeased the Ministry of Welfare because no one contributes to it. The Israel Blind Children can be assured of sponsors, scientists, artists. The Jewish Home for Retarded Children also has its own crowd, prominent people with retarded children or grandchildren. The Jewish Home for the Deaf is also solvent. But, in the States, no one collects at Jewish bakeries, supermarkets, kosher butcher shops, Barton's candy stores or Jewish booksellers for anything that is a combination of Jewish–Wayward–Girls. The Ministry decides to dissolve the home and even advertises it for sale. Today is the protest march of Street Workers and Streetwalkers.

Simha, a member of the Street Workers, leads the march with Hava strapped to her back, Hava's head wobbling. Terry carries a banner: WAYWARD IS THE WAY YOU WANT IT. Joan, the playwright and photographer, is busily recording the event. The press comes out. The specialists also arrive, Antoinette, the Shakespearean, and Gerda, the scientist. Hepzibah, the religious, is unwilling to march, but she stands on the sidewalk and quietly salutes her passing friends. Gloria, the redhead, is busily granting interviews. Deedee, the Irish-American, six feet tall with frizzy long hair and lanky build, is clad in a skimpy top and faded, torn shorts. The religious men boo her. One throws an empty milk carton. Another would throw a Coke bottle at Deedee but a policeman good-naturedly takes it out of his hand. Dahlia has come in from Beer Sheva, leading the group in song. She sings of the old pioneer days, of building The Land, working the fields, fishing the seas. Passersby, from an earlier immigration, are annoyed to find themselves singing with the protesters.

There was never such a unique parade. It was not a Day of Independence Parade with tankim and Skyhawkim. It was not like a Purim parade with children in costume or a March to Jerusalem with campers encircling the walls of the Old City three times and triumphantly entering the new city.

This is a young-to-old parade, a secular-to-religious parade, a whore-to-matron parade.

It is unbearable. The police cannot bear the traffic being stopped. The men cannot bear the women passing en masse. Young men cannot bear the tightly encased breasts of the wayward girls or the freely swinging large breasts of Terry and Vered. The married ladies pushing buggies cannot bear women without buggies, cannot bear women staring straight ahead and carrying banners, cannot bear heads uncovered, hair flying, hair curling, cannot stand smiles and teeth and sturdy stride.

The parade is stopped by a barricade. Terry and Simha, Deedee and Gloria climb over the barricade. On the other side are the Officers of the Peace with clubs, with truncheons. On the other side are the male members of the fire department with wide hoses. The leaders are drenched. While they are distracted and shivering, they are attacked. Simha falls and twists so that her baby falls on top of her. Terry's nose is swollen. Deedee's long, light hair is bloodied. Vered's breasts are bruised. The women stop. Gerda attends them. As she bends over weeping Simha, Gerda is beaten and dragged into a paddy wagon. Joan and the press photographers take pictures—no more leg shots and bosom shots, but bloody head shots. Rina and Shula, the wayward girls, are crying. Their parents cover their own eyes from the shame. Antoinette is cursing in Elizabethan English. Tova, the curly-haired actress from New York, has climbed onto a parked car and shouts to the crowd for its support. The owner of the car, which is covered with its night dustcloth, is horrified to see someone standing on his hood and knocks her down: "Do you know how much a car costs? Are you crazy? One scratch and you'll pay expenses!"

Mickey has arrived late to find her friends being beaten by men and cursed by women. She hesitates, until they are taken away to the jail in the Russian Compound. Mickey goes to the fruit stands for clementines, grapes, mangoes, sabras. She goes to the book kiosk for paperbacks in

Hebrew, English and German. By the time she arrives the women are booked and behind bars. Mickey's fruit is taken by the police. A matron takes the flowers and says she will deliver them to the cells when she finds a plastic container. The books are sent back with Mickey.

The women appear on the evening's television news. Vered's lover does not recognize her in the long striped robe and sandles, without makeup. Vered would not think of asking for *protexia*, special treatment. The rule is: One Does Not Ask a Lover for Help.

The toilets are terrible. No toilets, in fact. Holes in the floor. No paper provided. Antoinette always carries tissue and they divide it among them. The wayward girls are ashamed. No amount of Simha's soothing, of Terry's rhetoric will comfort them.

The guards come by, one even with flowers. She has found no plastic container, but they can hold the flowers in the cell or she'll put them in a glass container out front and lift them out periodically for the women to view. Joan's camera and tape recorder have been confiscated and are on the guard's desk, next to the flowers.

Messages are sent. The kibbutz, which has declared paternity for Simha's baby, is willing to pay her fine. Simha refuses to be isolated from the group.

Terry wants to work up their spirits. She knows some songs from early movement days.

This is the earliest song Terry remembers, when she herself was three years old. It was taught to her in Kinderwelt, Yiddish Socialist Nursery:

> One, two, three,
> Revolutionaries are we,
> Working for the working class
> Against the bourgeoisie.

She has many songs from her father's past, songs of the Spanish Civil War or of the guerrillas of World War II, but there are no songs that the women can sing to one another.

Dahlia from Beer Sheva is commissioned. Her guitar is at the desk with the flowers, camera and tape recorder, but Dahlia can sing a cappella.

Everyone has suggestions. Terry has rhyme suggestions: unite/fight; women/stamen. Antoinette wants the lyrics to be Shakespearean or Spenserian. Gerda wants a marching song without too much levity. Dahlia gets cross. Terry quiets everyone and explains that sound is preceded by silence. Gradually Gloria stops chattering, Tova whistling, Antoinette intoning.

Dahlia begins to hum. Her eyes shine. Her mouth opens. Her throat throbs. She sings a song without words to the women, a song of Mediterranean skies, trills of landscape, ululating Judean hills, a song of sounds that women make, lullabies and cries. La la-lee lee-la, sings Dahlia. The women hear the words she has not sung and weep.

"What is the name of the song?" they ask.

"The Women's Song."

"It's lovely," says Antoinette, "but it really does need words, dear."

"You are the queen of the words," says Dahlia. "You put them in."

"But I cannot sing," says Antoinette.


How does a night pass in cells? Hava is crying. Simha is uncomfortable. There are not enough mattresses to go around. Gloria is hungry. Tova is annoyed to be in the same cell with Gloria and thinks of asking for a change but Tova also wants to present a unified front.

They tell jokes.

Tova asks, "If men give out cigars when boy babies are born, what should women give out?"

"What?"

"Tampons, with little bands: 'It's a Girl!' "

The next morning the matrons bring in newspapers.

The embattled women are on the front page: Simha about to fall. There are clubs against Terry's face and Vered's chest. The story is picked up internationally. The party in power has to answer to major and minor opposition parties. The right wing wants to know why they allowed the women to march in the first place. The Communists tell of the reporting in the Soviet Union: OPPRESSION OF WOMEN IN THE SO-CALLED DEMOCRACY.

The women must be released.

They are brought into the judge's chamber. It is the period for Judge Malamud to preside, a serious, scholarly judge. He hears the case and dismisses all of the women. He condemns the police for excessive use of force. He warns the marchers to get permits the next time.

"No," says Terry to the women afterward. "That is the lesson. If it is permitted we don't make the headlines. We will march again and refuse to ask for a permit."

The women trust her but do not cheer. They are tired.


Some of them gather the next week for the march, some do not. But new women come. Hepzibah is with them. More of the wayward girls are out marching. Mickey, the divorcing woman, comes early enough to walk with them. Joan, the playwright from Manchester, is there, for the theater of it.

Dahlia sings her melody and the women hum with her.

"What are the words?" asks a watcher.

"There are no words."

"Strange song to march to."

Suddenly Vered's arms are grabbed. She is dragged from the group. The women try to cling to her, but the police protect her attacker. He is not really attacking her. He is shouting at her, they explain.

"What are you doing? For no reason, for no reason! Where are your brains? In your tuchas, in your breasts. You have a body and no brains."

It is Vered's fifty-year-old. He risks his career by

publicly pulling her from the crowd. The crowd applauds him. Vered cannot speak. Vered weeps.

Women long ago unlearned the words that preceded weeping, the incantations, anagrams, curses, witchcraft. Now, instead of muttering those words, instead of chanting them, they weep. Vered had once learned to be brave.


In Poland when her father died of overwork, Vered turned trustingly to her mother. When her mother died of overwork and of a broken heart, Vered took her younger brother by the hand, he who had turned so trustingly toward her, and came on Youth Aliyah to The Land. Vered did not allow them to be separated. She did not allow herself to cry when they had no visitors at the children's village or, later, at the agricultural school. She did not become enraged when her mother's only brother forgot his nephew and niece. She did not allow herself to be overwhelmed when her brother ran away from the children's village, but searched him out and, ever afterward, sneaked him into her bed at night.

She learned everything there was to learn, in every language, so that when she finished her army service and her university training, she could take care of anyone in any tongue.

She fattened on the troubles of immigrants. She ate at falafel stands or rushed into cafés for coffee and cake. Her bosom pillowed, billowed, cushioned the heads and hearts of newcomers.

When her brother was wounded in the war that is called The Earthquake, Vered took a leave of absence and sat by his side in the hospital. She sent X rays of his splintered fingers to all of the bone specialists. She helped to raise funds to send him to Switzerland for more treatment.

When she is now with him—tall, slender, curly-haired, the physical opposite of her—she holds his trembling hand, she carefully feeds his stomach that yet contains fragments of shrapnel. She enrolls him in courses in higher education and helps him with his papers. She phones his professors, without his knowledge, and warns them that it will take him longer to write the test with his wounded hand, but that he is too proud to ask for favors.

All this occupied Vered until her fifty-year-old entered her life. Now Vered is someone else. The shell is Vered, the flesh, the bolsters of breasts, but even the cunt is not Vered; it never felt that way before, contracting at odd and importune moments. The head never felt like Vered's before, distracted from the needy Russians, angry Georgians and spoiled Westerners. Her brother cannot easily contact her. Vered is always out. A woman with a lover is more and less than herself.

Her lover sends her notes: "I would swim in you."

The problem is that Vered has become a great pool of love, a reservoir, a sea of soothing movement. Yet Vered cannot call out to her lover, or write to him or phone him, or tell him that his energies feed her. He is the suckling. Her nipples are as sore as Simha's. Her cunt hurts, the tissues newly torn. Making love is not easy, is not always natural or spontaneous. Vered is both hysterical and lethargic. She wishes for a full belly, implanted by him, to hold him. She wishes for horrible things, for the death of his wife, for disaster to strike him so that he needs only her. She is the mistress, the ultimate in social workers.

Now her lover is shaking Vered's shoulders.

"Show her," says a toothless old woman.

"More," says the owner of the grocery on that corner.

The lover pulls Vered's hair. It has been loosened from its traditional *coo-coo*, pony tail. He shakes her face with the fistful of hair until her eyes blur and teeth rattle. He lifts her with difficulty, for he is smaller than she, as are many of the men in The Land. He tries to carry her to his car. Hands reach out to help him, from street urchins, from angry women holding their kindergarten children with the other hand. Everyone is there to help the lover, but the police have blocked off the parade from aiding Vered.

The press runs. The lover must decide. If he is photographed he will lose votes. He will lose the religious vote but gain the macho vote if he allows himself to be photographed. His wife will leave him. Will Vered be able to get home from the office in time to prepare dinner and attend to his laundry? He covers his face with one hand. The other is pressing into her breasts, those wonderful globes, goblets. He remains—for the press, for the censuring from his party, for that bed of a body.

What of Vered? Never in her life so humiliated. Will her brother see her being photographed—her last blood relative (the unknown uncle having died an uncounted time ago) and will he desert her? Will her clients see this man dragging her off and have no faith in her? It is all the pogroms and rapes that Vered has heard about, all the abuses in Poland. She stops kicking and screaming and crying. She is limp. She has passed out of her body. Over the parade there is a shadow against the sun, a shadow of striped robe, rising and lowering like a flag over the group.

"Vered!" cry the women and march on.

Vered's body is not Vered. The nipples harden and point automatically. The breasts heave when squeezed. But the learner of languages, the older sister, the office manager has left the body with its clown face, streaks of mascara, smudged mouth, blush-on rouge.

The lover, amid cheers and even the clapping of the male reporters, carries home his bounty.

The women march under the belly of the real Vered.


Wayward is given six months' extension. The Ministry of Welfare has had a wonderful suggestion from the Ministry of Religion. Change the name. It is no longer the Home for

Jewish Wayward Girls. It is now the Home for Jewish Future Homemakers, although no one ever calls it that.

Contributions pour in, also stoves, washing machines, irons, sewing machines. The wayward girls look at the equipment, at the cookbooks, domestic machinery and count the months until they are drafted into the army.

# 5
## Ceremonies in Dirty Old Women

The fields surrounding the stone house are full of surprises: poppies, old cisterns, boilers and rusting hardware, tiny purple clover, small yellow flowers, oil cans with leaping gazelles and Arabic lettering. Every field was once a battlefield. Every memory was once history.

If the women travel on roadways, cows graze one side, shot-up tanks rust the other. If they pass galvanized trenches, a flower climbs out of a crack.

"Something is happening to me," says Gerda. "I am becoming a dirty old woman."

Gerda is fifty-four.

The winter sun is still so bright that it pales golden domes, darkens stained-glass reflections, turns the Jerusalem stone beige, causes the apertures painted in bright blue to flake. Even the people become short shadows of themselves.

So the women stay in the stone house, comfortably and uncomfortably.

The most irritating person in the room is Gerda. She would be the final statement, bottom paragraph, summary of the life around her. She, the only descendant of her family, still competes with that incinerated memory. Her father was a scientist. Gerda must be a mathematician, statistician, physicist and geneticist. Her mother was sturdy and athletic. Gerda is a walker, climber and runner.

If Antoinette publishes a two-volume study of *Shakespeare's Women*, a work on Shakespeare as feminist, then Gerda must publish a long article, "Diseases in Shakespeare," including senility in King Lear.

Joan from Manchester is working on a play. Gerda is full of plots. Mickey, named for Mihal, King David's mistreated wife, is suffering a divorce. Gerda is full of advice and legal knowledge. Hepzibah and Simha have a talmudic discussion. Gerda bones up the night before. Dahlia has a new song. Gerda would sing one, also, but she has permanently ruined her voice with smoking. To the wayward girls she nightly relates her own mischievous ways as a child.

On one matter Gerda does not compete—in love. She talks too much, gestures too violently, paces the floor, smokes, does everything but lie on a mattress and let love know her.

She dreams.

"I dreamt the covers were violently pulled from my bed."

"Who pulled them off?" asks Gloria.

"I couldn't tell; it was dark; some grunting animal—a bear."

"Uh-huh," says Gloria.

"It's not what you think."

Another night.

"I dreamt I wore curtains and veils, billows and sails," says Gerda, "and set out on a raft upon the sea. But the raft buckled and bolted."

"Uh-huh," says Gloria.

"You're sick."

On Shabbat brunch, chomping on radish slivers and cheese:

"I walked near a tomb, the rock swung away and a dark tunnel appeared. I entered with some apprehension, as you may well imagine, and I had reason to feel so, for the ground was somewhat spongy, like needles in the forest, only waving their own tiny sea life, and the walls felt like skin. I heard breathing in all its forms, sighs, snores, gasps, groans, pants. I was walking in a mouth, my feet sinking into the tongue."

"Uh-huh," says Gloria.

"That's the last thing I'll ever tell you."

Antoinette is quiet. She has her passions that flip between pages. When young she wept with Juliet, now with Cleopatra.

Antoinette once said to Terry, "Everything one has to know about one can find in a book."

"Not quite everything," said Terry.

"Name one thing."

"Experience," said Terry.

"... Name another."

"Passion."

Antoinette is passionate. She sits demurely, her knees pressed together, hands clasped, ankles close, skirt proper, blouse buttoned, hair combed, lipstick following contours too precisely.

Antoinette dreams also. She dreams of her knees being spread, hands separated, skirt lifted, blouse unbuttoned, hair disordered, lipstick spread.

Who does this to her? It is not clear. A man? A woman? Both? She is ashamed to ask for identification.

Shadows pursue her. She often has to drop a book in the middle, she is breathing so heavily. She has given up D. H. Lawrence, Henry Miller and other moderns. When the characters head for the mossy grass under the tree, or when they turn down the silken coverlet or push their flat-bottomed boat from shore and let it rock in a cove, Antoinette bends the page, intending to return. She rises and makes herself a sensible pot of tea, bringing the pot to the kettle, never the kettle to the pot, dressing the pot cozily, setting out hot water and hot milk, sugar lumps with silver tongs, small silver stirring spoon and delicate tea napkins.

What to do? The weather is chilly but Gerda and Antoinette feel spring in their crotch. Winter is upon Jerusalem, but the skies are blue and bulbuls sing in the trees.

Antoinette takes off for a semester break. She goes to Eilat in the Negev. She spends the morning with lotions and creams and appears with her large hat, bath towel, one-piece suit with skirt attached, flip-flops. One does not see the flesh-colored paint on finger- and toenails, the pink dab at mouth. One does not smell, near the sea, the perfume, lilac or violet. Her towel is striped in crimson, black, chartreuse, yolk yellow, but the bathing suit is a plastic material in navy blue or black.

Oh, Antoinette, where are you?

A dust storm rises on the beach, blowing off her hat,

wrinkling her towel, sending pebbles into the crevices of her body. She scurries to correct nature, with a shoe holding down one side of the towel, books weighting down the other side, pins in her hat and pebbles surreptitiously picked out.

If Antoinette goes to the films, she tries to take her students and she chatters with them. If she goes alone she exclaims, cries out once or twice, clucks sympathetically, groans in pain. During the scenes of caressing, slow pan shots over throat, breast, hip, Extreme Close-Up of opened mouth, Antoinette blinks rapidly to keep from weeping.

The women in the stone house know it is time for matchmaking.

But with whom? With each other would be so easy and convenient—Gerda and Antoinette a pair—Gerda lanky, strident, Antoinette soft, pinkish, the fields of science and literature entwined, as C. P. Snow had envisaged. Their ages are compatible, Gerda's fifty-four to Antoinette's more youthful fifty-two. Politically and religiously they are not so far apart. Geographically they are both in Rehavia, one of the wealthier sections of the city where foreign embassies are located. The women in the stone house will not have to enlarge their company at meals or holidays.

But Gerda and Antoinette are antipathetic to each other. Gerda is bored by chatty Antoinette. Antoinette's eyes glaze over Gerda's Germanic precision and long-winded explanations. Gerda strides when she walks. Antoinette trips along, and Gerda hates to wait. Gerda is prompt, the watch set several times during the day to the radio. Antoinette's watch became waterlogged in the sink, and she counts on her students to knock on her office door, escort her to class, and to tell her when the period is over.

The women in the stone house must look elsewhere. They open the door of the house. Who, what will wander in?

A young American wanders in. He is asking directions to the Armenian Quarter. And can he have a drink of cold water? He drinks his water, sipping it slowly. It makes his teeth ache. He looks at the ring of women.

"What have we here?" he asks.

They introduce themselves. He shakes hands all around but bends to kiss the hands of Antoinette and Gerda. Simha and Terry exchange excited glances.

"It looks like I've made my fortune," he says and settles back. "Tell me about yourselves, ladies."

There is a babel. Gloria tells about California, Tova about New York, Antoinette about London, Joan about Manchester, Gerda about Germany, Deedee about Ireland and Crete, Simha about Jerusalem, Terry about the political situation in The Land, Rina and Shula about Wayward.

"Tell us about you," says Gerda graciously.

"You make me think of the time when I was sixteen and in New York," says the young man.

Expectations and titters.

"I was then accosted by a lady of forty on a Sealy mattress in Bloomingdale's. I was a stock boy and she a saleswoman. She would entice me when no one was around, 'Come over to the house. My husband goes away a lot. Come to my place and we'll play Hide the Wienie.' She once pulled me down on the mattress and I said, 'You wouldn't be satisfied with me.' She said, 'Lots of women would rather be tickled to death than stabbed to death.'"

Quiet in the house of women. Only Gloria looks into his eyes.

"When I was seventeen and living in Massachusetts, it was New Year's Eve. I was at a bar and there was this neat old woman among the guys—most of us eighteen passing for twenty-one. She was dressed in a conservative gray suit. I stepped on her foot and she bellowed, 'Get off my fuckin' foot.' Then she turned and grabbed me—you know where—'That's for steppin' on my fuckin' foot.' That from a little old lady!

"When I was eighteen and living in Connecticut, I had to have a pre-employment physical. The woman checking my vital statistics was wearing a gown that was thigh-high. She lifted her leg and told me to look into her eye.

Then she leaned back so that I had to lean all over her to see her eye."

A book in Antoinette's lap clatters to the floor.

"When I was nineteen and lived in Rhode Island, I was visiting a friend of mine with a beautiful mother. 'Where's your mother?' I asked him. 'In the attic,' he said. 'Let's see what she's doing,' I suggested. He was disinterested so I went alone. There she was in the attic jerking off with a Coke bottle."

"Get out," says Terry.

The young American sets down his glass, lifts his pack, walks slowly to the door, looking back at the women.

"Fuck you all," he calls, "great and small."

Simha decides that they are not going about this properly.


FORGETTING FALSE SELF-IMAGES

Clearly, demons have possessed this boy who must speak so disrespectfully of the women of his youth, to the women he presently encounters.

"He is a demon," Simha declares.

"How do you know?" asks Terry.

"Because of his time of arrival, on the eve of Shabbat. God terminated creation, and demons were created at the moment when all creation arrested."

"He didn't look like a demon," says Gloria.

"A demon can assume human form. He can drink water. He might propagate. He might die."

"What kind of a demon?" asks Antoinette.

"An injurious spirit."

"Sometimes," says Mickey, "you cannot see them for they are incomplete. They have wings but no shadow."

Gloria and Tova laugh.

"I know this," insists Mickey. "I was sunning on the beach near Haifa. Whoosh! I raised my head. Wings passed that close over my head and flew upward again. They cast no shadow. There was no body or head. And it was not a bird."

The women shiver.

"I will tell what demons do to you," says Dahlia of Beer Sheva. "They clog the throat. They make the nose run, the chest tight. I always know before I go onstage if a demon has entered upon me."

Gloria and Deedee snicker.

"What do you know?" asks Mickey. "There's more, much more. Exhaustion in the knees comes from demons. My stockings tear; my feet smell because of them. I'm careful with my feet. I bathe them daily, I powder them, I go to the pedicurist—"

"All right," says Simha. "We must rid ourselves of demons. There is the proper and the improper way."

"What is the improper way?" asks Gloria.

"It is forbidden in Deuteronomy to use 'divination ... an enchanter, witch, a familiar, a practitioner of the Ob, a wizard or necromancer.' "

"What is proper?"

"Name magic and oil magic."

Simha is the princess of the oil. She is the giver of names. First she rubs baby oil on Hava, into her insteps, wrinkled, folded legs, back of knees, crotch, under the arms, in the folds of Hava's neck.

"I name you Life and Breath," says Simha to her baby.

The women disrobe. Gerda is naked with arms placed modestly. Antoinette leaves on her panties and bra.

Simha brings out the bottle of olive oil. She whispers an incantation.

"To the genie in the bottle?" asks Joan.

"I am allowed to whisper over the oil in the bottle but not in the hand," explains Simha, "for the oil has the curing power and not my human hand."

The oil does work wonders. The limbs and necks relax. Legs stop quivering. Hands lie quietly in laps or at the women's sides. Chests breathe regularly.

There is another part to Forgetting False Self-Images.

"That is the telling of demons," says Terry. "You tell of your demons and I will tell of mine."

They are relaxed enough to listen without shock or interruption.

"I am thirty-nine," says Terry. "I always looked to older men so that I could be the younger, the innocent, the dependent one. Not long ago a client returned to visit me, a boy I had helped from the time he was thirteen until he turned sixteen. The boy was in the army now, eighteen and beautiful. Still hardly any hair on him—smooth face, pleasant odor, soft frills of light brown on head and crotch."

The women gasp.

"But he bit his nails. 'Doodoo,' I said, 'why do you still bite your nails?' 'I am sometimes nervous, Terry,' he said. 'Doodoo,' I told him, 'I will cure you of your nervousness.'

"I did. To this day his nails are so long I have to remind him to trim them or he'll hurt me."

The women react differently. Antoinette and Gerda are solemn. Gloria snorts. Deedee smiles. Dahlia roars.

"Find me a Doodoo," says Mickey. "I'll know what to do with him!"

The women say nothing. Mickey's laughter is also anger. Her husband knew what to do with her. He beat her. Now he is telling the rabbis at the rabbinate, in the divorce court, that he will be peaceful. They extend his time with Mickey another three months. "Peace of the House," they call this time. They admonish Mickey to take him in so he can prove himself. She takes him in. He disproves himself. Still, the old rabbis pull on their beards, their eyebrows, on the curly hair of their wrists and give him another three month extension for "Peace of the House," and another three months and another—and extend Mickey's pain.

"Little kids turn me on," says Gloria. "I have to watch myself when I bathe them."

"Sss! Sss!" the women hiss her.

"I'm being perfectly honest with you," says Gloria. "I like to have virgins. I do. Men dig it. Why shouldn't I? It doesn't hurt them. They don't bleed all over and cry and make a mess. They either come or they don't."

Antoinette covers her ears.

"I enjoy being a teacher," Gloria insists, "the pride of evoking response, the teaching of the cub scout the cub position, the goat the butting position, the puppy the licking position."

"Stop her," says Gerda. "She's a demon."

If only the women would listen to Gerda.

"Demons," says Simha, "can be found around one's bed. If you sprinkle ashes around your bed, you may find the footprints of a cock."

The women roar.

"A chicken," corrects Simha. "A rooster."

"Yeah, yeah," says Tova.

"Do you know where demons live?" asks Mickey.

They do not.

"In toilets. I was always afraid in the army to use the latrine. In wells, rivers, in some of the deserted Arab villages, in Crusader castles, in old churches."

"Where don't they live?" asks Deedee.

Mickey is mean. "Where it's nice and clean and Jewish."

"You mean there are no Jewish demons, just Christian?"

Mickey is ashamed. "No, no. Sure they're Jewish. They have Jewish names."

"Morris," says Tova, "Sam. Tilly."

"Their Hebrew names," says Mickey, "are *ashmedai*, boss of the demons; *shedim*, night workers; *mazikim*, hurtful spirits—like the demon who came in tonight; and *ruhim*, wandering spirits."

"That's a relief," says Deedee.

She keeps them on their toes.

Mickey says, "I'll tell you more. Knots in the hair—you

know what causes them? Demons. They tangle, they make rats' nests. That's their dirty work."

Gerda pounds on the table. A vase of wildflowers jumps.

"I AM A DEMON."

Rina and Shula, the wayward girls, stare.

The women are finishing the second part of the ceremony.

"A young man came to work in my lab at the university," says Gerda. "I fell for him. God help me! He was so good, sweet, so helpful, just like a girl. He was neat, never spilled a drop, always cleaned up after himself and the others, kept the best lab reports, in a readable handwriting too. Always asked if I wanted him to stay later or if I needed to be escorted to my apartment, phoned if I had the sniffles, phoned if an article of mine were published to congratulate me. I waited each morning for his arrival from class. I exhaled each evening when he left the lab. I watched him eating lunch so daintily that I had no appetite to eat. I watched him at the drinking fountain and my throat went dry."

She paused.

"What happened?" asked Joan.

"I didn't want him to know," says Gerda. "I had to protect him from me, so I gave him a bad grade."

"What did he do?" asks Terry.

"He left me a note, the only message I ever received from him. It said, 'Forgive me.' "

The room is quiet. Shadows dance—Shabbat candles against the wall, three figures dancing in wax.

"You weren't the demon," says Simha.

Rina and Shula are round-eyed. Do their mothers think such thoughts? They are sure not. These must be people from outside of The Land.

Antoinette's eyes tear.

"She, too?" asks Rina of Shula.

Antoinette brings books to the girls and reads to them aloud before they fall asleep. No one has ever read to them before. No one has ever tucked them in and kissed them. If she is dirty, can they let her pull the coverlets to their chin, kiss their cheeks, smooth their hair?

"I had a boy in Shakespeare—"

"What do you mean, you had him?" asks Gloria.

"—a few years ago. He was a bit careless in handing in papers on time and in his documentation, but he had the deepest, loveliest voice. He had trained at the London School of Drama. I would often ask him to read aloud and sometimes asked young women from the class to accompany him.

"One day, without my asking him, the student read Antony's death speech, last scene, Act Four, looking at me all the while: 'I am dying, Egypt, dying; only/I here importune death awhile until/Of many thousand kisses the poor last/I lay upon thy lips.'

"I was following in my text and found myself rising and walking toward him. I was somewhat dazed. It was late afternoon, early evening and had become dim in the class. He was shadowy.

"'Come to me, Antoinette,' he whispered.

"I walked like a somnambulist toward him.

"'Has thou no care of me? Shall I abide in this dull world . . . ?' I said it by heart and then swooned into his arms. The class was startled. You don't act out in a reading, you know. He embraced me quickly and released me. We were applauded, and I made light of it, joining hands with him and bowing."

Antoinette sits sighing in her panties and bra.

"What happened, Antoinette?" Tova asks gently.

"To protect him, to protect me, I gave him, despite only fair papers and average exams, *metsuyan*, excellent."

"Did you hear from him?" asks Tova.

"Yes," whispers Antoinette. "I saw him in the corridors of the English building. He was haughty. 'I earned that grade, Antoinette.'"

The third part of the ceremony.

"I name you Antoinette and Forget," says Simha. "I name you Hardener of Nails, Terry. I name you Mission and Christian, Deedee. You are Guide and Ride, Gloria; Anger and Laughter, Mickey. Gerda, I name you Test and Rest."

The last part of the ceremony, housecleaning.

## RIDDING ONE'S HOUSE OF DEMONS

"Demons," says Simha, "my thoughts reduce yours to shadows, to thoughts from the unborn.

"Leave these women or my womb will swallow you, and you will never be expelled.

"Leave these women, or I will call you by such names that if you have shape it will shudder from you. If you have hair, nails and teeth, they will fall from you.

"Leave these pure women, or I will curse you the black of soot, the yellow of chamber pots, the brown of donkey dung and you will be known as the refuse of demons."

Simha opens all the windows of the stone house and the doors, the door to the toilet where demons lurk around leaky plumbing, the door to the washroom, to the bedroom. She opens all cupboards in case demons are crouched with the onions or flattened between the dishes or hidden in a cloudy glass.

A great cooling Shabbat wind comes blowing through. Gerda's tears blow away. Antoinette's shoulders chill and she puts on her clothes. Gloria's hungers are sated. Terry stops biting her nails. Mickey forgets, for a moment, that her husband is allowed to keep his key to the apartment. Rina and Shula doze until Antoinette says, "Children, come for your bedtime story."

Terry and Simha are alone in the house. They pour wine and toast each other.

# 6
# Giants and Dwarfs

The eve of every Shabbat Simha plans a variation. She walks to a different hill to watch the sun setting. She follows a shepherd and the sound of sheep bells. She wanders into the religious quarter, the Hundred Gates, to see the Hasidim with their red fox hats welcoming the bride of Sabbath.

Simha is not a bride, but she is Shabbat. She sits in her room and reads a new psalm and explicates it line by line. She will take a new man unto her, for it is a *mitzvah*, a commandment and good deed, to make love on Friday night. She will welcome her women friends to her festive table.

All over the city men are at the bathhouse and women are shopping and cooking. The women board the buses carrying plastic baskets filled with parsley, dill, potatoes, barley, eggs and chickens whose heads stare upside down at the passengers.

Simha is cooking carrot tsimmes. A *tsimmes* is an event, an occasion. Simha slices carrots, browns them in butter, for the meal is dairy, cooks them in a syrup of one cup sugar to one cup water. Simha adds white raisins, pitted prunes, dried dates, figs. When one eats orange of carrot, yellow raisin, blackish brown prune, light brown fig, one forgets that it is not a complete meal.

Simha's roommate, Terry, is in Tel Aviv for the night. Simha has to decide with whom to share the Shabbat. Her kibbutz lover is too far away to be reached spontaneously—for a festivity, an announcement, a telling of the cleverness of their daughter, or even for urgings of the body.

Whom should she ask? She decides to ask the woman with whom she feels uncomfortable, the woman not from The Land, but from another, of different coloring, upbringing, the least mystical of her friends: Gloria.

Gloria arrives laughing and snorting. Simha has a revelation. Gloria is nervous. Therefore, Simha becomes calm.

Gloria has brought beautiful candles.

Simha puts on a shawl, a paisley shawl that her grandmother left to her. Simha covers her head.

"Lady of the flame," says Simha over the candles, "of the spirit and the smoke, I, Simha—"

"I, Gloria—"

"We are ready to light candles in honor of the Shabbat. Oh, my Lady, Bride, thus it is written that You have called the Sabbath a delight. . . . Melting, changing lady of the candles, melt among us, dwell within us."

Gloria's ways are delicate. Simha is surprised and chides

herself for having withheld love. Gloria lifts little Hava, who immediately begins searching for the breast.

"Lady of the Sabbath," says Gloria, "Creature of flame, bless me for I am alone, without parents and without offspring, no one to bless me, no one to caress me, no one to mourn after me. Lady, let it be that on this night I, too, become a bride. I, too, become a family."

Gloria and Simha kiss Hava. She smiles, the silly, lovely smile of unfocused eyes and focused mouth.

"Bride of the night," says Gloria, "keep Hava far from shame and grief."

Simha is even beginning to love Gloria. Thus it is with ceremony. The bride may not love the groom before, but she will after; the world is old before the Sabbath and newborn after. Hava's nappy is wet and warm.

Simha hurries. Soon Hava will wail.

"Let there be peace, light and happiness in our dwelling," she rushes. "In Thy light do we see light."

Hava is wailing. Simha does not like to nurse and eat at the same time. She nurses and Gloria eats—almost all of the carrot tsimmes. Simha watches carefully how Gloria goes back again and again to the serving dish, past the half mark, the two-thirds.

Can a hostess complain? She is descended from the culture of Sara and Avraham and their tent. This is the culture of hospitality to all the nomadic.

"You shit!" yells Simha, and puts her cloth napkin over the remaining tsimmes.

Gloria shrugs, then lies on the Arab rug.

"Is there cheese?" she asks.

There is, Camembert.

Gloria brings out a platter of biscuits and Camembert. She cuts slices of the soft cheese and puts a slice on each cracker until the cheese is neatly distributed in a wheel around the plate. Gloria eats one spoke, two, half the wheel, two-thirds of the wheel.

"You crap!" yells Simha.

Hava loses the nipple and begins to cry.

"Jesus!" says Gloria and she means it.

She may have been converted but she never lost her feeling for Jesus. There is no one here to compare him with—a lady of a melting candle, a father of the universe, a host of hosts? Compared to a Robert Redford-Jesus of blue eyes and golden beard, tall and gentle-handed. He does not have the Persian lamb curls on head and chest like these chunky Israelis. Jesus speaks in an English accent or Western drawl. He is a performer of good deeds, riding into the sunset.

"Who is that stranger?"

"That's Jesus."

Why did Gloria divorce Him?

"What's there to do?" asks Gloria.

"Let's sing," says Simha.

"I don't know those songs," says Gloria.

Simha is beginning to relax. Hava is across her lap, being burped. Simha is eating with her fingers, a carrot, a sticky raisin, a clump of prune or date.

"I feel wonderful when I pray," says Simha. "I pray for everything."

"Like what?" yawns Gloria.

"You're supposed to pray on eating fruit which grows on trees, on eating fruit which grows on the ground, on eating meat, fish, eggs, cheese."

"I know that," says Gloria.

Why did she come here to this dark, damp stone house with Simha so cheap she's even saving on lighting the naphtha heater?

"I pray after I smell fragrant woods or barks or odorous plants or odorous fruits or fragrant spices or fragrant oils."

Gloria thinks Simha does not use them very often from the smell of Simha's body.

"On seeing lightning, falling stars, lofty mountains and great deserts."

Hava is sleeping. Her nappy is malodorous.

"On hearing thunder, at the sight of the sea, on seeing beautiful trees or animals, even rainbows."

"Terrific," says Gloria.

"For everything," says Simha. "It's so wonderful. There's a prayer on seeing a sage."

"How about for a dumb guy?"

"No, but there's a prayer for someone strangely formed like a giant or a dwarf."

Gloria sits up abruptly.

"Do you know a giant or a dwarf?" she asks Simha. "Did you ever have to use such a prayer?"

"No."

"I have," says Gloria. "I could have used that prayer."

"Where?"

"In California, two summers ago. I was told by my Reform rabbi that I had to go for further instruction to Conversion Camp for six weeks. He would get me a scholarship. I put my studio apartment up for sublet. First I put an ad in the Temple news. Nobody. The suburban paper. Nothing. The *Los Angeles Times*. Everybody. I just had to pick. I chose someone with a deep, serious voice. I felt he could pay the rent. He had to be a radio announcer or a business executive here briefly. I made an appointment. In the meantime, I had to decide what to take for Conversion Camp—bathing suit and shorts or back-to-school dresses? Would there be dancing or should I bring my glasses, pencil case and notebook? Halter-top dresses or prayerful clothes? I had this on my mind when the bell rang. Two men, a very fat, six-foot-four man and a very small five-foot man.

"The small one asked, 'Gloria?' He had the deep voice.

" 'Yes.'

"They both came in, carrying their luggage.

" 'Wait,' I said, 'nothing's been settled.' They pushed me aside.

" 'This will do,' said the little one.

" 'Yes,' said the big fellow in his tenor voice.

" 'We'll take it now,' said the little one.

" 'I'm not ready to leave yet,' I said.

" 'You are,' they said.

"I decided I was.

" 'Six weeks in advance and two weeks' security,' I reminded them.

"They acted as if that were a big surprise and not in the ad.

" 'That's not very trusting, Gloria,' said the little guy. 'We'll give you the six weeks. Here's my card. If you find a thing wrong, we'll make restitution. Maybe it will be more than two-weeks' advance. Maybe a month's.'

"That wasn't very comforting.

" 'Sorry,' I said. 'It's not a deal.'

" 'Harry,' said the little one, and nodded at the closet.

"Harry opened the closet and pulled my clothes from the hangers. He looked for a suitcase. I wouldn't tell him where it was, so he stuffed my clothes and shoes into paper bags.

" 'That's it,' said the small fellow.

"I began to cry. How can you deal with freaks? And, in this world, I'm less freaky than some.

"The little one said, 'I hate sentimentalism.'

"Then he and Harry threw my bags of clothing out of the studio apartment. When they came toward me I decided to just leave with the grocery bags. Who knows what they intended?

" 'Where's the key?' Harry asked.

"I had thought to get out without leaving the key. The little one came to my chin, reached out two hands, pulled on my nipples, leaning backward as he pulled.

" 'On the hook over the sink,' I cried. 'In six weeks, I'll be back.'

"The door slammed."

Simha is round-eyed. Hava is snoring, droplets of milk wetting her mother's skirt.

"What happened in six weeks?"

"I was afraid. I called my landlady to meet me there with her key. She knocked. No one answered. She turned the key in the lock. There was the apartment, clean but freaky. They had painted it black and put stars on the ceiling, thumbtacks with phosphorescent paint. The floor was sanded and waxed, the windows washed, fresh sheets on the bed, my key over the sink."

"My God!" says Simha.

"The landlady looked around. 'They've improved the value of the property,' she said and increased my rental."

"Is that it?" asks Simha.

Why should a tale end? Why should a good book conclude?

"Yes," says Gloria. "They never bothered me again."

"What did you do in Conversion Camp?"

"I forgot."

Gloria is cross. Too long in one room.

"Let's go for a walk," says Gloria.

"Is it damp outdoors?"

It is chilly but clear. Simha dresses Hava in layers, undershirt, nappies, nightgown, sweater, bunting, blanket. She herself takes only the paisley shawl. Simha is always overheated and suffers in the summer.

They go into the night. Their steps lead downward through shuttered shops. Their shoes echo on cobblestone. Few people walk at night in the Old City. They come, before they anticipate, to the remains of the outer Temple Wall. The stones are warmly lit and textured. The Wall reduces Simha and Gloria. The Wall is a giant and they the dwarfs.

"Ah!" they say.

Gloria and Simha cover their heads and walk to the Wall. Hava stirs. Simha takes off her paisley shawl to cover Hava.

"Cover your head!" calls out a woman, a sleepy member of the Religious Police.

Simha continues to walk toward the Wall.

"Wait!" calls the woman. She has some *shmata*, an old rag, for Simha to put over her head.

"How do I know if it's clean?" asks Simha.

"How do I know if you're clean?" asks the Religious Policewoman.

Simha turns from her and gathers a prayer book.

"Blasphemer!" shouts the policewoman, as Simha prays to the Wall, says the prayer one says upon seeing large mountains.

She pulls on Simha, tugs at her elbow. Simha's elbow shoots out at the woman's eye.

The woman covers her eye, "Prostitute! Goya!"

Simha is finished praying and Gloria is still at the Wall whispering into the stones, perhaps prayers she learned at Conversion Camp.

There is singing and shouting and great laughter. Simha looks over the barrier separating the men's side from the women's side, an ugly plastic *mehitzah*, division, stuck in the courtyard in front of the Wall. It happened suddenly one night after the Wall was liberated. No one has liberated it since.

A yeshiva is dancing in golden robes. All of the members, young and old, are dancing facing the stones so as not to turn their backs to the Wall. It is a lineup of linked arms, beards, jiggling side curls.

Simha knows the song they are singing. Her heart lightens, her voice rises in song. She does not notice that the Religious Policewoman has thrown the shmata over her head.

The dancing men stop.

"WHO IS SINGING?" thunders their rabbi. "It is forbidden for a woman's voice to be raised in song."

Simha sings the louder, all of her favorite Shabbat songs, "Leha Dodi," "Shalom Aleihem," all the tunes. The men begin to sing to drown her out. She can raise her voice louder than duets, trios, quartets, quintets, crowds, until the Religious Policewoman begins to pull Simha's hair.

"It is forbidden to distract the men," says the policewoman.

Simha is holding on to the mehitzah. Gloria joins her. Gloria does not know the songs, but she knows how to join in anger.

The rabbi shakes his finger at them; yet, at the same time, he is not allowed to look upon them, so he protects his eyes with one hand and gestures menacingly with the other.

"I am the bride," says Simha. "I am Shabbat. I take you to bed with me in white coverlets. I feed you from my table. You would know me and yet you pretend not to see me. But I see you. I stare at all of you."

The men shrink back.

"The Evil Eye!" they scream.

Simha shakes the mehitzah until it rattles and the chains holding the separate partitions together clang. Gloria shakes it with her. The men run to hold it tight. Simha rocks back and forth shaking that which separates her from the side with the Torah, with the bar mitzvot, with the dancing and the singing, two-thirds of the courtyard—like Gloria's eating of her Shabbat food. They want more than their share, those on the other side of the partition. They want the tsimmes, the food, the event, but only they can participate in it.

Simha stops abruptly, so that the policewoman falls backward and Gloria is left to rock the partition alone. Simha puts her shawl over her head and stretches out her hand to the men.

"Blessed art thou," she intones, "who varies the forms of thy creatures."

She gives the prayer one recites on seeing giants and dwarfs.

The rabbi gathers his disciples. Their robes are badly in need of cleaning, it is now clear. Their fur hats are askew.

Some are really too young for such elaborate costumes which hang from them. Some are too fat and their wrists show at the cuffs. Some are full of acne and blackheads and even the beards, mustaches, side curls don't cover the noses and foreheads.

The court is cleared. The policewoman goes back to her booth. The bluish green shmata lies on the court stones. Simha and Gloria hold hands as they walk back through the deserted Old City.

Near the Wall a soldier passes them and calls out. His Uzzi machine gun is reflected in the city's lighting of historic sites.

# 7
# The Feeding of Demons

Hepzibah and Terry are in the North. Hepzibah lives in Haifa. It took her a long time to bring the women into her life. Now she is bringing Terry into her home.

Terry is in Haifa conferring with the mayor and the welfare superintendent of the North. Hepzibah is shocked by the subject of the conference: the high rate of illegitimate pregnancies among the young girls of the religious, poorer communities. Only the girls, their parents, their boyfriends and the street workers are aware of this. The communities will not admit it, and the religion rejects it.

Hepzibah is always dependably cool. Today is different. Hepzibah is trying a new wardrobe: a brightly colored chiffon head scarf, frivolous shoes, transparent stockings, a long skirt with a floral pattern, a less than opaque blouse, earrings, and nail polish. And she is trying her husband with her first private friend.

There is activity in the kitchen, the kitchen that comes equipped in pairs: a milk sink and a meat sink, two sets of gas burners, two small ovens. But, in this perfectly equipped kitchen, everything is going wrong. The meal is to be a full Israeli lunch of chicken soup, chicken, egg pastina, grated carrots, grated red cabbage, and a cake made without dairy products. The chicken is dry, the soup greasy, the egg pastina pebbly, the carrots and cabbage watery, the cake both flat and soggy. Hepzibah's eyes also begin to water.

Terry enters the house after her meeting. She passes under the plaque above the entrance: You are Entering a Pious Home. Conduct Yourself in a Seemly Manner.

Everything is seemly. The view is perfect, the house situated halfway up the Carmel mountain overlooking the harbor. The children of the house are properly fulfilling their duties, two sons in the army and an obedient youngest daughter at home.

But the meal and the youngest daughter are in rebellion. Hepzibah has to request the daughter's help several times. To each request there is no reply as the girl lingers in her bedroom.

The husband, a teacher of military science, appears. He removes his hat and within it is another hat, his yarmulke. He looks at Terry.

"How do people tell if you're a man or woman in those pants? And with boy's hair? Did you never think of marrying? How do you fulfill yourself? Do you think there is really such a science as social science? Can you not see it is a false science, unlike chemistry and physics? Do you really think you can change people by giving them things? Do you think you know my wife away from her life? Do you realize you are dooming your race to extinction by not marrying and procreating? If everyone were like you, the Muslims and Christians would overrun The Land."

Terry, on her part, has been curious about meeting Hepzibah's husband. She wonders if she met him before in a story by Hepzibah.

Every Sunday, the first workday of the week, Hepzibah has made the trip down from Haifa to Jerusalem to spend a night with her mother. The mother refuses to move because her late husband's grave lies on the Mount of Olives. It had been desecrated by the Jordanians, but, with the reunification of the city, the mother found a bit of tomb standing. She goes regularly to address her glad tidings and complaints to this broken tooth.

Hepzibah visits the mother. They cook together. It is the mother's only real meal of the week. It is Hepzibah's only time to be a daughter. The mother strokes Hepzibah's cheek. Hepzibah sits at her mother's knee. About seven in the evening the mother begins to doze.

It was at such a time a year ago that Hepzibah grew weary of sitting there in the dusk. She heard about the Writer's House in the Old City, where adult education courses were taught.

Hepzibah, with her false fringe of bangs under her heavy scarf, her long-sleeved blouse, her opaque stockings, walking shoes, and sweet vacuous smile, arrived at the class.

"Sit down," said the professor.

Hepzibah listened to the writing of the other students. The men wrote of their coming to The Land, of their times in the camps in Europe, in the army camp in this land, of their work, of wars fought and comrades lost. The women wrote of their families, their daily lives and their memories of parents.

But not Hepzibah.

"Who is H.?" asked the professor the next week.

Hepzibah half-raised her arm. The teacher did not look at her when he returned her paper. "You are a writer," was the only comment on her story.

The class brought out a small magazine, *Friends in the Writer's House.* Terry picked up the magazine and read quickly past the war stories, always the same, and the camp stories, also the same horror, until she came to the only unsigned story: H. Terry read with excitement then took the magazine home to Simha and the women who visited the stone house.

## H.'S STORY

A young bride marries a much respected, much older groom. He is a learned scholar and rabbi, while she, twenty-five years his junior, has but finished girls' religious-training school.

The first night the bride awaits her groom. She undresses. Her hair has been shorn. She lies on fine cotton sheets monogrammed with her new name. A slight breeze coming through the window stirs the sheets.

Still the scholar has not come to the bridal room.

The bride nibbles her nails and knuckles. The scholar is deep within his texts.

The bride develops acute hearing, awaiting his footsteps. She hears only the grunting of mating dogs, the scream of cats in the courtyard. She dozes and dreams of plants opening and closing, of birds mating in midair.

She awakens frightened. The bed is uneven. She is sure there is someone under the bed, perhaps demons, demons who had surrounded the bridal canopy with the temporary faces of relatives. She is unable to look under the bed but feels them rolling upon each other. She is too frightened to open her clothes closets for she knows they will tumble out.

Long hours later the groom comes to the room. He smells of tobacco. His shoes are dropped heavily on the floor. He takes off his suspenders and drops his pants. He has no underwear; under his shirt he wears *tzitzit*, the fringed vest. His bottom is bony, his knees knobby, his fingers heavy.

Everything is a pinch that comes near his hands, a blow that presses against his knees, a scratch that rubs against the long toenails. He falls asleep immediately, while the young bride's eyes remain open and her ears catch the tittering of demons.

Terry wrote a fan letter to H., care of the magazine. She received a brief, formal thank-you in reply. Again Terry wrote and invited H. to visit. One day there was a knock at the blue door of the stone house.

"You are not far from my class," said H.

H. is smiling, smiling and spilling the soup and apologizing.

Her husband says, "Are you nervous before your friend? What kind of friendship is it that makes you nervous?"

Hepzibah serves the meat too soon, while they're eating the soup, and forgets the salad. She rises and knocks over a bottle of wine. The linen tablecloth is stained. Hepzibah lowers her head to mop it up, still smiling.

Terry is staring at Hepzibah's daughter. The daughter has pushed the food away.

"Eat," says her father. "Who'll want a skinny bride?"

The father himself is skinny, his food encapsulated in the belly.

"Ēma," Rahel says to Hepzibah, "why do you wear that

thin scarf, those stockings, that gaudy skirt? It is immoral. Look at my stockings."

Her ēma doesn't have to look. She knows about the stockings. She bought them for Rahel, the opacity recommended by the religious girls' school.

Rahel has long, curly hair. She will not have to shear it off until after her marriage. Yet Rahel is brushing it back from her forehead, knotting it, twisting it, pulling on it, picking imaginary strands of hair from her chicken soup.

"This hair, ēma," says Rahel, "is too heavy. It binds me. It hurts my neck to carry it, and it falls out on everything."

Her father says, "Don't draw attention to your physical attributes."

Terry looks at Rahel. Rahel is a fog behind the steaming chicken soup. Her light brown hair begins to dissolve in the brownish wallpaper behind her. Her body is concave, the little breasts facing downward toward her lap.

"Why not?" says Terry. "Why not draw attention to your physical attributes?"

"Ah hah!" says the husband. He uses carrot stick and celery stick as foils in his attack upon Terry. "That's it exactly. Each reference to the body erases a reference to the spirit. The body is ephemeral, the spirit everlasting. That hair on my daughter's head will fall out, her teeth decay, her body lose its suppleness. . . ."

Rahel gives a cry and falls forward, knocking against the gold-rimmed soup bowl.

"See. She already overdramatizes," says her father. "You will get no dessert until you finish your other courses."

Rahel is not thinking of dessert. Her mouth is open, gulping.

Hepzibah rises in alarm to clasp Rahel's shoulders.

"What can it be?" asks Hepzibah.

"She is too sensitive," says the father, "like Hepzibah. That's why women are forbidden to join a minyan or handle the Torah."

"Rahel," says Hepzibah, "let me help you to your bedroom."

"Don't touch me!" cries Rahel, lifting her head from the table. There is grease on her hair. Her cheek is hot from the heat of the bowl. "Not with those painted fingernails. Don't lean against me with that transparent blouse—"

*"Motek,* sweet one," begs Hepzibah, blushing deeply. Her smile trembles.

Rahel flings herself into her room. The husband forbids his wife to join the daughter.

Hepzibah clears the table and Terry begins carrying in dishes.

"Don't shame me, Terry," says Hepzibah. "You're my guest. Let me clear."

Terry dismissed must rejoin the husband.

He is preparing for her. He begins to smoke his pipe without asking her permission. Terry opens the front door.

"Are you hot?" asks the husband.

"No. I dislike the smell of tobacco."

"There is much in this life one dislikes and that one must get used to. Accommodate yourself to the world around you."

Terry is wearying of this man and his usual argument.

"Let the world accommodate itself to me," says Terry.

"Are you something special?" The man is amused.

"Yes," says Terry.

"You suffer from swollen pride, also, one of the more grievous sins."

"So do you or you would not have to terrorize your wife and daughter."

"Do I look like a dictator? Let me tell you something, young lady. I could have been a führer, but I chose to be a scholar, teacher, and family man."

Terry is bored, but not her host. He has only begun his life's story.

"I helped found The Land. I rid it of the English vermin."

Terry inhales.

"I was a member of the terrorist gangs. Those who were hanged in the prison at Acre were my comrades."

His bearing is soldierly.

"I was a courier," he says, "who rose in the ranks to the highest position. At every cost my identity was kept secret. When the English arrested the leaders of The Land on Black Shabbat, no one knew I was one of them. To the Mandate I was a series of names, a platoon of people."

He laughs shortly.

Hepzibah returns from the kitchen. Her husband's tale continues to fascinate her.

"When the State was declared, I was on the ship landing at Tel Aviv. I knew what the State needed. My ship was full of ammunition and brave heroes who would unify The Land. But that bastard ordered the Haganah to fire upon us. Ben Gurion sank our ship with its ammunition. Ben Gurion caused the deaths of my brave comrades. I, of course, escaped. They could never afford to lose me. I, who had to live underground during the Mandate, now had to live underground those first years of the State. And now in my house, I am insulted and declared an enemy."

Hepzibah backs away from conflict, into the kitchen.

"It's time for me to leave," says Terry.

She is regretful. She had hoped to spend the night here. It is inconvenient for her to journey to Jerusalem at this hour.

"You had no business coming," says her host, "and stirring up trouble."

He expects her to comfort him, this man deposed of his state and setting up his kingdom in the house. She cannot comfort him, though it be an act of mercy.

Nor can she help him understand her. Should she tell him of her paining heart, worries, fear that she will be called upon by the women one last time and not have the strength to respond? He would swell as she shrank.

"What are you?" asks the teacher. "An independent woman? You know what an independent woman needs? To be squeezed between someone's legs. I could do it—anyone could do it—your independence would be squeezed out of you."

Hepzibah appears in the doorway and puts her finger across her lips signaling to Terry. Rahel stares from her bedroom door.

"You couldn't do it," says Terry, "and that's why you squeeze the life out of everyone around you!"

Hepzibah starts forward. The military scientist raises his hand to strike.

"And that's why you have to command ships of ammunition. You have little of your own."

He does strike. Rahel begins to sob and runs to the toilet room. Dry heavings for she ate nothing.

Terry, in shock, prepares to leave. No one notices. Hepzibah is holding Rahel's head; the father is wetting towels with cold water.

"She's like this night after night," says the father. "She eats nothing and tries to empty her poor stomach even more."

Why is he confiding to Terry, his opponent? Because he only respects his opponents. In his dreams he is having a love affair with Ben Gurion.

Rahel is helped to bed. Terry stands with her raincoat and briefcase. The meeting at the mayor's office was also stormy. The day is full of weather. The day is endless.

Hepzibah has retired into her bedroom. The father knocks softly, opens the door and closes it behind him.

Terry is uncertain what to do. Rahel is cringing on the bed.

"Have you *shepat*, the flu, Rahel?"

Scornfully, "*Lŏ*." No.

"What have you, Rahel?"

There is a whisper. Terry cannot hear. She goes closer.

"A baby."

Terry stiffens. "How do you know? You don't bleed?"

"*Lõ.*"

"Nausea?"

"*Ken.*" Yes.

"Has a doctor examined you?"

"*Lõ.*"

Terry asks the question she often has to ask of her wayward girls.

"Do you know who impregnated you?"

Rahel presses her face into the pillow and nods.

"Do you want to tell me?"

"*Avi,*" whispers Rahel. "My father."

Terry trembles. She sometimes hears this answer. But does not expect it in this house. Should she ask further or leave?

Terry prepares again to depart.

"Don't leave!" cries Rahel. "He's everywhere with me, on the school bus he sits next to me. His knees rub mine. In school he is there and he stares at me. He wants me. Everything wants me. In the summer, at the beach, the water wants me."

Terry slowly exhales, and lowers herself to the bed.

*"In my reading there are hands grabbing me into the book. Why else would I always have to stay and finish until the last page—even if I don't want to? Why do I read all night? Why do I dream of him?"*

*Oi v'voi*, trouble and pain, chaos and void, and out of this created God the heavens and The Land. And this Land was created with trouble within and without its borders. And, also, created God laughter and lunacy.

"I can't eat," says Rahel. "If I eat, the baby will be forced out of the belly. If I defecate, I'll lose the baby. So I won't do either."

"Rahel, do you know what it is to be impregnated?"

Rahel looks vague.

"Nothing can enter you, Rahel," says Terry, "without your knowledge. No dream, no seat partner."

Rahel's chest begins to heave again. Information can be more easily dismissed than fear.

Terry sighs. Social work. Why didn't she practice the piano harder? Why didn't she have more pleasure at the Rubiner Academy with her dance?

Forget it.

Terry goes into the kitchen and comes back with chicken left on a dish and with a glass of wine.

Rahel makes gagging sounds.

"It's for the child," says Terry.

She places the food and wine at the foot of the bed.

"Rahel's child, sleep and awaken. Let the light roll away before the darkness, and the dark before the light."

Rahel smiles and waits for more. Terry tries. If only she were Simha.

"Wine to blood, meat to bone. Eat with us, or eat alone."

There is a sound, not of the sphincter muscles, not a grumbling of the stomach, but a popping.

Terry wonders. Was it anorexia? Gas pains?

Rahel sits up and grins, a bright child's grin. "The baby's gone."

Rahel's hair curls around her sweet forehead. Her hands separate the white meat from the chicken breast. She nibbles. She wets her lips with the wine. She lies back and is soon asleep.

Terry has a sharp longing for her family in Jerusalem, Simha and Hava. It is a sensible family, no incestuous dreams, no shouting and soothing. Terry's is an ideal home.

Hepzibah and her husband are at Rahel's door. Hepzibah is smiling.

"Shalom, Terry. It was such a pleasure having you here at last."

The husband shakes Terry's hand.

"A pleasure," he says.

What is this? H. cannot dwell in this house!

Hepzibah steps outside of the door.

"Terry," she says. "We thank you, Rahel and I. We are both fiction writers until we can change circumstances."

H. does live there.


Haifa is beautiful. The bus follows the curve of the mountain, down through the lights of the valley. At the bus station Terry boards for Jerusalem. The driver rides along the Mediterranean past sunset and into darkness on his way to the City of Cities.

# 8
# Mourning for Vered

Vered's brother looks at the sea. He is drinking beer in Jaffa, watching the sunset. He wants to eat something but everything in this restaurant with a view is too expensive. He drinks a Maccabee. He drinks another. His hurt hand relaxes on the slate table. He fills the ashtray with butts.

"Yonah sailed from here," he says. "How did he do it, the clever fellow? He invented the fish. It was a ruse to leave The Land."

Who could afford to leave? People with relatives outside

of The Land. He had no one, parents dead in Poland, a well-to-do uncle who ignored his niece and nephew when they were children and died before they became adults.

He orders more beer and begins to mumble. Gray waves hit against the breakers. One small fishing boat returns to its moorings. The sky is vast, a lighter gray than the sea, with slashes of pink rays. Vered's brother stares at the table.

"I'll go to Nineveh," he cries out. "I'll go to Tarshish. I'll go anywhere."

A priest from the Catholic church emerges from the door hoping to find a passing Catholic or any interested tourist. He speaks only French and says to passersby: "Dieu vous bénisse."

"No, thank you," says Vered's brother.

"A storm arose," says Vered's brother, "and the sailors said to Yonah, 'What is thine occupation? . . . what is thy country? and of what people art thou?' And Yonah said, 'I am a Hebrew, and I fear the Lord . . . who made the sea and the dry land.' "

Vered's brother has a dangerous trait. He becomes maudlin. He is a hero who can hold off tanks, can take days of strafing and bombing, can withstand the loss of his entire battalion. But he is a weeper.

"He made the sea and the dry land and wars and the bloody earth. He made sisters who are whores. He made orphans. He made men alone and afraid in the belly of this fucking world."

The waiter, with his white dish-towel apron, takes away the empty Maccabees.

"More?"

Sure he wants more, but he has no more cash. Just enough for the bus. He will charge groceries until his stipend comes from the government. The corner grocer calls him The Soldier, The Hero. When the sale is completed, the grocer says, "All honor to you."

Vered's brother buys biscuits and cheese, tomatoes and long cucumbers, dried fish and fish spread, beer, wine, fruit. When the bill totals more than a few hundred lira, the shop owner turns the slip so Vered's brother can see the total. Nothing is said between them.

Above the kitchen counter Vered's brother has photographs, brown photos of his mother and father, photos of himself and Vered, he a little boy and Vered embracing him, he in the uniform of his youth movement, he in the children's village, in a school play wearing the crown of Solomon, in his uniform, a photo of his tank, snapshots at the sea with Vered. In the couch area of his room are several photographs of Vered with her light eyes, turned-up nose, Polish wide cheeks, bosomy, full figure. All the pictures of Vered have been taken down from the wall and are piled on the couch.

Vered's brother sits next to them. His hand is shaking, his stomach sore from the beer. There is little that eases his pain. He cannot do the assignment for class. He cannot concentrate on the reading and the report is impossible for him.

For weeks Vered either is not at her home or, when he does reach her, she's distracted. His classmates saw her photo in the newspaper.

"Some piece," they told him.

She is being carried under the arm of the Knesset member like a long loaf of French bread.

Vered's brother tries writing a letter to the Parliamentarian care of Knesset but it is too difficult for him. He thinks of asking to speak to him when he phones Vered, but he's too shy.

Vered's brother is a quiet fellow. No teacher ever had to tell him, "*Shekit!*" Quiet! He enjoys sitting next to Vered at concerts or at the Habima Theater in Tel Aviv, or on a towel at the beach. He does not need to open his mouth. Vered has understood without his having to say.

Until now.

The hazel eyes, large, expressive, curly-lashed eyes of Vered's brother overfill with tears onto the photos of Vered, wrinkling the paper, spreading the dust.

Oh, Vered, his lost sister! His duty is clear.

The brother cleans his small room, weeping as he does. He looks in his drawer for a dress shirt. He finds an old tie and his yarmulke. He digs into a trunk for a jacket. He wipes his shoes with a cloth from the bathroom.

He has washed his face and hands and sprinkles water on his hair to comb it smooth. It leaps back. He dunks his head under the faucet and brushes it. The hair is flat and wet but greasy.

He puts on the *tallith*, prayer shawl, that Vered bought for his communal bar mitzvah in the agricultural village. He has his own *sedur*, prayer book. He is lovely to behold.

"She is unable to say it for herself, Lord," he says, and begins with the portion of the Hour upon Leaving the Spirit. There are two prayers to be repeated three times and one to be said seven times. He rends the right lapel of an old jacket and whispers blessings to the Judge of Truth.

Vered's brother removes his shoes, goes into the bathroom to cover his only mirror, takes the pillow from his armchair.

"As for man, his days are as grass; as the flower of the field, so he flourishes. For the wind passes over it, and it is gone."

Prayer brings back memory. A few Rosh Hashanahs ago he and Vered went to the Wall on the first day, and to the beach on the second. It was warm and they both longed for sun. Their six-day work and school week exhausted them. There they were at the beach of Natanya, floating on rubber animals that they had borrowed from children. They heard calls, whirling down from the embankment above them. It was an Orthodox family turning their pockets inside-out, emptying them of sins. The sins were hurled upon the sacrilegious bathers. The following year the war struck.

Vered's brother finds a handkerchief that Vered had given him. He blows his nose.

"I will not abandon your soul to the grave," he promises.

But she has to be judged: "All thy deeds are written in the book."

He tries to light a match, those Israeli matches that blow out as they're being lit. Her photos burn with difficulty.

"May she come to her place in peace."

For a week no one sees Vered's brother. His professors have Vered's number and one concerned fellow calls to inform her that the brother has missed an important test.

"Then he must be ill," says Vered.

Vered goes to his little room, climbing six winding flights of stairs. The stairs adjoin an elevator that has not worked in years. The landlord no longer promises. There is an extra key in the hall lantern case, outside of the apartment.

The room is dark. Vered clicks the entrance light. On a cushionless chair sits her brother, eyes open, staring, lips cracked and tongue parched. He is strangely dressed in crumpled but formal wear. There are ashes at his feet, ashes on his forehead and his jacket is rent.

"My brother!" she screams.

He sees her but does not see her.

His lips open with difficulty.

"You are dead to me," he says hoarsely.

"Why?" whispers Vered.

"You have shamed us both beyond bearing."

"My darling!" says Vered. "My only darling, my blood, my past, my dearest life."

He is deaf to her.

She makes a little vegetable soup from withered vegetables in the refrigerator and brings him a bowl.

He is blind to her.

She cleans away the ashes and tries to take off his dirty clothes. He is immovable before her.

"My brother," sobs Vered. "Are you dead?"

It is of no use her being there. But of what use is she elsewhere, she the social worker, the one who places immigrant families in apartments, jobs, towns? She cannot leave. She sits the night near his chair. With dawn the room looks dustier.

"My brother," says Vered. "Give me strength. Love me and I'll leave my lover."

The brother is bleary-eyed. He looks vaguely upon her, she the clod, dust in the dawn.

He closes his eyes. For thirty days he can go to no entertainment, for a year to no concerts or plays.

"Let me help you to bed before I go," begs Vered.

Of his own accord he rises and stretches out on the sofa bed. Vered brings the quilt from the trunk, the last of the possessions of their late mother. Her brother is cradling his sore hand and beginning to sleep.

Vered descends the six flights along the ghost of the elevator, spiraling down the metal shaft.


Vered goes to Jerusalem that very day.

"My brother is dying!" she tells the women in the stone house.

A brother must, at all costs, be brought to life.

"Bring him to Jerusalem," say Terry and Simha.

"I cannot move him. It's as if he were in a coffin."

"These sad, young men," says Terry. "Too many wars for them."

"No," says Dahlia. "He needs another Vered."

Everyone is visiting. There are days like that when Tel Aviv and Beer Sheva converge upon Jerusalem.

"Let's see his picture," says Mickey.

Vered is reluctant. Mickey is too cynical. Her brother doesn't need a Mickey. But maybe Mickey needs Vered's brother. Would that be a mitzvah?

"Too skinny," says Mickey. "I'd embrace him and his ribs would crack."

Antoinette and Gerda look at the photo.

"A melancholic, I should say," says Antoinette.

"Unhealthy-looking chap," says Gerda.

"I would frighten him," says Tova. "Too American and speedy."

"I've never been with a circumcised man," says Deedee. Gloria just laughs.

"Let us see!" say the wayward girls. They giggle shyly.

Dahlia takes the photo from Vered.

"Oooh ah!" she says and puts the snapshot into her blouse. "I will go to him," says Dahlia. "Give me your key."


Vered's lover is looking for Vered. His wife is consulting a lawyer. His children are nervous about speaking to him on the phone. Vered has not been home in two days. He phones the police to see if she's been in an accident. He will not leave his name. He phones the large hospitals. She has not been admitted. She could have eloped with an immigrant, that bitch! Some Russian or South American would do anything to get an apartment with an extra room, a little closer in to a big city.

He dreams of her. He rocks the bed. He goes to the Knesset and votes against abortion reform. He votes against the secularization of marriage and divorce. He is considered a Liberal.

Dahlia takes the jitney to Tel Aviv. She is hardly aware of the six flights of stairs in the apartment building. She reads the door plates on the way up, one an optometrist, another a lawyer. She reaches into the lantern case and pulls out the key. It is still warm from the bulb. She does not knock but opens the door. She clicks on no lights in the darkened room. She hears soft breathing and is unafraid.

"*Bō*," she whispers. Come.

She flicks her lighter. The brother is awake and stares at her. His senses are sharpened from his fast. He is not insane. He is bereft.

"I am your sister," says Dahlia, "your mother, your love."

She pulls him from the cushionless chair.

Dahlia unties the halter top. It falls. Her breasts are already pointing.

"I am here to quench your thirst," says Dahlia.

She unzips her long skirt. Her panties are bikini. Her waist, stomach and hips are full.

He cries out.

"I am here to give you life," says Dahlia.

He falls upon her and eats until he is sated. When he awakens her arms are around him. She does not need to sleep. He loves and sleeps. In the dawn she is gone.

He knocks his body around the room looking for her. He opens the door, no footsteps down the stairs. She is not in the bath.

She has left him a note on the kitchen sink.

"I am alive. Vered is alive. The Land is full of love for you."

He washes and tries to shave without using the mirror. He finds another jacket that is not torn. He goes to class. His teacher gives him a date for a makeup exam. His pain in the hand and in the belly is sharp but he's alive.

That night he stretches out on the couch. The door opens.

"I am Mihal from Haifa," says Mickey. "I want a man with whom I can be gentle and who will treat me softly. I, too, have been badly wounded."

She kisses his hand. She kisses his stomach. He caresses her heart.

The next day Vered's brother studies in the library. Nothing distracts him. He holds his weak hand with his stronger and writes two reports.

That night he hears the lantern being opened, the key inserted.

"Do not be afraid, Vered's brother," says Tova. "I, too, am your family."

Tova tickles his chin with her curly hair. She lifts his sore hand and the fingers move stiffly through her curls.

The next day he begins to look for part-time work.

It is early evening of that day. A large woman and her baby enter the room of Vered's brother. The baby is placed carefully on the chair without its cushions. The woman comes to him.

"I will give you sustenance," says Simha. "I will give birth to you."

She presses down her nipple and the sweet, thick fluid squirts into his opened mouth.

Vered's brother stocks his refrigerator at the corner grocery. That night his door is opened.

"Laughs?" asks Gloria.

She saunters in. Vered's brother laughs.

He replaces the cushion on the chair, removes the cloth from the bathroom mirror.

On the sixth day, when the beasts of the earth were created and cattle and everything that creeps upon the earth, and male and female created He them, there is a fumbling at the door. There is some trouble with the lock. Deedee enters, blinking in the dark.

"Something different?" asks Deedee.

The following day Vered's brother begins to sing.

The night of the seventh day the door opens. It is Vered.

"Come in, my sister," says her brother. "I have been expecting you."

They lie next to each other. They are family. They are the past. They both can live.

"Send him away, Vered," says her brother.

"I did," says Vered.

The ex-lover has begun to look more closely at his young secretary. Life isn't bad. Some lock their doors. Some open theirs.

The women in the stone house have performed their good deeds. They are Temple Priestesses, renewing themselves and saving lives.

# 9
# Dahlia in the Desert

There is a time when the storks fly from Northern Europe to East Africa. This summer, rolling out of her sleeping bag in the Sinai, Dahlia sees a stork standing with a broken leg.

Dahlia sighs. Storks who land in the Sinai are too tired to fly on, too worn to eat or drink. They die of exhaustion.

Dahlia is in the Sinai to rest. She has sung everywhere in The Land, at the kibbutzim in the north, army camps on the borders, parochial and public schools, before immigrants in development towns, at weddings and bar mitzvot in Tel Aviv, at the amphitheater in the artist's village of Ein Hod, at a caravansary in Jerusalem. She sang before the war and during the war. She sings after the war. She sings songs like "I'll Meet You at Ten Minutes Past the War" or "My Brother Yehuda." All of the songs from this war are sad.

Dahlia's career opportunities are also sad, or foolish. In the musical, *You Don't Have to Be White to Be Jewish*, Dahlia played a Falasha from Ethiopia. Her face was blackened, her auburn hair covered with an Afro wig. Dahlia passed the posters for the show pasted on every fence and kiosk, but could never recognize herself in the cast. In another musical by the same composer, *The Hin-Jew*, Dahlia wore a sari, a straight black wig and browned her skin. Her big number was "Eating Deli in New Delhi." The Indian immigrants did not come from their moshavim and development towns, nor did anyone else. Yet a third time the same composer and producer tried for a hit. It was a South American Songfest for television, with Dahlia imitating Carmen Miranda, the South American Bombshell. Dahlia's lips were broadened and reddened, her soft hair covered with a basket of fruit. She was introduced as Dahlia, the Beer Sheva Bombshell, and sang sambas in Hebrew.

The stork is expiring at Dahlia's feet. She pours water from her canteen into a plastic container and forces the stork's bill into the water. The stork slowly drinks. A good sign. Dahlia pulls dried fruit out of her rations. The stork eats a bit, then falls back, the leg dangling, the head sideways in the sand.

On a nearby dune Dahlia is being observed. There are shadows of the sun, humps of mountains.

"If I don't get to the *yam*—the sea—I'll be covered with the dust of the year," says Dahlia to her friends in the stone house of the Old City. "If I don't lie under the sun, I'll turn white as death."

What can the women do for her?

"I don't want eyes," says Dahlia, "if I only see cement and stone buildings and never a tent."

She lives in Beer Sheva next to sun and tents and close to the Red Sea. But Dahlia has no time for leisure. During the day she works or sleeps in order to work at night. She is the palest person in this frontier town. She travels to Tel Aviv and sees the cement buildings crumbling in the salt air, their color fading as soon as the paint is applied. She sings in Jerusalem, in a sarcophagus of stone buildings. Here and there, in the old City of David, is a black Bedouin tent like a fly speck in the landscape.

"I must have a *hafsakah*, an intermission!" cries Dahlia.

The women contribute to Dahlia's intermission: water canteen with strap, sweater, jacket, clogs, towel, soap and soap dish, toothpaste, Vaseline for dry lips, map of the Sinai, metal plate, cup, knife, spoon, pot, Sterno, matches, rice, powdered milk, dried fruits and nuts, canned Argentinian beef, split peas, toilet paper and even a little money.

Dahlia heard about this cove, which is invisible from the road, when she sang at an army base near Sha'arm es Sheikh. A soldier made a map for her, and the stork must have seen that map. The next day Dahlia force-feeds the stork her Argentinian beef.

The sun is unbearably hot, the nights terribly windy in this cove. Everything has to be weighted down. Dahlia allows herself limited sun, lying nude in the landscape of dunes, slopes and slides like the shapes of her own insides. Or else she covers everything: gloves, scarf across her face, jacket, long pants, socks, shoes, sunglasses. She builds a fire at night in the shelter of a mimosa tree, out of brush and thorn bushes.

The mountains are dromedaries in the sharp shadows of evening. The rocks are outlined and cast long shadows.

Dahlia is joyous to be alone and she is also lonely. So it is with passionate women. It is a blessing and a curse. To eat lustily, drink gustily, rock back and forth in someone's arms is a blessing. But to have the skin enflame, the eyes dull over, the mouth dry in longing is a curse. To laugh noisily, to dance, to sing, that is a blessing, but to have dull stomach pains from lack of love, to weep for no reason, to bite one's nails, knuckles, pinch one's wrists is a curse. To love easily is a blessing. To be easily hurt is a curse.

The women in the stone house talk about needing someone's body.

Tova tells Dahlia, "I finally need a fuck and I pick up a fuck, and I tell you, it isn't worth it."

Dahlia needs friends, passionate friends. She looks for them among the customers at part-time jobs—the record shop and movie theater where she is the cashier. She tries out the sax player in the wedding band. Tova is right. It isn't worth it.

Vered introduced Dahlia to one of her clients, a handsome Georgian whom Vered had placed in Beer Sheva. That client was no noble Prisoner of Zion, escaping from the Union of Soviet Socialist Republics for Zionist principles. He had been arrested in Georgia as a petty thief. He follows the same profession in The Land, first stealing Dahlia's time, energy, then borrowing her little bit of money, eating her food, weighing on her heart. A thief is a thief.

The stork will die. Dahlia hesitates, then takes her long chicken knife from the pack and unwraps it from its cloth covering. She knows what to do. She has seen it done at kibbutzim and conservation sites. She holds down the stork, avoiding the snap of its bill, and cuts its leg off at the knee joint. The stork bleeds but only a little, and goes into shock. Dahlia gathers brambles for a rough coop.

Dahlia in the desert is being watched.

The whole trip she was watched: coolly staring Arabs in the cafés of Al Arish; vendors of a desert suk, a pitiful market that sold bushels of shriveled oranges and potatoes with bad spots, and had huge black beetles crawling among the produce. A white donkey watched her while she slept. The next night an Arab woman and her camel watched all night over her sleeping form.

She knows that mountains watch and rocks observe. She discovered this climbing Mount Sinai. ("There are seven Mount Sinais!" said the guide proudly.) The rocks were peculiar. Dahlia thought someone was smoking behind a rock, but it was only a thin stream of fog. She thought ribbons were decorating another rock, but it was streams of shadows. She thought a rock was talking, but the rock seemed to have stopped the echoes in the valley. She lost her path and the guide, and she backtracked to retrace the smoking rock, ribboned boulder and speaking stone. When she reached the top of the mountain, where she was promised a vision, she found only a tiny chapel and the discards of tourists, moist orange peels and dropped flashbulbs. She jarred herself down the seven thousand steps Christian monks had cut into the mountain.

Everything in The Land has its own jarring.

The next day the stork rises. It stands on its only leg. It continues to eat.

In Dahlia's childhood things ran away, her father from her mother, her mother from responsibility, calling Dahlia *mamele*, little mother. Dahlia had a dog whom she named No Name and a strangely striped cat she called No Face. Each disappeared. She also had two canaries who mysteriously fled their cages. Only recently did Dahlia's mother tell her that the canaries had died of pneumonia.

What to do if you long for visions and your only visitation is from a stork? Yet Dahlia is not alone. The few trees around shake. She thinks, at night, she hears the snicker of a camel.

Dahlia goes to the sea. The fish are friendly. She offers them dried bread and leans over the water. The fish come to eat out of her hands, the big angelfish, yellow and blue, the parrot fish of green and purple with its mouth like Carmen Miranda.

Life is passing her cove. She can tell by the droppings: chestnut dung from camels, beans from goats, black drops from sheep, eels from sheep dogs.

The stork is hopping. Each day it hops the more. And Dahlia calms, forgets her full- and part-time jobs. She needs less and less to eat. The days are long and have their proper weight.

The night breeze blows over Dahlia. Only she and the stork of the interrupted voyage live together.

"Mother," she will say when she returns to Beer Sheva, "I am a strong and beautiful woman. I sing because I want to. I love because I have to. Do not make me afraid of myself or of the world. If a man leaves me, I will not mourn him for the rest of my life."

There is a shadow over her tent. Midafternoon. Impossible.

A figure. She could cry out but doesn't. Only some wind and water sounds and the stork's clacking bill.

Two men in striped robes, the elder pudgy, the younger, sixteen or eighteen, slender. They bow to her. The younger extends his hand in handshake. Another shock. Bedouin men don't do that. They speak to her in Arabic. Of course she understands. They are formal and polite. Will she join them? the younger asks. It is his father's will. Their tent is not far. He gestures but Dahlia sees nothing in the distance.

She rises to gather her gear. The men have already gathered it neatly for her. They tether the stork to the mimosa tree and leave it water and fish.

Their camel is with them, drooling and bad-tempered. The father hits the camel's nose with his stick. The nose has welts upon it, but the camel is precious to them. There are many words for the different ages of the camel in their tongue. Dahlia has a rocky ride on camelback. The camel can trot at great speed but the father holds on to its reins.

The tents are soon visible in the small oasis. They are under the date trees. The dates have ripened. Dahlia is helped from the camel and looks longingly above her. The son, a prince, really, lifts his robe above his knees and climbs the tree, knocking off dates for her. They are the sweetest she has tasted in The Land.

They are beginning the Ceremony of Hospitality, the Ritual of Grinding Coffee. Neighbors will hear the drumming and will know the mukhtar has company.

The coffee maker has blue eyes and light hair, no surprise in this land of descendants of Crusaders. They offer Dahlia first a small amount of bitter coffee, a thick fluid that barely covers the base of her ceramic cup. The mukhtar, the older man, shows her the cup wrapped. For her, the honored guest, he unwraps this cup. The bitter coffee will reduce the heat of the day inside of Dahlia. The grinder plays a song, holding onto the wooden pestle at different heights and beating into a hollowed-out log.

From behind curtains shelled nuts appear. She sees slender hands, a woman's hands, pass them.

"Who is she?" Dahlia asks the young son.

"My mother."

"May I meet her?" asks Dahlia.

No one hears her. She is given pillows to recline on.

"This is how Ibrahim *avānu*, our father, lived," says the mukhtar.

Dahlia is getting sleepy.

"Yes," says Dahlia, "but I am the daughter of Sara and not of Hagar."

The stripes on the rugs run together. The coffee maker is working rhythmically. Dahlia dozes. Someone covers her with a camel's-hair rug. It is dark. The stars expand and contract as she looks out of the tent.

The mukhtar is there.

"You sleep quietly," he says.

He touches her shoulders. His hand is soft. His son leaves this partition of the tent.

Dahlia stands in the opening of the tent. The mukhtar turns toward her.

"I have been watching you," he says, "in your cove."

Dahlia reddens. In the evening when she is all wrapped or in the morning when she bathes?

"You are young and strong," he says, "though not so young as my wife when I married her."

"How old was she?"

"Thirteen," says the mukhtar. "I made of her a woman."

All of the flippant remarks Dahlia makes to men are inappropriate here. She would ask, "Did she make of you a man?" but everything is beyond its effect—the sounds, shadows, words even have their shadows. A sigh has meaning. One's eyes have meaning.

The mukhtar's eyes are dark and the whites are bluish by lantern light.

"Are you afraid to be here?" he asks. "You see, we have done nothing to harm you. It is against our laws to harm our guests."

"And if I were not your guest?"

"Why would I do anything to you?" he asks. "You have done nothing to hurt me. Ask for anything, whatever you wish. I am your host. Food, fruit, liquid, company—or even, I myself—even that much you may request."

He is not handsome. He is short, a hair shorter than Dahlia. He is not a desert-lean Bedouin but has spent much of his life in oases. His complexion is pocked, yet his lips are shapely and red, and his eyes as warm as the coffee. He does none of the vulgarities of the *chakchakim*, bruisers, pressing her leg, grabbing a breast. Everything here is gracious, leisurely.

They stand in the flap of the tent and do not touch each other. Dahlia looks away from his eyes and feels his breath across her face.

"You are kind," says the mukhtar. "I have seen you with the stork."

What else? Did he see her go behind the hills to defecate? Who is he? And how old is he? Is he as old as her runaway father? Could he be her father? Or maybe he is only as old as she—thirty—marrying at thirteen and with a son sixteen.

"I am only here on holiday," says Dahlia.

She is becoming nervous. Voices are whispering behind the veiling that divides the room. The mukhtar excuses himself, goes behind the separation. The voices cease utterly. He returns smooth-faced.

"What does a mukhtar judge?" she asks him. "What decisions do you have to make?"

He seats himself and indicates that she, too, can be seated near him.

"We have the tribal council," she says, "but I preside and make the final decision."

"What do you decide?"

He does not really want to speak. He answers out of politeness.

"One of my people was drafted into the army," he says. "As soon as he left, his wife was approached by another man. He did not gain entrance into her tent but he did present himself there. She repulsed his friendship. He returned the next night. She was frightened and came to tell the mukhtar. I, in turn, called a meeting of the tribal council. The husband had heard of the situation. Though his wife was unharmed and was not even tempted, the husband demanded reparations. A large sum of money. My people do not have money. He asks for four hundred lira for his honor. The tribal council wants to interview the wife, though I am opposed to this. She comes to the council weeping. I look at her carefully. Is she weeping from fear of the council? Of her husband? We discuss this over many cups of coffee.

"I decide, at the end, that the husband can expect some money, but for himself not so much as he wants or the men will try to make money from their wives. You know the way, accusing other men falsely. I say that the trespasser should be fined four hundred lira. For this much money he must go to work in Beer Sheva. The husband is to be awarded one hundred lira and the remainder goes into an emergency fund for my people."

"That is justice," says Dahlia.

"I also speak with those wanting divorce or to add another wife to their household," says the mukhtar. "Neither is as easy as once it was." He sighs. "Now the wife must agree."

There is movement behind the curtain.

"I think my wife disagrees," he says, "but the body has its longings, the heart its desire, and my wife cannot be allowed to interfere with these."

Ach, he is a gentleman. Ach, maybe he would be a lovely lover. But it is too confined within the tent, every sound discernible from gasps to sobs, all within this perimeter.

Dahlia's body begins to long for this mature man, this reasonable judge, this person of experience and delicacy.

She hears a soft "Ai!" from the women's section. The mukhtar rises. She hears a great slap. No response.

Dahlia becomes frightened. She remembers all the gentlemen she's known: the sweet beach boy who took her out on the boat and tried to rape her. She threw his flippers overboard. He socked her but dove in for the flippers, and she was rescued. She remembers the cars that picked her up when she was tramping from city to city, the concerned men, their question as to her destination, their assurance that they knew exactly how to reach it, then the detour and sudden stop. She remembers the polite member of the audience who presents himself backstage. Can he get her a late dinner? He has his car. Once she is inside, he forgets his offer.

The mukhtar returns, smiling a bit coolly.

Dahlia is scurrying around, collecting her gear.

"Is there nothing here you wish, my guest?" he asks.

"I wish to return to my stork," says Dahlia.

"By and by," says the mukhtar.

"Then I wish to know your son," says Dahlia, "your young son."

The mukhtar pauses a second, smiles politely. He calls. The son appears without his shirt. The mukhtar speaks rapidly in a dialect of the region. The boy looks startled then amused. He bows to his father and to Dahlia.

"Not here," says the mukhtar. "Take her to her place of origin."

The boy leads her to the cove on camelback. Dahlia is not sure this is her cove until she sees her stork standing there on its one leg. The boy laughs.

In the wind the young prince helps Dahlia construct a primitive shelter. Outside this wind-breaker, the camel makes the stork nervous; the stork makes the camel mean-tempered.

This is for the boy, the Ceremony of Initiation. The ingredients of such a ceremony are one lovely young boy, one loving and experienced woman.

It is necessary to have a bottle of olive oil. This aids in exorcising the demon of nervousness. The initial body rub is brisk, followed by a more languorous application.

In the initial rite one should avoid reflections—mirrors and eyes. One should also avoid laughter and chatter.

This is a time of body prayer.

The boy will never forget this rite.

In the morning the boy and his camel are gone. It might have been a mirage but for the camel dung.

She rises and runs to the sea to wash herself. She returns to the stork to untether it. The stork begins to hop. It hops to the water's edge.

"*Motek*," says Dahlia, "sweet one, do you intend to paddle in the water with one oar?"

The stork spreads its wings and ascends.

"Go in peace," says Dahlia, "to East Africa."

# 10
# God Counts Her Tears

While Dahlia was in the desert, Mihal was in the season of the flowering almond. She walked through the bridal bouquet of pink and white trees on her way to divorce proceedings.

The presiding rabbi had warned Mickey's husband the week before, "There is a saying: 'Be careful not to cause a good woman to weep for God counts her tears.' "

The tears had accompanied Mickey's testimony.

She was asked the usual question of identification: "This is your baal?"

Yes, that was her baal, that pouting boy, *baal* the word for the ancient god, the master and the husband.

"What did he do to you?" asked the tribunal.

"Everything there was to do, he did."

"Everything is nothing," the stern rabbi said. "You must be specific. We don't go about this lightly, you know."

She knew. All the unhappily married women in The Land knew. For the husband always has to agree to the *get*, the divorce. And he got, don't worry, he got.

Sometimes he got to keep the wife celibate. Sometimes he got to keep the children. Sometimes he got to keep the money.

Mickey and her friends meet and weep. And no one counts their tears.

About one matter is the rabbinate curious.

"Was it consummated?"

"Yes, but. . . ."

"It's a simple question. It was or it wasn't."

But, the brutality of it. When the consummation of the first night was over, Mihal knew she had been right to guard her virtue. She wished she still could.

Why would anyone believe in Mihal's innocence? Who would think she had come to the marriage a virgin, with her shiny black hair, dark eyes, large hips and breasts, small waist, gliding walk, wicked humor?

How did she remain a virgin? Hawk-eyed parents, that's how—a handsome, courtly father and a squat, sallow-complected mother each guarding her for their separate reasons.

"What specifically angered you?" asks the rabbinate.

Mickey whispered. Her voice, usually boisterous, sank into her chest.

"The neighbor."

"How old was the neighbor?"

"A child."

"What proof have you?"

"My word."

But there are two sayings among talmudists: "If you listen to a woman too long, you begin to stink," and "Better to burn the words of the Torah than give them to a woman."

So they did not listen to her. Instead—

"Mihal," asks one of the tribunal, "have *you* committed adultery?"

They look upon her closely.

"The shattering of the wedding glass," intones one, "symbolizes that one act of unfaithfulness forever destroys ... the home."

But it was her *baal* who had shattered the wrapped glass under his heel, grinning proudly at his friends.

If Mihal had only read over the marriage service ahead of time, she would have known what was coming:

"Thou ... who hast made man in thine image ... hast prepared unto him, out of his very self, a perpetual fabric."

Perma Press. A shmata, that's Mickey.

Still the rabbinate dawdled. Still she cannot leave this city. Still her husband's time with her is extended. Still she is not protected in her own apartment. Still he is married to her. And waits to be bought off. And waits to tease.


One night he shows up at her parents' house, knocks softly on the door, begs their pardon for disturbing them, and invites Mickey to dinner. He is courteous to her and treats her as he never did in their marriage.

The next night he shows up again, contritely asking if he can be allowed to see Mickey and can he take her for a ride?

"Go, go," beam the parents.

He caresses her and kisses her more passionately than he did any child-neighbor. Mickey is shaking.

"I will do nothing more to you," says her husband, "until

you return to our marriage bed. I will not love you in the car."

She is tempted.

The husband prepares his case. He quotes Talmud to her: "He that has no wife cannot be considered a whole man."

She goes to the apartment with him that night. He tells his snickering brothers to leave.

On the bed he caresses her limbs. He kisses her over and over until she calls his name. He gently enters her. Is she, as the benediction said, truly in the Garden of Eden?

His and her lawyers are told, and the case is dismissed.

A month later he is beating her and breaking the wedding dishes at the Sabbath table.

"He isn't a son of Adam," says her mother, holding the cracked china.

Mickey is an unclean thing now, a forbidden thing like the weasel, the mouse, the tortoise, the chameleon, lizard, snail, mole. She is an abomination.

Mickey's skin breaks out into lizard scales. Mickey's face swells. She can hardly see out of her eyes. She feels she has a shell upon her back. She creeps, slides, scurries and hides.

Her mother does not bawl her out. The house is like a hospital, ointments, messages, tiptoeing, whispered consultations.

A dermatologist in Jerusalem.

On the bus to Jerusalem Mickey meets Hepzibah. Through Hepzibah, Mickey goes to the stone house and encounters the women.

Gradually her face clears. But now she has the frown of her mother. Now she smokes constantly and has the stained teeth of her father. Yet she can say anything to these women and they have heard it from another's lips or recognize it as the truth of women.

"I am crazy!" sobs Mickey. "I still long for him."

The women know they have also been crazy and longed

for that which demeaned them. They were so trained.

"I cannot even move to Jerusalem," says Mickey. "The rabbinate won't let me. I have to stay in Haifa and give the marriage a chance."

Mickey never stops talking about herself or about men. She is seeing the attorney. She once hesitated when he offered to drive her to his apartment. Now she expects it of him. He does not bother offering her food, wine or music from his stereo as he did before. Mickey is slipping away from women.

She has begun auditing classes at the university in order to meet boys. She sits languidly before the professor. She may follow him to other classes. She sits in the *merkaz*, the plaza in the center of the Carmel, at an outdoor café, flirting with the waiter, a boychik. She calls out to *pushtakim, chakchakim*, to all the bums that pass. The street is full of people getting off buses, going into the supermarket, the boutique, stopping at the newsstand, the flower shop, the banks. She asks people where they came from. She asks them their destination.

Hepzibah finds her there one afternoon when Hepzibah goes to the merkaz to shop. She blinks. Is that Mickey? Her fingers like sausages, wearing a smock to hide her stomach and hips. Is she pregnant? Hearing her, Hepzibah knows Mickey is just fattening on her anger.

Hepzibah stands at Mickey's little table. Mickey turns to look at her, fiercely then tearfully.

"The worst," sobs Mickey, "the worst thing yet has happened."

Hepzibah does not know if she wants to hear, but she knows she must hear.

"My father," says Mickey. "I left my door open for him. I called. . . . I lay naked on my bed waiting for him as he entered my room."

Hepzibah keeps her calm expression.

"Mickey," she says, "we are leaving."

Not just the café. The city.

It is Yom Rishon, the first day of the week, Sunday, when Hepzibah shops, cooks for her family and goes down to Jerusalem to see her mother.

"What will I wear?" asks Mickey. "Nothing fits me."

"We'll find something," says Hepzibah.

"Where will we go?"

"We'll find someplace," says Hepzibah.

Hepzibah takes Mickey to her mother's Jerusalem apartment. There Mickey is fitted into old lady clothes, a wraparound dress and crocheted shawl. Hepzibah's mother looks closely at Mickey. She makes gruel and spoon-feeds it to Mickey, spilling a little on her chin. The mother wipes it off with a cloth napkin, patting the cheek and chin clean.

"*Vos ist dos?*" asks the mother in Yiddish.

"She lost herself," says Hepzibah.

H. takes Mickey on the bus to the stone house in the Old City. The women are gathered laughing and drinking Nescafé. They do not, at first, recognize Mickey. When they do, they know not to ask, "What is this?"

Mickey laughs a nasty laugh.

Simha has heard such a laugh before. She rises and goes protectively to Hava's buggy.

Mickey stands against the damp wall. She will not sit on the bed, on the Arab rugs or on the pillows.

"I will not touch anything in this room," says Mickey. "There is nakedness in this room. It is forbidden to uncover your nakedness."

Simha closes her blouse.

Mickey laughs and loses her breath at the end of the laugh.

"Jesus!" says Gloria. "A looney."

"No," whispers Simha. "It's something else."

"Is she a religious fanatic?" asks Deedee.

"Not she, exactly," says Simha.

"The societal pressures on her," says Terry.

Mickey's voice is upon the women: "Thou shalt not uncover 'the nakedness of thy father.... It is an abomination.'"

The women who have been reclining on pillows, loosely clad, sit up and fasten belts and zippers.

"'Neither shalt thou lie with any beast to defile thyself ... neither shall any woman stand before a beast to lie down thereto.'"

It is enough. Simha rises.

"We need a tribunal," she says to the women.

She looks for the tribunal in the eyes of her friends and selects her roommate Terry, Antoinette the Shakespearean, Tova the actress, Dahlia the singer, and Hepzibah the religious. The others are requested to leave.

Gloria says, "Selection time is rejection time."

Deedee wonders if she's set aside because she's Christian. Gerda thinks she's not chosen because of her age—fifty-four to Antoinette's fifty-two. Joan, the playwright, knows she's left out because she's so quiet. Rina and Shula, the wayward girls, are shooed out, escorted across the street and told to go to sleep.

The left out depart, not far, to an Arab restaurant that keeps late hours.

"The land vomiteth out her inhabitants," says Mickey, watching them leave.

"Dybbuk!" yells Simha. "I'm coming after you!"

Simha makes a sudden rush at Mickey but Mickey eludes her and cackles like an old woman. Mickey's face suddenly seems to be toothless, her neck sinewy, her hands clawlike.

Simha explains to the startled women, "It's the spirit of someone, probably, who could not get a divorce and has been wandering from meeting to meeting with the rabbinate throughout the years. She cleaves unto Mickey."

The women are awkward. What is their duty?

"You are eyes to stare back at the Evil Eye," says

Simha, "for that is an evil eye within Mickey. You will cleanse your hands and say the proper prayer and then lay pure hands upon Mickey."

"Do you need black candles?" asks Tova. "I saw it in a Paddy Chayevsky play."

"No," says Simha. "That's showy. This is business."

"Do you need someone especially pure?" asks Antoinette.

"I have her," says Simha. "A virgin. You."

"Do you need someone experienced in these things?" asks Terry.

"I will become experienced," says Simha. "I need will to fight will."

"Why do you need me?" asks Dahlia, the singer.

"To sing to the dybbuk."

Hepzibah sits apart and says nothing, watches everything.

"Dybbuk, name your favorite song and Dahlia will sing it. Name your favorite dance and we will dance with you."

The dybbuk calls out the name of a Ladino lullaby.

"Ladino?" asks Tova.

"How does it go?" says Dahlia to the dybbuk. "Start me off."

Mickey's mouth opens. An ancient, out-of-tune crone's voice is heard.

"I got it," says Dahlia, slapping her knee. "My mother's cleaning lady sang it. This dybbuk's Sephardic, Rumanian maybe."

Dahlia sings the Ladino lullaby, the language of Spanish and Hebrew that traveled during the Inquisition from Spain to Eastern Europe and to Africa.

The song is so sweet that the dybbuk weeps.

"I kiss you," says the old voice of the dybbuk. "Young lady, I kiss you."

Simha says, "Dybbuk, we bring you joy. Do not live in that cave of Mickey, in that place of wail and woe."

Mickey's hair covers her face: "'And if a man take a wife and her mother, it is wickedness; they shall be burnt with fire.'"

"Dybbuk," says Simha, "what did I do wrong?"

The dybbuk begins to gag. "'If a man shall lie with a woman having her sickness ... he hath discovered her fountain ... she hath uncovered the fountain of her blood; and both of them shall be cut from among their people.'"

"Dancing is wrong, I think," says Simha. "Dybbuk, are you hungry? Fresh vegetables, fresh bread. Everything in this house tastes fresh."

The mouth opens. The tongue shows. From inside the bloated body of Mickey, the voice says, "I have not sat at anyone's table. I have been hungry for years, thirsty for months."

The tribunal quickly spreads food on the table, cutting the tomatoes into wedges, slicing the cucumbers, unwrapping margarina, unscrewing the jar of preserves. They put out everything they have in the refrigerator.

"Come to the table, dybbuk!"

The dybbuk rushes to the table. She does not use plate or fork. She uses both hands. She gobbles the food, crouching, spitting up, eating, even chasing the crumbs around the table. Nothing is left.

"I'm still hungry!" wails the dybbuk.

"What are you hungry for, dybbuk?" asks Simha.

A murmuring comes from the dybbuk, "Mmmm, mmm, MEN."

Tova wants to giggle but Simha is so grave that Tova desists.

"Antoinette," says Simha, "speak to her. Tell her it is possible to live with friends, books, work."

Antoinette is nervous. She is usually shy. Also, she hates ad-libbing. All of her lectures are carefully notated on three-by-fives.

"I'm not too good at this," she whispers to Simha.

"Use your will," says Simha.

"Excuse me for addressing you. I'm Antoinette. I'm sorry, but I don't know your name."

"Magda," says the dybbuk.

"Rumanian, I tell you!" says Dahlia.

"Magda," says Antoinette. She stands as if at a lectern. "Do you like to read, and, if so, what do you favor?"

A whisper. "Before. Before this. Romances. Light history."

"Ah," says Antoinette, "then you know about feeding a book through yourself, about talking to others who have read the same book. Magda, this is happiness."

"More," says Magda.

"Magda, there is talking to friends about one's feelings. There is watching the sunset from this doorway. There is music, Magda. There is dancing."

"Ah!" sighs Magda.

Antoinette's throat is getting a little dry.

"More."

"There is phoning someone, Magda, and the person being about to phone you. There is excited chatter. Eating together and the calm talk that follows meals. Shopping—"

"Oh yes," says Magda.

"Going to the Old City to look at rugs and jewelry. Selecting the pieces to make up earrings. You use your friend's eyes for a mirror."

Magda touches her ears.

"There is remembering songs together, from old films—"

There is a strange sound. The dybbuk is sobbing? Choking? Laughing, rusty laughter.

"More," says the dybbuk.

"I'm tired," Antoinette says to Simha. She is beginning to sag.

"It is dangerous to stop," says Simha.

Antoinette begins to tell a joke but her voice is lost. Not

a comprehensible sound comes out. She has taught two long seminars today. She has been with the women all evening. She has no words left.

"I stay where I am," says the dybbuk. "I will never be alone again."

Simha puts on her shawl.

"Dybbuk!" she commands. "I order you out of Mickey. One last entreaty. Mickey is young. Do not age her. Mickey has joy yet. Do not cause her to weep. Mickey is slender. Do not bloat her."

"No," says the dybbuk. "Here I stay."

Simha sighs, then sternly, "Magda, if you do not leave the body of Mickey, I will excommunicate you."

Magda shrieks with laughter. "You have no power. You think you're a rabbi, my master? A woman can never be a master."

"Magda," says Simha, "I am the spirit of the prophet Miriam."

Magda laughs raucously. "She was given leprosy instead of prophecy."

"Do not use words to defeat me. I am Miriam. I predicted the exodus from Egypt before the birth of Moshe. I predict your exodus from the body of Mickey."

"I remain," says Magda. She speaks with certainty.

Antoinette's voice has returned. She likes high drama, Elizabethan confrontation between the spirits and the mortals.

"Magda," she says, "you are utterly alone, despised, a creature of caves and dark tunnels, a creature exiled from the green earth. You are the most friendless and abandoned in all eternity."

"You are not of the tribe of humans," says Simha, "of women."

A terrible wailing, a thrashing about of Mickey's body. Mickey's eyes look helplessly as her hands become bloody from beating the stone walls.

"I remain," says Magda. "I will cleave forever. You cannot separate me. You cannot separate from me."

"Dybbuk," says Simha, "if you do not fly out of the throat of Mickey, you will dwell eternally on borders of lands, in warfare, knowing no peace, speaking no tongue."

"I stay," says Magda.

Simha sits down exhausted. Terry pours her wine. Simha says the blessing over the wine and drinks. Hava is restless and gets up for a late feeding. Mickey is frozen against the wall. The women huddle around the warmth of the nursing daughter and mother, the holiest of families, the original holy family.

Hepzibah has been silent, watching and smiling slightly. Sometimes she suppresses her usual pleasant expression.

"What should I do, Hepzibah?" asks Simha.

"You must divorce them," says Hepzibah.

"Yes," says Simha. "That is it."

It takes about twenty minutes to nurse. Simha does not change the diaper. Hava will lie in wet warmth for the moment.

Simha calls upon the tribunal to attend her, as, once more, she approaches the dybbuk.

"Magda," says Simha, "you are before the divorce court. I am divorcing you from Mickey."

Magda begins to sob heartbrokenly. "No one gets a divorce," she cries.

"This is a fair tribunal," says Simha. "Is it your will, your need to obtain a divorce?"

"Yes," says Magda. "It always was, since first I was married to that man, years my senior, of habits vulgar. Oh, to marry again, someone my age, tender, whom I could love, with whom, maybe, I could bear children! But this man would not let me go, and the court would never grant me a divorce. I ran from him. He was well-to-do and had connections. Police took on extra jobs for a few lira. They found me quickly. I ran, the next time, with a young man. We hid. I was found. The young man was taken from me and not seen again in The Land. I said to my husband, 'If you do not separate from me, I will separate from myself.' He only grunted. I walked into the Mediterranean where the undertow was strongest. I did not have to swim far off."

"I'm so sorry, Magda," says Antoinette. "My dear, I couldn't possibly have known!"

"It is unbearable!" cries Tova.

"Magda," says Hepzibah, "may you rest in peace."

"This is a psychological possession," says Terry. "But it's so convincing that I'm moved to tears."

"Magda," says Dahlia, "I'll lullaby your tired spirit to sleep."

Mickey's shoulders sag. She yawns.

"Magda and Mihal," says Simha, "we are declaring you divorced in the tradition of our nomadic people, the way of our Bedouin ancestors. Magda/Mihal, repeat after me three times, 'I divorce you.'"

The mouth of the women opens. No sound issues.

"Magda and Mihal," says Simha. "I order you to obey me. Cleanse the defilement from you. Say, three times, 'I divorce you,' and the name of your husband."

"Aren't we supposed to have his shoe for her to spit into?" asks Tova.

"Hush."

Like some vehicle in the distance, or a call far off, or an animal crying on the mountain, there is the approaching sound.

"I divorce you." It clarifies. "I divorce you." It is shouted. "I DIVORCE YOU."

Mickey is lying on the floor. Carefully the women approach. Mickey's eyes flutter. She looks up into the face of the tribunal and smiles.

# 11
# Count the Stars
# and Give Them Names

Only the Holy One knows the number of stars and their names. Others have tried.

To Deedee, the sky is the battlefield of Irish kings, the flash of shield and dagger.

When Simha sees a falling star she blesses Her from whose womb it fell, that monthly red dropping.

H., in her writing class, tells tales of the frightened young maiden peered at by the eyes of the world, voyeurs, animals in the dark.

Mihal becomes depressed at starlight. She retires early to cold bed sheets in the home of her parents.

To Dahlia, when singing in town, the stars are blinding footlights into which she automatically smiles.

Antoinette rushes into the dark with quotes—of star-crossed lovers from the differing households of fair Verona or, from *Julius Caesar*, of "the strange impatience of the heavens ... dreadful night/that thunders, lightens, opens graves." The drama of Antoinette's life lies between book covers of the night.

Chain-smoking Gerda glances up at the ashtray of the world with its glowing butts.

Gloria, the redhead, sees the night sky as a dressing room mirror. She knows that she will act out her fantasies during the third act.

To Terry the stars are numerous as the seats in Parliament, whose height she would attain. She will fight the enemies of wayward girls, the party of Vered's lover.

Vered sees her lover dimming.

To Rina and Shula, wayward girls, it is ethereal gossip, the midnight press, models and movie stars. It is yet another world from which they are excluded.

To Joan and Tova, it is bright figures on the firmament, flaring and paling, people as conqueror, citizens unhoused. It is their drama, *The City Between Us*, of Jerusalem Jew and Jerusalem Arab. No one in the city is about to help the production of such a work.

To mourners in The Land, the stars are relatives ascending from wars. The heirs of the biblical names, Yitzhak, Shlomo, David, Yehoshua, rise at night wearing yellow badges with stars of David.

To children of development towns, they are the glinting eyes of the enemy, crossing the border once again to attack.

To the young Bedouin prince, lover of Dahlia in the desert, the stars are the first night of his loving, shining on nipples and swells of hip and belly. He searches for Dahlia, not in the Sinai, but first in Beer Sheva and then in Jerusalem. With him he brings a friend of evil counsel.

All the stars converge at Purim time, the season for the breaking of laws: the law against drunkenness, transvestism, and the law against teaming together unlike animals. Rather than matched teams, one can see along the highways and streets of the city a tall horse and a colt unevenly dragging a cart.

On this day in their little stone house do the women gather to play the games of chance, to deal the Priestess of the Tarot, the Empress of Justice, to throw dice or move the cup across the Ouija board.

On this night the women are drinking. From Simha's kibbutznik has come cherry brandy, made by his father. Each time he visits there is a present: a fresh fruit basket, a coffee cake, nuts, sturdy dresses for little Hava. Once he came with a wooden *haleel*, a shrill flute, and sang a shepherd's song to his shepherdess so sweetly that Simha threw him into bed as the last note died.

Tonight she drinks his cherry brandy and her nipples redden and glow.

Terry is the champion of the Ouija. The women clamor to pair with her.

"Ouija!" demands Terry, "from what land came you, what language speak you, and what tidings bring you?"

The Ouija is overwhelmed and replies fully under Terry's firm hand that rushes around the board spelling out the spirit's name, tongue, century of birth and message.

"Ask about me," says Simha, wetting her lips with brandy.

"What will happen to Simha?" asks Terry.

The cup darts to NO several times, moving from the center of the board, where Terry forcefully places it, to NO on the right-hand side.

"Why won't you tell us, O Spirit?" asks Terry.

"NO!" says the Spirit.

"Are you a Spirit of Peace?" asks Terry.

"YES."

"Have you come in friendship?"

"YES."

"Then you must reply to our questions. What will happen to Simha?"

Terry's hand is unmoved, no force pushes it.

"I demand to know," says Terry.

Slowly, slowly the cup slides: B-A-D.

"Something bad will happen to Simha?"

"YES."

"What? Please, Spirit of Peace, tell us what to expect or to avoid."

The Spirit is dispirited, tired, stubborn, who knows? Limp. Perhaps it is a limp male spirit.

Simha spills her precious brandy. It is sticky like blood on her skirt.

Deedee has been dealt the Hanged Man card.

Antoinette says, "I don't know if I would take the Tarot seriously. After all, it's medieval Christianity."

"I'm Christian," says Deedee.

Antoinette picks up the cards and tries once again. The Hanged Man stares at Deedee upside down.

Rina and Shula, the wayward girls, use the *dreidel*, the square spinning top, to shoot for nuts. A new wayward girl, Robin the Runaway, watches. Rina, the Sephardic almond-eyed, wins all the filberts, walnuts and the almonds. Shula, the Pole, loses everything every turn and spits at Rina.

Terry tries her own turn with the Ouija.

"Spirit," she asks, "are you there?"

The cup jerks too fast.

"YES."

"Good," laughs Terry. "An eager Spirit. Who are you? Name yourself."

The spirit scoots and darts around the board, stopping at every consonant: BCDFGHJKL—

"Come on, Spirit," says Terry. "This is noncooperative behavior. Name yourself."

The spirit goes through the remaining consonants of the alphabet.

"Are you a Spirit for Peace?"

The spirit doesn't reply.

"Spirit," asks Terry, "will I do what I want to do?"

"NO. YES. NO. YES."

The spirit is insane.

"What do all the consonants in the alphabet stand for?" Terry asks Mickey, who is well acquainted with the properties of spirits.

Mickey gasps. "For Satan," she says.

"Satan can also answer my questions," says Terry. "Satan?"

"YES."

"You know what I want to do."

"YES."

"Will I succeed?"

"YES. YES. YES. YES. YES."

The hand keeps jerking until Terry forcibly stops it.

"I must want it very badly," says Terry.

The women pour more brandy. It is according to the law that they do so. It is written that one must drink until the good cannot be distinguished from the bad.

At this time men can have the curliest of wigs, smear their mouths with lipstick, stuff their chests with stockings and rags, borrow earrings for unpierced ears, shadow their eyes.

At this time girls tuck hair into caps, mustache the hairless skin above the lips, charcoal in sideburns, speak gruffly.

At this time Dahlia's Bedouin lover has entered the city of Jerusalem, accompanied by a strange figure, a swarthy Jew wearing a long, black caftan, a fox fur hat and a false beard.

For this season Simha has been busily baking. The

women have brought noisemakers and plastic hammers. The *greigers*, noisemakers, grind, the hammers squeak at the mention of certain villainous names and deeds.

Simha takes *Ozni Haman*, ears of Haman, from the oven. The women eat of Haman's ears, three-cornered, folded-over dough, covering poppy seed or apricot, piled high, looking like the browned, dried ears of a defeated enemy army.

As the visitors from the desert search out the stone house, a parade passes: Moshe Dayans, little police, American cowboys and Indians, small brides carrying dried bouquets and clinging to their mothers' hands, gypsies in Moroccan jewelry, a Russian cossack, a young girl in her brother's rolled-up pants, a clown with an orange face and billowing stomach. Somewhere amid these strange beings the Bedouin prince will find the familiar arms of his beloved.

"There are two possibilities," begins Terry. All learned discussions in The Land begin thus. "We are what we choose."

This is the holiday of determining what is to happen to the people of God and to those who plan their demise.

"We are our politics," says Terry, "and all decisions are political. Queen Esther was a political animal."

The new wayward girl, Robin, is an American, a truant young American, the despair of her parents, and now the responsiblity of the Home for Jewish Future Homemakers.

All three wayward girls reject this assessment of Esther. They know Esther after years of Sunday school drawings. She is themselves. She is a Moroccan beauty like Rina with black slanty eyes and a Yemenite necklace of silver coin. She is a Polish blonde like Shula, with blue eyes and wide cheekbones. She is an American movie star, unlike awkward Robin.

The women must hide their worries from the girls for Wayward is once again in danger. This is called the politics of destruction. When something unpopular or uneconomic— a river, meadow, village—is saved from destruction, that means destruction is only postponed.

"Take it all the way back," says Simha, "into the politics of exile."

Hepzibah strokes Robin and moves her closer to the naphtha heater. She pulls Robin's feet out of the Danish clogs and warms the cold toes.

Robin is unhappy. She is in exile, not an American and not yet Israeli, not furthering her English and not learning Hebrew.

"The exiles had two choices," says Simha. "They could mourn forever by the rivers of Babylon for there they sat down, or they could sing and play the lyre for their captors, 'they that carried us away captive required of us a song.' If they endeared themselves to their captors, they could exist in the land of their exile."

The wayward girls hear laughter and parading. They stir unhappily, with no real alternatives, too old to parade, too young for parables.

"Now we come to the story," says Terry. "It begins with Queen Vashti, who had ascended to her throne three years before. And it came to pass that two alternatives were presented to her."

The girls settle. "Once Upon a Time" is really enough of a preface.

Terry says, "Vashti could be queen of all Persia and rule, with Xerxes, the hundred and seven and twenty provinces, or Vashti could be a woman of dignity. She had to choose."

"Tell it, tell it!" says Rina.

This is the dirty part.

"There came a time, the year four hundred and eighty-two Before the Common Era, when a great council of war occurred."

"What?"

"The planning of Xerxes' campaign against Greece."

The girls boo and sound their noisemakers against Terry who would change fairy tales into history.

Terry continues calmly. "The princes from the hundred and seven and twenty provinces were there, from India to Ethiopia, from Persia and Media, all gathered at Susa, the winter palace of Xerxes."

Rebellion in the group. The changing of names for accuracy is not allowed in legend: "Ahaseurus," the drunken king, into "Xerxes, son of Darius the Great"; "Shushan the Palace" into "Susa." If legend is changed in the slightest, it is no longer legend.

"And there reigned Queen Vashti, hostess to the princesses of all the provinces."

All right.

"Now, also in this palace were seven wicked chamberlains, seven powerful princes and seven obedient handmaidens."

That's better.

"At the very moment when Queen Vashti was entertaining her company, the seven wicked chamberlains appeared, bearing the word of the king. The queen of all the land shall appear disrobed and shall parade before the princes, who represent the extensive holdings of the king."

"Did Vashti do all that?"

"She refused," says Terry.

"Then what?"

"The seven wicked chamberlains reported back to Xerxes that the queen had refused his commandment."

"Wow."

"Now Xerxes had two alternatives. He could have made light of Vashti's disobedience or he could have made a political issue of it. He chose the latter."

"What did he do?"

"He turned to the seven powerful princes of his kingdom and asked their advice."

The girls wait.

"Then spoke Memucan, the most powerful of the seven.

"'All women shall despise their husbands,' said he. 'Vashti not only insulted the King but the princes and the peoples of these provinces.'

"Now, at this point, Xerxes had no alternatives. Once he asked for advice, he had to follow it."

"What happened?"

"He forever removed Vashti from his presence."

"That means he killed her," said Shula, spitting.

"But now Xerxes could have ended it, or he could have enlarged it. He enlarged it. When men are planning war, everything is enlarged. When men are planning war, they are also planning the subjugation of women. Xerxes sent letters to the hundred and seven and twenty provinces, in the language of each and every province, that men are the rulers of their household."

The noisemakers grind. The hammers squeak.

"All right," says Terry. "Who came then? Who was the scab?"

"Who?" asks Robin.

"Esther," says Terry grimly.


Somewhere in Jerusalem the wanderers are walking. The young Bedouin looks with delight upon the festive city. His costumed friend carries a toy hammer. The streets are full of the sound of the hammer, like animals penned up, squealing. The streets are too crowded and the "Hasid" perspires under his black coat.

A bus returns from the big parade in Tel Aviv. Holiday people descend. One person is helped down the steps by parents. It is a hermaphrodite, half-bride, half-groom, half-veil, half-black yarmulke, one white heeled shoe, one black leather lace-up, part of the outfit a white wedding dress, the other half a black tuxedo. One half of the mouth is lipsticked; the other half mustached. The child limps with uneven shoes.

There is an uneasy mixture in the air of danger and safety, victory or revenge, love and lustfulness, engorgements and fasts.

A large dog walks alongside the young Bedouin and his companion. The dog has patches of fur missing from its hind legs. The visitors do not notice him at first, but the dog is persistent and too large to be ignored. They shoo him away. Dogs are not pets in this land. The dog sees the gesturing hand and whines. Food is a gesture. He is hungry.

The visitors cross a busy avenue. The dog follows. At the next street corner is a soccer team. Schoolboys are playing by lamplight, bouncing the ball off their knees, heads, kicking the ball. Cars honk and try to pass, but no one wants to break up the national sport.

The dog barks sharply at the visitors. The sound startles them. The visitor in caftan raises his arm and brings his toy hammer down on the dog's head. The dog grunts. The yellow and blue plastic bounces between his ears, but does not squeak. There is, instead, the sound of hitting bone. The dog goes down, falling behind a parked car.


Terry continues her narrative.

"What did Esther have going for her?"

"Beauty?"

"Nice dresser?"

"Youth?"

"Piety?"

"Modesty?"

"Intelligence?"

"Virginity," says Terry.

"Not like little Hava," mourn the wayward girls for Simha's pierced baby.

"Esther had two alternatives," says Terry. "She could live under the protection of her cousin Mordecai, or she could compete with the young virgins of the hundred and seven and twenty provinces."

"Compete! Compete!" says Shula.

"Be on radio and TV," says Rina.

"She did compete and what happened?"

"She won the beauty contest!"

Simha objects. "It wasn't so easy," she says. "According to Apocrypha, she hated the uncircumcised Persians, she hated her ruler. She even hated the regal crown and never wore it in private. She called it her menstrual rag."

"Honest?"

"In truth!"

"What happens when she becomes queen?"

"She finds out Haman, the adviser to the king, wants to kill all the Jews."

"Esther has two alternatives," says Terry. "She can decide to remain safely anonymous or to declare herself as one of them."

"She was passing," laughs Gloria. "Funny, you don't look Persian."

"Two choices again presented themselves before her," says Terry. "She could make her declaration quietly or she could tie her fate in with that of the exiles."

"What did she do?"

"She heeded her cousin Mordecai, who said, 'Think not ... that thou shalt escape in the king's house, more than all the Jews.' "

Contented sighs. Known fact repeated is reassuring. Every Greek tragedy must end tragically. Every heroine must perform heroically.

"Once again," says Terry, "she must decide. She can either send a message into Xerxes, the king, and hope it will not be stopped by Haman, who wishes to kill the Jews—"

Grind. Squeak.

"Or by the seven wicked chamberlains, who wish to continue their influence with the king. If she does not send a message, she must make another plan."

"It wasn't easy."

"She was a shy girl."

"Inexperienced."

"She had to think about it."

"She had to fast on it."

"And so did her seven handmaidens."


In the German Quarter of Jerusalem, the visitors hesitate near the felled dog. The soccer team interrupts its game. Black clouds of flies gather between the dog's ears. The visitors walk quickly away.

The soccer team kneels in concern. The dog slowly rises. He is bleeding badly; he is limping. He limps off, a swarm of flies following. He will return to the vacant lot from which he came. No one fed him there or gave him drink, but no one bruised him. He will sleep if the flies let him be.


"What did Esther decide?"

"It was the month of Adar," says Terry, "a time of waters and floods, a time when night is longer than day and the moon defeats the sun. It was the time of the new moon, and the seven handmaidens were indolent from fasting. They lay on rich coverlets, their bodies illumined by moonbeams. In their hands were stone statuettes, a woman of the moon, her face Semitic, her slanting eyes outlined, her nose thin and long. On her mouth was a mysterious smile. Her hair was braided and covered with veiling. The body of the statuette was naked, the hands held up her breasts. The belly curved in the moonlight. The thighs were thrust forward. Then did Esther learn of her foremothers."

"Who was her mother?"

"No one in this tale had a mother."

"What?"

"They were the children of fathers. Xerxes is descended from Darius; Haman, the enemy, from the house of Mannedatha; Mordecai, the cousin, is the son of Jair."

"And Esther?"

"Esther is of man born. She is the daughter of her father Abihail, not the descendant of her mother."

"How did she learn of her birth?"

"From the seven handmaidens. Her origins went back beyond the generations when her family was carried away by Nebuchadnezzar, king of Babylon. The source of Esther is Ishtar, born of sea foam, the goddess who nightly rides the heavens in a chariot pulled by the tiger."

"Ahh!"

"Esther's ancestor was the goddess of night and of love. Her ritual was pleasure."

Hepzibah is silent.

"Then what happened?"

"She had two alternatives. She could either ignore her origins or she could act upon them. She could ignore the fact that once her powers were vast and her influence wide, or think only that her statues are broken and her name whispered. She could ignore the fact that once she was queen of heaven, mistress of the fields, and the great destroyer, or act upon that knowledge."

"She was a good Jewish girl," says Hepzibah.

"Yes," says Terry, "and so she prayed to the new moon to help her make her choice."

Simha continues, "They danced by moonlight, covered with light, 'as with a garment,' as Psalm 104 says. The heavens were a curtain, the clouds the chariots of the maidens, the winds wings. They danced while the world bedded. They danced until the world rose."

Terry says, "When they had done with dancing, Esther

made her choice. Confrontation. 'Now I will go in unto the king,' said Esther, 'and if I perish, I perish.' "

"But she didn't!" cry the girls.

They are ecstatic. Bedtime stories, a Moon Purim, up late, drinking brandy, warmed by these women. If only tomorrow would not come with disappointed parents, disapproving teachers, arresting officers and a government that withholds support.


The Bedouin is explaining Dahlia to his companion.

"I will have no other," says the young prince. "She is the only woman I love, that I will ever love."

"She will soon be like all other women," says his companion, "skinny, toothless, pocked with disease, sagging from childbirth."

"I must have her," says the prince, for his father, the mukhtar, and his mother, of whom he was the only male issue, had denied him nothing.

His companion had, some time ago, left the tribe, its places of gathering, its oases. He had gone from Sinai into Africa.

He returned with a message.

"We are wandering Arabs," he cried out one night in the mukhtar's tent.

The sound of the grinding of coffee echoed for meters around as the tribesmen gathered.

"We are deprived of our land. We must take it upon ourselves, each of us, to deliver the land."

To distract him, the mukhtar sent the wanderer with his son on this romantic search.

Dahlia sang late at the Khan, a former Turkish caravansary. Tourists were there, talking during the singing, bothering her after the concert. Dahlia returned to the stone house in bad temper.

She is smoking too much and her throat has become

raspy. She is eating too much and her hips have broken through the seams of her costume. She eats ten of Simha's Ozni Haman. She drinks half a bottle of the cherry brandy. She lights up a cigarette, rests on an Arab rug and exhales.

"Ah! I needed that."

She attends the Tale According to Terry, dozing, smiling at the young girls, and touching the hands of her favorite women.

There is distraction. Joan, the playwright from Manchester, and Tova, the American actress, would confer with Dahlia.

"Be in our play," says Tova.

"What play?" asks Dahlia.

"*The City Between Us*," says Joan.

"I never heard of it," says Dahlia.

"That's because we're just writing it."

"How can I be in a play that isn't written?"

"We've written in a part for you."

"I'm not a South American Carmen Miranda?"

"No."

"I'm not a Falasha from Ethiopia?"

"No."

"Who am I?"

"Dahlia."

"There's no such character."

"Shh!" says Gerda to this offshoot group.

Terry frowns. How can she ever accomplish anything? Deviationism everywhere.

The young girls are trying to overhear Dahlia, the star. Once she gave them tickets for a performance. They knew who she was because her voice was the strongest and carried the chorus, but never could they have recognized her.

"The play is about Jerusalem and the pain of its inhabitants," says Joan.

"Jerusalem *is* a pain," says Dahlia, "a pain in the ass.

You should have seen my audience tonight."

Tova tells her, "It's about the people who have lived here for years. We're writing songs—"

"Not 'Jerusalem the Golden'?"

"No, 'Jerusalem the Torn.' "

Dahlia drags on the cigarette and coughs.

"You write it, I'll sing it."

Tova reaches for the cigarette. "Not with that throat."

They wrestle and giggle.

Antoinette tries to distract. "Think of the drama of the event, the elevated prose, the dialogue."

"Of our play?"

"No, of the Book of Esther."

They are brought back to the occasion.

"This has the stuff of Shakespearean drama," says Antoinette. "Royal families, lands to conquer, court intrigues, assassination attempts and the attempts thwarted, wiliness, seduction of women, clowns and humor, the wise cousin, the wicked counselor, the drunken ruler and the beautiful queen. It has portents and prophecies. It should be an opera like *Samson et Dalila!*"

Antoinette has set the stage. Terry continues calmly.

"Esther approaches the king dressed in her finest."

"What is she wearing?" asks Rina.

"Oh, a very nice dress," says Terry.

Disappointment.

"Royal apparel," says Simha. "She has learned from the goddess to expose her breasts. She ties bands under them and around her neck. She hides her garb under a silver robe. When she appears in the inner court, the king looks up annoyed. Esther's robe opens. She is pointing at him. He points his scepter back at her."

"That's disgusting," says Vered, "before the children." She's become prudish.

"That's counterproductive," says Terry.

The Tale is a great success.

"Xerxes says to his queen, 'Ask what you will and it shall be given you, even unto half the kingdom.'"

"Wow," says Robin, "a real fairy tale."

"Maybe that second half belonged to Vashti," reminds Terry.

They sound the greiger against Terry who would remind them of the unpleasant at the height of the tale.

"What does she say?"

Every Israeli knows the whole script.

"She says," Terry continues, and the others join in, "'The adversary and the enemy is this wicked Haman,' for he would cause Esther and her people 'to be destroyed, to be slain, and to perish.'"

The happy grinding of the noisemakers. May all enemies be given a headache.

Terry concludes. "So Haman is undone and the three of them live happily ever afterward."

"The three?"

"Xerxes, Esther, and her cousin Mordecai, who has taken Haman's place as the king's adviser."

More noisemakers. A woman sandwiched between men.

Terry: "And Esther made no more choices. They were all made for her."

Silence.

Deedee says, "Once there were two alternatives. I could stay at home, the good girl, the supporter of my mother and brothers and sisters, or I could travel into danger."

Rina and Shula say, "Once we had two choices. We could stay at home, good girls, or we could go on the road into traffic."

Dahlia says, "Once I had two alternatives. I could stay at home, the good girl, and feed my mother, or I could go on the stage and arouse every unholy passion."

Mihal says, "I had two choices. I could stay in my marriage, a beaten wife, or I could try to strike back at the beater."

Simha says, "Once I had two choices. I could have stayed home and married, or I could make new births and new prayers."

Hepzibah says, "I had but one choice and I took it."

Gloria says, "I had two alternatives. I could have stayed in the Midwest and questioned nothing, or I could question everything and travel from the Midwest to the Mideast."

Antoinette says, "I had two choices. I could have quoted Shakespeare in my beautiful native land, or I could bring him here to the desert."

Terry says, "Once I had two choices. I could have stayed home and sung revolutionary songs, or I could sing them in the streets."

Joan says, "Once I had two choices. I could have stayed in Manchester and written in a familiar tongue, or I could come here, forever the foreigner."

Tova says, "I had two choices. I could have stayed home as Gittle, the good girl, or I could come here, change my name and find a new definition for good."

Gerda speaks quietly. She is smoking and coughing. "Once I had two choices. I could have mourned forever after my family in the crematorium, or I could rise from their ashes."

So the lots were cast.


A strange figure passes the visitors to the city.

"What is it?" asks the Bedouin prince.

"An insect," says his companion.

It is a ladybug, black spots on red wings, a little cap with antennae.

"Did they make it themselves?" admires the Bedouin. "It is truly unique."

Not so, another bug passes, holding its mother's hand, and a swarm of them with red wings and black spots fly before the visitors.

"It is not unique," says the companion. "It is a plague."

They begin asking, in a more organized fashion, for the Khan Theater. They have learned that Dahlia is singing there. At the Khan they are told by a member of the cast, "She is at the little house on the small street in the Jewish Quarter of the Old City."

And the prince goes forth with gladness of heart. And his companion goes forth to cause mischief.


Simha wipes the scattered poppy seeds from the dish.

"And the spirit of Vashti prevailed, as well as the courage of Esther, for women have only one choice."

Simha rises. Hava is whimpering in her basket. She is getting too large for it. Simha has bedecked Hava with festive apparel. She brings her forth, wrapped in a colorful shawl, a tiny bracelet around her fat ankle. Hava peers nearsightedly at the family of women.

Simha is of the caste of Cohen, the priestly caste. Because it is a festive holiday, there is recited the blessing of the priest. Simha sings that chant that was sung in the Temple of Jerusalem. The melody is ancient, the form playful—three lines consisting of three, five, and seven words.

Simha holds Hava up in her arms. The light from the naphtha heater glows through the grate. Simha bounces Hava.

> Shehena bless thee,
> Shine Her face upon thee,
> Turn Her face unto thee in peace.

As Simha sings "*shalom*," peace, there is a running in the street, a scuffling outside of the door. There is a pushing and shoving. The door gives.

"No!" says the young prince.

"Which is she?" asks his companion, throwing off his black caftan, the long coat.

"Don't do anything!" begs the Bedouin.

"We cannot allow a Jewish woman to defile the tribe," says the companion.

The women are screaming. Terry rushes the door with a chair.

The wanderer jumps aside.

"*Which is she?*"

Dahlia has been dozing from the brandy. She sits up.

"There! There! Not there. Not there." The young prince would defend her. How? By pointing to another.

He points to Simha who is standing, the presiding priestess.

The companion calls to his God, to the God of his provinces, his tents and trappings. His hammer strikes at her forehead and misses. It hits, instead, the infant in the flowered shawl. A weak cry is heard. Hava's toes jerk and droop. The ankle bracelet dangles.

The men, of course, cannot escape. The young prince does not want to, once he sees the horror on the face of his beloved. The companion does not struggle for he has committed his holy act.

Gloria, Tova, Deedee hold them. Gerda punches them. Hepzibah goes for the police. The quiet streets of the Old City, the deserted streets, are filled with the wail of the siren and the wailings of the mother.

The *Megillah*, the tale, is told. In the legend there is relief from the enemy, sorrow is turned into gladness, mourning into holiday.

In life, only some of this is possible.

# 12
# Kiss the Lip of the Sea for Me

When Hava died Simha said the prayer, On Seeing Falling Stars. But prayers did not satisfy. Curses were needed.

Simha's mouth was an O—moan, bone, soul, alone.

Simha's chest heaved words like breath/death.

Simha's breasts were stones that hung from the neck. Milk hardened in them. Simha's stomach digested nothing. Her bowels clanged shut. Simha's eyes were dry as the cornea of an old woman. Her menstruation began heavily.

The woman floated in the heavy air of the house. Mickey

washed the baby, every crack and crevice. She bought a soft brush to brush its light hair. She covered its bruise with a bonnet.

The wayward girls, Rina, Shula and Robin, brought gifts for Hava, a rubber doll, a squeak toy, a teething ring.

Antoinette brought a charmingly illustrated *A Child's Garden of Verses*, which she had intended for Hava's bedtime. Hepzibah read aloud, "*El moley rahamim*, Lord, full of compassion," but Simha stopped her with a glance.

No psalms, none of David's *mēzmorim*, nothing sacred, no instrument plucked, no harp or lyre, for under Simha no Rock solidified and over her no wings sheltered. The Lord looketh away and tooketh away. The Great Hand was careless, palms wet, allowing slippage.

The kibbutznik came on the long journey from the north to sing a last lullaby.

Hava is to be wrapped in a shroud and carried to the Mount of Olives, where for four hundred years Simha's family had their ancient view of the city. Generations lay in a stony circle, like teeth in a mouth, father-to-son, and here is mother burying daughter.

The women bear the shrouded child on their shoulders through the streets of the Jewish Quarter, out the Dung Gate toward the Mount of Olives. One day the Redeemer is to come through the gate and enter the Temple court. Then will all the stones churn, then will shoulders overturn mounds, then will a parade follow Her through the streets— a parade of faintly cheering ghosts and the shouting living.

Arab workmen have prepared the shallow grave.

Hepzibah says, "May she come to her place in peace."

"And what of me?" wails Simha.

Each of the women and the kibbutznik put a small stone on Hava's mound. Not Simha. She lies across the grave.

"I am a stone," she says.

The women pluck grass and scatter it on the grave.

Hepzibah says, " 'They of the city shall flourish like the

grass of the earth. . . . the Lord wipeth away tears from all faces.' "

Not so.

The kibbutznik and Terry walk the long way back holding onto Simha. The others trail. When they come to the stone house, Simha hesitates at the door and will not enter. The wayward girls lead her across the strip of road to their house and seat her near a window.

"Water," requests the kibbutznik. He wets the cracked lips of his beloved with droplets.

"I do not accept this," says Simha at last. "Neither death nor life."

Nor can the kibbutznik who has learned to accept everything. He had accepted loneliness and found company; he had accepted long walks and sports and found exercise in bed. He had accepted the idea of marriage but found an independent woman. He had accepted paternity, but what is a father without his child?

For the week of mourning, Simha refuses to return to her house. Nor does she sleep or eat or attend services. She sits on her hard chair, feverish from her engorged breasts.

There are more than ten women, enough for a minyan of angels, a dozen doyennes, thirteen lunar maidens, fifteen friends. It only takes one to pray. She cannot pray and will not entreat.

This week Terry does not organize, does not work, does not campaign for the coming elections, does not force attention upon Simha or order in the stone house. From Wayward, Simha can see Terry watering plants. Terry nods at her gravely and does not linger.

Each of the fifteen women is saddled to a different horse, reined to another life: Terry to action; Gerda to molecules and numbers, exactness and abstraction; Gloria to self-glorification; Deedee to deaths and resurrections; Antoinette and Joan to the word; Dahlia to the note, Mickey to passion and regret; Hepzibah to the soul, Vered to responsibility; Tova to performance; among the wayward girls, Rina and Shula to respectability and Robin to confusion.

The reins have slipped in Simha's large hands. Her hands were chalices and her eyes praised all wonders. Now she is dulled, her hands dry and limp in her lap. The kibbutznik is getting stiff sitting by her. He is used to an early schedule, rising with the cows. Now he sits and dozes and startles awake.

So is the city dozing and startling.

Jerusalem cats are fighting fiercely. A Moshe Dayan cat with one eye growls. In the rain yesterday a woman in the Old City hung her dripping clothes on the wet balcony. This morning a goat brays, chickens and kittens trip over one another in someone's garden.

"I need a chicken for dinner tonight," a young wife says.

"I just saw one walk into the court," says her husband.

Balloons of gas are expiring in housing projects. Women are rinsing their hair with henna. Someone is playing first the recorder and then the oboe.

People are rude and sweet. Someone asks a bus driver where the Old City is.

"Am I a taxi? If you want to know, ask a taxi," says the driver.

The passenger's startled hand drops all of his change onto the bus floor. The driver stops and everyone scrambles to help the man.

Someone is washing fruit carefully so the family will not get cholera. Someone is buying a kilo of light green pears, an avocado, an eggplant and large radishes. Someone is buying lemons for a salad dressing.

Everyone is talking about money.

The sun alternates with cloudy days. The sun shines on the rose-colored city in the morning. The taped voice of the muezzin is heard loudly in the stone house. So are the voices of birds.

Jerusalemites shiver at night.

The phallus of the YMCA casts a shadow over the city. Across from it is the King David where people eat glazed strawberries on cake.

In various quarters of the Old City children carry unbaked falafel loaves on their heads. Little Armenian girls with large eyes and tiny earrings lead smaller children by the hand. A Baptist tour is going through the Stations of the Cross. Everyone has something in the Old City: embroidered, quilted, striped. Braids of prayers entwine over the separate quarters.

In the stone house statues of women sit. In Wayward nothing untoward happens. A figure never leaves the window, staring at the doorway of her house as if someone would crawl in, staring at the dust-filled blue sky, as if someone were flying by.

Someone does crawl in. Someone does fly by.

It is Shlomo Sassoon with his yard goods.

He is carrying dark purple materials and transparent black Indian cloth, edged in gold. The gold is tarnishing green. He sets down his wares and requests a ladle of cool water from the clay water jar.

The water jar is empty. Terry is startled. It was filled earlier. The ground around it is dry.

" 'The depth of the well is dry,' " says Shlomo, " 'as are all streams and brooks, even the river coming from Eden.' "

Across the little road Simha is looking hollow-eyed at the dozing kibbutznik. He swam in her water. He fished therein. And the water creature grew from fish to amphibian. And was expelled in the stream coming from Eden.

In the stone house Shlomo Sassoon's scarves wriggle out of the case. They float and fly and dive, kites, butterflies, model airplanes. He is enshrouded in a fringed black scarf like a tallith.

"Is there a fan on?" Shlomo asks Terry.

There is not.

"There is a disturbance," says Shlomo, "a whirring in

the air. A stirring. See how my scarves float?"

The room is ribboned.

"Is there a hive on the roof?"

Terry does not think so.

"There is a gathering, a droning," says Shlomo. "Small wings are tapping against carapaces of skin."

The scarves are whispering. Some are faintly wailing, a baby's nasal Whah. One is hissing terrible things:

> I eat them,
> the fat worms of fingers and toes.
> I eat my way through the nose.
> I hate that which lies in the crook of the arm,
> that which creeps, which is smooth-fleshed,
> all that is an abomination,
> for I am covered with scales and scabs,
> with pits and boils.
> I hate pink pads of feet,
> for I am callused and horny-toed.
> I hate what suckles for I drink brine.

The scarves are tired. They sag to the floor. One or two heave and sink again.

"Action must be taken," says Terry. "This is irrational but there is discontent in the air."

"Maybe there should be another funeral," says Rina.

"Maybe we should dig her out and put her back again," says Robin. She had done that numerous times with her goldfish and cat.

"It has never been done," says Hepzibah, "uprooting the dead, for they grow as the living do. They root into the ground. They extend into branches, travel along underground rivulets. The dead are busy. It is a sin to disturb their work."

"Hava is decomposing," says Gerda.

The children are startled. Gerda persists.

"It would be disagreeable to exhume her. As a scientist, I cannot endorse this."

They turn from Gerda.

"If Simha could have given her the last bath," says Mickey.

"If Simha could have given her the presents," says Robin.

"If Simha could have held her to the breast one last time," says Vered.

"If Simha knew there were deaths and resurrections," says Deedee.

"If the death could be restaged," say Joan and Tova.

"If Simha could sing a last lullaby," says Dahlia.

"If we could have another ritual."

But what kind? Simha was their lightning in clear weather, their claps of thunder on dry days, the moon in daytime.

A scarf snakes across the terrazzo floor.

"'And the spirit of God hovered over the face of the water,'" says Shlomo. "'And He divided the waters from the waters.'"

Terry begins to understand.

"Shlomo says that we must make a firmament between heaven and earth," says Terry, "between reality and unreality."

Shlomo turns to her. He remembers her. His eyes light up. That bed behind the curtains. He was the waterpipe she blew through. He slides on his scarves, crossing the floor to her. But when Terry is in action, nothing intervenes.

"It has to take place at water, at the sea," says Terry, "for some reason."

"It began there," says Antoinette.

"How the hell do we all get to the sea?" asks Gloria.

In a little country with a seacoast, don't worry, one can get to the sea.

"No one wants my wares?" asks Shlomo, repacking his case.

"Not now, motek," says Terry, "not in a house of mourning."

With a twirling and a winding, an undulation like a fish's tail, Shlomo Sassoon is out the door and around the corner of the stone house.

There is Simha standing at the doorway.

"I must go to the *yam*," she says, "to the sea."

Terry goes to Wayward for a phone.

"I must have the bus," she tells the Ministry of Welfare, "to take the wayward girls on an excursion."

The bus dispatcher begins to shout. It is normal to react thus.

"They are restless," says Terry. "I may not be able to contain them."

A bus is ordered to leave for the Old City.

Nothing comes on time in this land. So, also, the bus is late. And the driver is a fool, and a bad-tempered one. He even loses his way out of the city but would not think to ask the women.

"Alley cat!" he calls to a driver whose car he has just forced against a curb. "Where is the Road to the Sea?"

The driver gets out of the car to fight. The bus driver opens the bus doors. Terry pushes to the front.

"I have been trained to drive buses, tractors and trucks in the army," little Terry tells the driver. "I can also read any kind of map. If you do not do as I tell you—"

He is half-in, half-out of the door.

"—I will lock you out of the bus and drive it to the sea myself."

He grumbles and backs up into the bus. He looks to the kibbutznik for support. The kibbutznik is dozing. The driver releases the brakes and turns on the news, full volume.

Terry is at the helm again.

"It's the news!" he shouts. "Are you an isolationist?"

"Nahag," she addresses his occupation in a megaphoned

voice, "this is a bus of mourning. You are taking us for a burial. If you commit sacrilege, desecration or profanation, the spirit of the dead will wail in your ears forever and will drown out all events."

The nahag turns down the radio. He puts on his jacket and straightens his cap. He is a man on a mission, but he cannot help being curious, nor can he help noticing the hair of Gloria, red as King David's, burnished like a shield, or like one of the wild flowers it is forbidden to pick along the roadside.

"Hey, *Gingy*, Redhead," he whispers, "who died?"

"Our baby," says Gloria softly.

Terry directs the nahag eastward, down from the Judean Hills to the lowest spot on earth, the Dead Sea.

Immediately Simha spreads her arms and rushes to that barren area. The mountains of Jordan are jagged on the other side of the sea. The sea is blue. It is a painful sea. Every bruise is cut by the salt. Every wound throbs. All orifices gargle in the saltwater.

"*Yam, yam,*" she cries, "I didn't see you for such a long time!" There is the beach, the *safat yam*, lip of the sea.

She races in with the long skirt that has not been changed all this week of mourning. The kibbutznik runs after her. He is short but speedy.

The driver yells, "Hello! Hello! Watch out there!"

The women stand on the beach like driftwood.

Simha's knees are wet and her skirt looks like knickers. Simha's breasts are wet, as when she was nursing. Simha's head is submerged. The kibbutznik splashes after her. The head bobs up, the breasts, the knees, the feet. In the Dead Sea no one drowns. The swimmers are matzoh balls floating on chicken soup. Simha stares at the sky above her, at the mountain range in another land with its apertures of caves.

"What is she doing?" asks the nahag.

"Drowning herself," says Gloria.

"She found the right place to do it," says the driver.

The kibbutznik paddles in wide circles around her. The women are getting chilled, for the desert cools in the late afternoon. But still they stand.

Simha closes her eyes and folds her arms over her wet blouse, as if she were on a pallet. The kibbutznik steers her into shore.

The women line up, pallbearers. The nahag debates between going back to the bus to listen to the news or watching this beach show.

Simha is stretched out on the sand.

"Ah," he says to Gloria, "it is *her* baby."

The kibbutznik is wringing his hands. Direct action he understands, not circuitous.

Terry stretches on top of Simha and kisses her mouth.

"There are tears on her lips," says Terry.

"It is the sea," explains the nahag.

Terry rises from Simha. She goes to the edge of the sea and wets her lips. She beckons to the women.

"Go to the lip of the sea, kiss it, bring salty lips to each other," says Terry.

They do.

"Now say, 'I accept salt in our lives and in our friendship.'"

They repeat this.

"Two," says Terry, "gather a handful of sand. Say, 'I accept the shift of the sands in our lives and in our friendship.'"

They do this, except for Simha, her anxious lover and the shocked driver.

"Three," says Tova the actress. "Look at the waves. 'I accept continuity and change in my life and in our friendship.'"

They are a chorus.

"Four," says Joan, the playwright. "We have stood here from low to high tide. 'I accept tidal changes in my life and in our friendship.'"

The waves strum. The waves drum.

"Five," says Gerda. "Imitate the whisper of the waves. 'I accept mysterious rustlings in my life and in our friendship.'"

A gull shrieks.

"Six," says Mickey. "Hear the call of the gulls. 'I accept demonic laughter in my life and in our friendship.'"

A vessel is going to Jordan.

"Seven," says Deedee, the traveler. "Watch a passing vessel. 'I accept direction and destination, departures and ports of call in my life and in our friendship.'"

A boat rocks on the sea.

"Eight," says Vered, the social worker. "Locate rope or a moored boat. 'I accept moorings in my life and in our friendship.'"

The waves are slight, the waves pucker, curtsy, bow.

Dahlia is there. "Nine," she says. "Dance on the sand."

The women join hands and run in a line along the ripple marks of the waves.

"'I accept leaps and boundings in my life and in our friendship.'"

"This isn't bad, you know," the driver confides to Gloria. He has joined hands with her to run along the beach. He stops to pick up shells.

"Misses," he calls. He whistles shrilly.

They are startled.

"Number ten. Pick up driftwood," says the nahag, "the insides of shells, whatever is washed ashore of the salt sea."

They do as he has said.

"'I accept the leavings of the sea in my life and in our friendship.'"

Terry looks at him in surprise. Gloria stays close to him.

"Wait," says the show-off, "that isn't all. 'The sea giveth and the sea taketh.'"

Simha sits up. They all stop.

A flock of birds flies from Israel to Jordan.

"Eleven," says Terry softly. " 'I accept flights from my life and in our friendship.' "

Simha is shivering.

Terry finds a mollusk broken in two. She brings the halves to Simha.

"Twelve," says Terry. "Find a shellfish divided in two. 'I accept being broken in half in my life and in my friendship.' "

She gives Simha one of the shells. Their palms meet.

"Thirteen," says Terry.

She is on her knees embracing Simha.

"Unlucky," the driver whispers to Gloria.

"No, lucky."

They are holding hands.

Terry says, "Accept support. Sit in the crotch of a tree, lean against a branch or accept an embrace. 'I accept firm embrace in my life and in our friendship.' "

Simha clings to Terry, then to the kibbutznik. The women embrace each other. Gloria and the driver begin kissing passionately.


That night, in the early hours, on the last day of mourning, the kibbutznik, the cowherd, milks Simha.

# 13
# Swear a True Oath

In this Chapter the Thirteenth all will come to right.
Allotments will be fair, time apportioned and justice
preside.

A baker's dozen is a lucky thirteen. One pays the
Baxterie for twelve and receives thirteen loaves.

The lucky day for the women in the stone house is
Friday the thirteenth. All over the world, in the Diaspora,
women shall dwell on the thirteenth floor. In that space
between twelve and fourteen of every hotel and office

building, are women crouching, sleeping, eating cheese-cakes, bathing, paring their toenails, reading puzzles, working math problems, bearing down in childbirth, fondling one another.

Some are having sunlamp treatment, others massages. Some are ritually cleansing themselves. Some are examining their vaginas for three days consecutively, to see if there is no issue of blood so that they may return to the bed of their husbands.

Some are reading difficult books, some are looking at *Bride* magazine. It is a world of long hair, short hair, eyebrows, unshaven armpits, bushy or light crotches, thick hair on legs, or smooth or prickly legs. Hair is everywhere—in the wastebasket, wires of hair in the sink, floating in the toilet bowl, clumps of hair in the trap of the shower. They are furry animals of the forest lying tamely between floors.

Despite this lucky number, one does not like thirteen at the table, and the wages of the hangman are thirteen pence halfpenny. Disagreeable people are said to be in their thirteens.

How can definite numbers be so indefinite? Because calendars flip whole years and days are not days. The Roman, French revolutionary, eighteenth-century British and the Hebrew calendars have no time in common.

Women in the Gregorian world are in day until midnight. Women are in daytime in Israel until sundown. It is past sundown and the women in the stone house of the Old City sit and work on the political campaign.

Literature to be distributed is piled on the floor. Some of it is idealistic: *Return to our origins, an egalitarian society.* Some is informational: *Money spent on training our daughters is less than one-fourth of that spent on training our sons.* Some of it is illusory: *Tax the rich.* Some is strident: *Girls in The Land are untrained and illiterate. They are fit for only two things, marriage and whoring.* Or, *Do not have daughters if you do not want daughters. Drown them, but do not send them out into the streets.* Some is pleading: *Practice birth control. Practice vote control.* Some attacks special interests: *Divorce the rabbinate from the state.* Some attacks the ministries of internal and external affairs: *Peace with our cousins. We have no alternative.* Some of it attacks the ladies of Hadassah: *If we accept American money, we must accept American advice.*

There is something in every pamphlet to offend everyone. Even the women. Hepzibah will not touch the pamphlet attacking the rabbinate. Gloria will not distribute the pamphlet attacking American money contributions. Simha cannot look at the pamphlet about the necessity of peace between Jew and Arab.

The Bedouin and his companion languish in jail. The mukhtar comes to visit Dahlia.

"I am not in favor of killing babies. I am a loving man. You know. It is not possible that you forgot. Or that you forgot my son."

Dahlia is not allowed to see the young Bedouin. She sends him fruit. It spoils awaiting clearance. She sends him a message. It spoils in censorship.

One night, after a rare rain in Beer Sheva, Dahlia comes out of the theater to find a silent, veiled woman awaiting her. The woman lifts the silver coin chain that she brought as a bride to her marriage, and wraps it around Dahlia's hands.

"For my son," whispers the woman in Arabic, "to buy him back."

Dahlia's hands tremble. The coins rattle. The prince's mother stands regal and dry-eyed. Dahlia replaces the chain around the mother's head.

Dahlia goes to Jerusalem to prepare herself. She pours ashes on her head, rends the collar of a blouse, wraps a mourning shawl around her. She spends the night on the steps of the stone house. When Simha opens the door in the morning, she finds the supplicant.

No word has been spoken between them since Hava's death.

"Slahee-lee, forgive me." Dahlia prostrates herself on the stones of the street.

"Rise," says Simha. "It is a sin to humiliate yourself."

Still Dahlia lies prone.

"I have waited for you to come so I could tell you that the accidental needs no forgiving."

Simha would embrace the singer, but Dahlia grovels.

"I have to ask more," says Dahlia.

"No," says Simha. "I am only human."

"Forgive another," says Dahlia.

"No," says Simha.

"An accident needs no forgiving," says Dahlia.

"I am not a saint," says Simha. "Allow me to hate. Hatred is my child. I carry it in my arms. I nurse it. I bed down with it at night. I rise with it in the dawn."

"Distinguish between them," says Dahlia. "Hate one and not the other."

Simha is panting, holding her chest.

"It is written that the sufferers of violence cannot avenge themselves for the pain is too close to them," says Dahlia. "Only the priests can decree. You are both, Simha, the sufferer and the law, the priest and the subject."

"I will love you or hate you for this," sobs Simha. "We may never speak again."

"I would be in mourning all of my life," says Dahlia.

Simha closes the door behind her.

"We will walk to the Russian Compound," she says. "I will carry nothing to the prison, no key, no money, only my sorrow."

So it came to pass that Simha testified as a witness for the young prince. Justice Malamud presided and sentenced the prince to two years and his companion to life, the two separated forever. The young prince will be eighteen when he is released. He will leave the prison at Ramle, kissing the dear friends he has made there. He will go into the desert like Ishmael, longing for his old Bedouin companion and hating his own land.

Terry is making enemies.

Who are her enemies?

The religious are her enemies, for they would not limit birth, or the power of the rabbinate.

The administration is her enemy for they would not be exposed for wrongdoing.

Men are her enemies for they would not share power.

Women are her enemies for they have adjusted to discomfort.

Warriors are her enemies for she is a pacifist.

Pacifists are her enemies for her ways are martial.

Who is this politician, this citizen of the city?

She is small with dark eyes, a straight nose, full lips. She is small with staring breasts, a soft belly, hairy crotch. She is small with brains that scratch and whine at the confines of her head. She is delicate with callused hands. She smiles with grave eyes. She devastates with dimples.

Yet she is offensive, not in odor or stain, cigarette-brown fingers and teeth. Not with voice, raised or reasoned. Not with hair, wild or combed. Not with hands, calm or gesturing so flamboyantly that people within reach are burned with the rushing butt of her cigarette. Her mind is searching for its way out of the room, out of the tiny land. Her mind is a terrorist—at borders and corners. Her mind frightens.

In the past she was a good girl. She mouthed the slogans of her father but shopped with her mother. She set the table at night for dinner. She had highest marks in Handwriting and Deportment. She had lower marks in Citizenship and History. She had average marks in Math.

She wore good-girl clothes, stiffened petticoats and long flannel skirts cartooned with felt poodle dogs. She wore ballet slippers or high pointy shoes. She always smiled. She never screwed. Screwing, after all, had to do with the Mechanical Arts, in which her marks were average or less. It had to do with the fitting together of parts, with engineering, and how could she, tiny, ever be invaded without being torn and split in two?

One day she stopped being a good girl. Her Handwriting became more cramped, her Deportment went downhill, her Algebra improved, as did her knowledge of all things technical, the repairing of light fixtures, plumbing valves, her own internal valves.

She began to love men. She began warmly to love women. One day Terry found that to love men a lot was to love herself less, for they were pleased to let her bathe, comb, wash and feed them. They were pleased to let her shop for them and place their clothes in the cleaners. It gave them pleasure if she typed for them, wrote letters to their mothers and raised their children.

Terry became shorter yet. She walked with head forward, eyes to the ground. Her voice was whispery and lispy. Her toes turned inward. Her fingers fidgeted each other.

Her heart had become a compact in which one man at a time saw himself reflected, a savings bank where they could withdraw from her account. Her stomach turned sour. She began to shout at her mother, her father and the lovers.

Then she discovered that her place of loving and caring was not the heart, that uncertain pump which the Diaspora celebrates, nor the liver, where feeling and power are located, according to The Land. It was not in her head, which developed sinus trouble during damp weather. But in all of her: the dark eyes, the dimple to put a finger into, the straight nose to trace, the raspberry lips that needed no coloring. All of her was for thinking and for loving. She did not circumscribe her thoughts or her amours. Old men like Shlomo Sassoon were made nimble by her. Young men like her client Doodoo were natured by her. Women like Tova and Joan were caressed by her. A religious like Hepzibah was understood by her. A singer like Dahlia was applauded by her.

Perhaps, adding up all of her loves, she would have a constituency.

Her bitterest enemy is the former lover of Vered, a member of Parliament.

Guess who now upholds the dignity of the family, the honor of womankind, the protection of children and of the innocent? Vered's former lover.

A former lover is everything a lover is not. When he hears the name of his late beloved, a growl starts deep in his chest. Instead of a pelvic reaction, fists clench. Instead of dreamy eyes, there is the determined gaze into the family future. Instead of the sensual, there is the sentimental. The lover tears at the mention of "mother," "family," "country." Instead of the exploratory, the former lover comes home to a familiar address.

Vered's former lover has reconciled with his wife. It is he who brings Shabbat flowers. He baby-sits so his wife can have evenings out. He gives her time and money to shop.

He leads his political party into liaisons with the National Religious Party. He is against abortion or birth control. He is one of the organizers of the Male Gynecological Conference, whose purpose is to praise traditionalism and treat infertility.

Vered's former lover has introduced legislation to ban antinational marches, to reduce the age of imprisonment for young girls found soliciting. He is active in the government's plan to balance the budget and would reduce costs first by phasing out the Home for Jewish Wayward Girls. Already meals are cut to once a day, linen service is eliminated, the telephone removed and the television set has been given to a poor deserving family.

The *Jerusalem Post* praises him. He is photographed with his family in a photograph so contrasty that he is a shadowy bulk looming behind his wife and children. The reporter quotes him on the subject of the approaching Male Gynecological Conference:

"'Women, leave your bodies in our hands.'"

Terry girds for battle.


## THE CEREMONY OF GIRDING FOR BATTLE

It is written in the *Iliad* that warriors must swear a true oath with two lambs, goatskin of cheering wine, fruit of the earth. The women decide, however, to be like the Nazarene Samson. They consecrate each other at the place of their meeting, the little stone house. They swear that they will abstain from wine and strong drink or even fresh grapes or raisins. None of these women warriors will shave their armpits or legs. Their hair shall grow from eyebrow, chin and wart. They shall avoid contact with dead bodies, nor eat, any unclean thing.

There is great argumentation over the latter. Does that mean Hava's grave on the Mount of Olives must be avoided? What if violence should ensue in the upcoming battle and their comrades or opponents are killed? When they eat, is meat a dead body?

They argue into the night, the next day, again a night. They decide by consensus that:

Hava's spirit is alive and her graveside can be visited.

That they will be passive resisters in the war ahead.

That they will eat no shellfish in the Arab restaurant or "white meat," pork, from the Not Kosher butcher shop, or anything which creepeth and crawleth upon the earth.

The warriors gather. Simha gives them drink of cold spring water. They drink from the ladle and swear a true oath, to live on in golden Jerusalem or to sail across the Mediterranean to other lands and never forget this city. They swear to be arms and legs of one body. They swear to be one heart and one liver, feeling and power.

For Hepzibah they cover their heads with kerchiefs, tied tightly, to honor the power under which they fight and to prevent their hair from being pulled.

Terry is the first to rise. She is the smallest but the loudest. Her shoes have platform soles and stamp across the room.

Gloria is there, nervously trying not to giggle. Irish Deedee is there for all her ancestors, her aunt who fasted to death in a British prison, her grandmother who lost sons in battle.

Tova is there, the kerchief lumpy over her curls.

Dahlia is there to sing the women into battle. She drums marching feet on her guitar and the women hear armies assembling and the great horn blown. They know their enemy will stumble from wine and overmuch eating of meat. The women will be lionesses in pursuit.

Mihal is so wrathful that she has sharpened her fingernails, heedless of the resolution to be peaceful.

Vered is there, the gall of her lover.

Simha is clad in black with charcoal marks between her eyes and around her mouth. She is the tallest, Strife, who will tread upon the enemy.

The wayward girls come with goatskin drums. They recite The Psalm on Girding One's Loins:

As a wall of warriors,
As a cloud of wrath
As waves unceasing
As a chorus,
A host, a din
They turn toward the setting sun.
They turn toward the pale moon.
They turn East to the Mediterranean,
North to the source of the Jordan,
South to the Dead Sea.

They turn with the chill wind of winter.
They turn with the scorching hamsene of summer.
They are taut as bows,
unerring arrows,
shiny as unsheathed swords.
They are armed
and ready for battle.

What is the name of the monster, the enemy? Not Humbaba, the monster of *Gilgamesh*. More like Humbug, the Male Gynecological Conference.

The women of the Independent Party send in a message. "Let us speak."

There is laughter from the hall. Hissing. "Denied."

The women of the Independent Party send in another message. "Let one of us speak."

There is a laughter from the hall. Hissing. "Denied."

From inside of the hall, knee slapping, guffaws.

The women of the Independent Party march in. "We will speak."

From their blouses they produce banners.

WE ARE OUR BODIES

RETURN HEALING TO THE ORIGINAL HEALERS

MIDWIVES, NOT DOCTORS. HERBS, NOT ETHERS

A transformation occurs. Not one woman is recognized as the gentle sex, the tender sex. Not one male gynecologist remembers seeing so many women's faces. Not one of those suited gentlemen, with or without glasses, with or without hair, with small or large penises, with empty or filled testicles, remembers seeing so many women erect, not in stirrups.

From the dining tables cloths are snatched up and thrown over the invading army. They are the Evil Eye, these women. They are the shouting mouth. Veil the eye, muffle the mouth.

These men of smiles and offices, of nurses and families, of hospitals and beds have turned into the monster Humbug, sucking in their breath like a giant fart, rushing like bulls at these ghost-covered women. Under their feet the floor trembles, chairs crash, tables knock together.

Terry and Simha look like dustcloths over furniture, like the haunting memories of these men. They shake loose from the tablecloths and rush the platform. At the microphone is Vered's former lover. His voice is shrill. Something is wrong with the mike. It whistles.

"Kill"—whistle—"the women."

"Get"—whistle—"the bitches."

Whistle—"Fuck"—whistle, whistle—"the whores."

Ah, so that's it! That is what politicians and male gynecologists think of Independent women.

The hotel summons the police. The press follows.

Vered's lover has thrown the metal water pitcher from the speaker's platform at Vered's head. She ducks. The pitcher knocks out an eminent infertility expert.

The melee is duly recorded and the informed public reacts. It elects Terry to the Independent Party seat not for her platform, not for her party, but for giving battle.

"All honor to the soldier," people say. She is at the borders. She guards their home.

Comes the day of the new Parliament. Terry goes down the aisle to take her oath of office. The members of the National Religious Party, the Likud, Labor, the Communists and all the splinter groups whistle and wink.

# 14
# The Bird and the Thieves

Robin, at fourteen, plays truant from her life. She alights on edges and ledges, balconies, doorsteps, windowsills.

Her family is in disarray, the school disagreeable and the intensive language classes incomprehensible. The Home for Jewish Wayward Girls is filled with girls from Europe and Africa, several inches shorter than she, yet more developed in every way.

She circles the Walled City, studying the peripheral life. It is here that she comes upon Stephanos, Hannah and the Word of God.

They sit outside of the Walled City. When the finger of God points they go witnessing.

Stephanos chooses carefully. He speaks only to the young.

" 'I will show you the river of the water of life, bright as crystal, flowing from the throne of God.' "

The witnesses themselves are in late teens or early twenties. They sit on haunches, the girls dressed modestly, head covering, long skirt, wrist-length blouses. The boys wear button-up shirts and yarmulkes with their jeans. Each witness has both the Old and New Testaments.

They sit every day at a different gate to the Old City, the Jaffa Gate, Damascus, Dung, the Lion. They murmur, " 'Enter the city by the gates.' "

They look for young tourists carrying knapsacks, who gaze into other people's eyes for a home.

" 'Enter the city by the gates,' " warns Hannah. " 'Outside are the dogs and sorcerers and fornicators and murderers and idolators and everyone who loves and practices falsehood.' "

That is not only true outside the gates. Inside the gates Robin watches the dismantlement of Wayward. Each day another item is missing: an attachment on the kitchen faucet that suds dishes is taken away and given to Boys Town. The vacuum cleaner cannot be found. Drapes are taken down and brought to the cleaners. They are not rehung.

"There will be redemption soon," smiles Stephanos.

Robin stops. His hair is curly, eyes dreamy. She herself is frizzy and self-conscious. She would wear cap and coat all seasons if she could.

"What?" Robin asks.

His eyes are blue, hers brown. He is slender, not nearly filling out the Sears Roebuck blue work shirt. She is thin, not slender. She cannot decide whether to pull her hair over her ears and hide their protruding or to push her hair away from her ears, for it is warm in the sun. Her face is erupting again and she is miserable. So she walks the shady streets of the Old City where everyone else's face looks greenish and shadowy also.

"Shalom," says Hannah from the ground. "How're you doing?"

"Fine," says Robin.

They introduce themselves, Stephanos, Hannah. Her name?

She blushes.

"Robin in the States. Here they call me Tsiporah, bird, a feminine bird."

"I can see why," says Stephanos.

"How do you like it here?" Hannah asks.

Robin makes a hand gesture. *"Kaha-kaha,* so-so."

"Why kaha-kaha?" asks Stephanos.

"Disconnected?"

"Lonesome?"

They question Robin with concern. She nods.

"Listen, are you free to lunch with us?" Stephanos asks.

He takes her arm. She looks at his smile, his clear eyes, the curly hair.

"Sure," says Robin.

The young people go through the Christian Quarter to a narrow stone house with an ancient wooden door. Once they have closed the door on the dirty street, they find the house large, well furnished and clean.

"A guest for lunch," says Stephanos.

Arab women bring in soup bowls, silverware, and an earthen pot of stew. The children say the blessing over the bread before they break bread together.

The house is quiet with its thick walls and darkly draped windows. The outside stays outside, the screaming cats, beaten donkeys, fighting children.

"What do you do here?" Robin asks hesitantly.

"We study."

"What?"

"How to live with God."

They all smile at her, their faces tan from the Jerusalem sun.

"We groove on God," says Stephanos.

Some of the members of the house drift from the table.

"We're high on Christ," says Hannah.

"You do look happy," says Robin/Tsiporah.

"It wasn't always this way."

"What do you mean?"

It is so quiet here.

"I went through the same thing you're going through now," says Stephanos.

"What?"

"The hypocrisy, right?"

"Right."

"The changes."

"Right."

"Without meaning."

"Yes."

"It wasn't enough," says Hannah.

"No."

"I was still sad," says Stephanos.

"Yes."

"And into the usual things," says Hannah.

Robin/Tsiporah waits.

"The dope, the traveling, the screwing."

"Oh."

"I will never go back to what I was," says Hannah.

"No."

"And my mother doesn't know where in the world I'm at."

That interests Robin.

"How did you get here?" she asks.

Robin's tongue feels a crooked tooth. She needs braces, but cried in the States when her family suggested it and cries now when they don't.

"God sent us," says Hannah.

Others in the house are busy. In the Reading Room several are comparing texts in various languages or exclaiming over a poetic section.

"'I saw heaven opened, and behold, a white horse! He who sat upon it is called Faithful and True. . . . His eyes are like a flame of fire and on his head are many diadems. . . . He is clad in a robe dipped in blood and the name by which he is called is the Word of God.'"

"That's the name of this house," Hannah tells her. "The Word of God."

"Cool," says Robin.

An older man with dark skin and thinning hair comes down to meet her.

"Shalom," he says. "What is your name?"

"Robin back home, Tsiporah here."

"As we all have been given new names," says the man smiling kindly.

"I was Shelley," says Hannah, "for a Grandma Sarah and for Shelley Winters."

"I was Robert," says Stephanos, "for Reuben and for Robert Cummings."

They laugh together, pressing hands.

"Listen, Tsiporah, come back tomorrow."

Can she once again get away from Wayward? Skip school? Fall even further behind at the Hebrew language training? One day away and she missed the Future. Now they all know the Past and she still stumbles in the Present.

When tomorrow arrives Tsiporah worries that she will not find the house in the crowded quarters of the suk. But here are Hannah and Stephanos near the Damascus Gate to lead her in.

They each kiss her tenderly. Tsiporah jumps, runs, backtracks as she walks between them.

The older man is present at the table. He blesses the fruit of the vine. Would they like wine? The wine is warm, the day is warm. None of the young people wants wine at noon.

Tsiporah sits smiling, but Hannah becomes serious.

"This is not what will be eaten on the day of final judgment," she says.

"It isn't?"

"No. On that day, if the house of God is not recognized, we feast on 'the flesh of kings, the flesh of captains, the flesh of mighty men, the flesh of horses and their riders, and the flesh of all men, both free and slave, both small and great.' "

Stephanos turns to Tsiporah.

"Save yourself," he pleads. "You have yet time."

Tsiporah does not stay long this visit.


"Hash, the best?" a whispered voice.

"Nice, that's very nice what you have there," says a man looking at Tsiporah's newly formed breasts.

She walks stiffly, not thinking. She is descending steps and soon stands before the Western Wall.

"Hey, how's it going?" asks a young man.

He is thin, relaxed, his head brilliant in a flowered square yarmulke.

"Fine," says Tsiporah.

"I can see that," says the fellow.

Why is he so friendly?

"What are you doing on the eve of Shabbat?" he asks her.

"Why?"

"Listen, if you want a total experience, I have a friend, this Hasid, who's having an *erev Shabbat* at his house."

"Who's going?"

"The kids who want to come."

"Where is it?"

The young man is efficient, pen and paper ready, an address near the YMCA.

"I'll tell them to look for you," the young man says, "if you promise definitely to be there."

"I'll try definitely to be there."

"I'm Moshe, you look for me."

"I'll tell them at the Home."

"It's not for the Home."

"I'll tell my parents."

"It's not for your parents."

A secret. Two secrets.

Also, the Home is full of secrets. Rina and Shula tell private stories to one another in order to keep them from Robin. Or they tell Robin what happens to them on the street, things Robin would rather they had kept secret—leg things and hair things, juices running, tongues and mounds.

The phone is locked. She cannot call her parents, although for the past two months when she phoned they would say, "Yes, what happened?" If she said, "Something bad," they said, "Wouldn't you know it?" If she said, "Something good," they said, "Who would have believed it?" Her parents cannot handle her. She is not the proper size for them: laps spill, embraces cannot encompass.

Her new family is in the stone house. Terry is the shortest and most energetic, Simha the tallest and, since Hava's death, the most distant. Antoinette and Gerda seem alike to her although of different heights and accents. Gloria, whose beauty she adores, ignores her. Joan and Tova are working on a project and keep assuring her they will need her, but she doesn't know when. Hepzibah says little on her visits from Haifa but warms Robin's toes and rubs her wrists when the naphtha is out. Dahlia croons to her, but she does to everyone. Vered, the social worker, talks to Robin as if to a client. Deedee, who has frizzy hair like her own, is her favorite; Mickey, ill-tempered and impatient, her least favorite.

At night she dreams of none of them. She is in her crèche, the States. Her old friends become dear. The boys she knew, her age but half her size, have grown in stature. She writes sentimental letters to them, to old teachers, to neighbors, even to her grade school principal who once complimented her on her thick braids. In the dream they chatter and beckon. There is so much catching up to do.

The next Shabbat Tsiporah wears a proper dress and carries two white candles. The girls are in the kitchen, preparing a pot dinner. The Hasid is still asleep. The boys gently awaken him.

"Shalom," the girls greet Tsiporah, blessings on her arrival.

When the Hasid comes into the room Moshe is with him. The Hasid is freshly washed and his beard still damp. He kisses his way around the room. Moshe whispers to him when he comes to Tsiporah.

"Tsiporah, little maid," he says and holds her against his chest. "You light the first Sabbath candle."

After the blessings for the grain taken out of the earth, Moshe begins a Hasidic song. The group makes a round of the two lines:

The heavens will be joyous and the land will rejoice,
and the sea will thunder in its fullness.

"Children," says the Hasid, "we will eat and dance our way to the Wall and tell stories there."

Evening is as golden as the desert. Goatherds gather their animals who have strewn the path with dung. The group walks past archaeological digs and new foundations.

The Hasid pauses as they reach the Wall: "Heaven will not have golden gates, my friends. It will have golden stones."

His hands float into the air.

"What day is this? Sabbath. Shabbat. It is our glimpse of heaven."

"Yes."

"When the Lord made the world, on this day he rested. This day of meditation and singing is our preview of heaven."

"Heaven."

"Our most sacred holidays can only be comprehended by multiplying Sabbath a thousand times."

Wow, what an idea! Tsiporah is in ecstasy.

"And so I say, children, 'Good Sabbath, Shabbat Shalom, Shabbat Shalom, my children.' Wish each other a glimpse of heaven."

The Hasid turns to the nearest girl, wishes her a good Sabbath and kisses her. The girl turns and kisses the boy beside her who kisses Tsiporah. Tsiporah turns to Moshe. Moshe lets the kiss fall full on his lips. Tsiporah will never leave.

The Hasid singles her out.

"Come, little bird. Come live with us, and we will tell each other wondrous tales."

It is like dating. Everyone is asking her out.

Before this no one wanted her. The language of The Land does not want her. She cannot comprehend what she hears in the street, the school, the air shaft that led off the bathroom in her parents' apartment. She cannot bear what she understands of the conversation of Rina and Shula.

If she learns one word of Hebrew, if she lets it on her tongue, she will be stuck here in The Land forever. With each word she learns, she loses one in English. First her name. Then all salutations. Then the names for food, like bread, milk, butter. Then the names of new people will fill her mouth.

Nothing is like what it was. This is not home, her parents' apartment with square rooms and loosely fitting large windowpanes that rattle whenever a plane flies overhead.

Her parents are not like her old parents. They have no friends and are busy going from agency to agency about their business.

The girls her age are not like the fourteen-year-olds at home. They're like eleven-year-olds, jumping and giggling. Even though they study English at school and hear it on TV and at the movies, they understand nothing she tells them.

If only Tsiporah could take flight. One of the Russian girls in her Hebrew language class tried. She had been separated from her boyfriend, whose family was not allowed to leave Kiev. The girl stepped in front of a car, but the driver swerved. He knew enough afterward not to bawl her out, but to say over and over, "It will be good."

So, Yom Rishon, Sunday again, Tsiporah skips her school, her language classes and roams the Old City. The air is still and then swirls with sand as the wind rises. Word of God people are leaning against the wall of the walled-in city. Neither Hannah nor Stephanos is with them, and the group does not approach her.

A few feet away is Moshe, at the orange juice stand, paying his half-lira.

"Want some juice, Tsiporah?"

The juice vendor is cutting the oranges. He has mucus hanging from one nostril. He does not rewash the glasses.

"No, thank you," she says.

"I had a feeling you'd be coming down today for a little soul fixing."

They walk and talk, Moshe and Tsiporah. They walk into the garden of the Church of the White Fathers, a French order. They sit on a bench and speak about the state of Tsiporah's soul.

"We'll walk more as soon as it cools," says Moshe.

German tourists come into the garden. They take pictures of the trees, of the White Fathers; they aim at Moshe.

"Forbidden!" he says.

The Germans do not stop. They focus their close-up lens, adjust the speed of the film.

Moshe walks out of the garden, his fingers spread, his image behind his hand.

They walk into Mea Shearim. Darkness comes. Moshe must return to the Hasid.

Tsiporah is not tired. She is excited. She walks long distances alone, to concrete playgrounds, on unpaved roads where dogs bark tiredly. The hours pass and few are walking, a couple, a Third Year Abroad American carrying a bottle of Stock Arak, a man heading home late, staring at her. She passes a pale man with black circles under his eyes. He is leaning against his Volkswagen.

"My car's not working," he tells her.

"I'm sorry."

"Yeah? Who're you sorry for? Me or my car?"

"Both."

"That's fair. Don't go away."

She sits on the curb.

"I just need to talk to somebody," he says. "That's a simple enough request. You're not doing anything special now, are you?"

Tsiporah moves from the curb to a higher stone ledge.

"My car's not really broken."

She is listening and also dozing.

"Well, if you're too sleepy to stay, you can go. Don't let me keep you from anything."

"It's OK," she says.

"I've been in The Land three months already," he says, "and haven't found anybody to love me."

He looks at her earnestly.

"What do you think of that?" he asks.

"That's too bad."

"Do you think it's my fault?"

"Oh, no, probably not."

"What do you mean probably?"

"I didn't mean probably. Certainly not."

"Certainly not what?"

"I forgot."

The young man leaves her abruptly for his car. He does have trouble starting the motor.


Morning again. Tsiporah walks back toward the Old City, maybe Wayward to sleep. At the Jaffa Gate the Word of God people are out with guitar, drum, oriental finger cymbals.

"Hannah!" she cries. "Stephanos!"

They regard her severely.

"Where have you been, Tsiporah?"

"I met this knockout Hasid."

"Moshe's Hasid?"

"Yes!"

"Little Tsiporah," says Stephanos. "Tell her, Hannah."

"He wants you to be careful," says Hannah.

"You're an innocent," says Stephanos. "People prey on innocence."

"But he's very nice," says Tsiporah.

"The lecher or his pimp? Which is nice?"

"What are you saying?"

"Moshe pimps for the Hasid. The Hasid has an appetite, especially for pre-pubs. He likes them. He eats them."

"Don't be gross," says Hannah.

"Tsiporah," says Stephanos, "didn't we break bread?"

They broke bread.

"Haven't we been straight with you?"

"Very straight."

They walk slowly, helping her, for she's sleepy from the long night. At the door of the Word of God, the man is waiting.

"How many guests today?"

"One, so far," they say.

"We've met her before, haven't we?"

"Yes."

"How many times?"

"Twice."

"Then this is the third time."

They eat silently.

"Family," the man says, "this is Tsiporah's third visit."

"Ah," say the young people around the table, "the third visit."

"Tsiporah, come here," the leader tells her.

Tsiporah has trouble getting the heavy old chair out from under the table. It catches on the oriental rug.

"Tsiporah," says the man, "you are either one of us now or you are against us."

"Oh, I'd never be against you."

The table empties. The Arab women clear the dishes. Tsiporah is not yet dismissed.

"We have only so much time, Tsiporah," says the leader.

"I know," says Tsiporah, "but I promised. I've got this appointment—"

"You have a higher appointment."

"Where?"

"In the hereafter. 'There will be a tree of life with its twelve kinds of fruit, yielding its fruit each month.' "

"One tree has twelve kinds of fruit?"

"It's allegorical," says the man.

"I think I need a little more time."

"Hannah, Stephanos, be with her. Don't lose her."

"I'd like to walk outdoors," says Robin.

The house is dark, the furniture heavy, the drapes concealing and its inhabitants hidden.

They walk her to the Holy Land Souvenir Shop not far from the Wall. Crèches and crucifixes, dolls cradled by tender Mary, Christ in painful grimace on the cross.

Moshe's face is reflected in the shop window.

Is he a pimp?

"Tsiporah, get away from them!"

He loses his yarmulke grappling for her. Stephanos is strong, taller than Moshe, although Moshe is wiry.

"They steal!" yells Moshe.

Stephanos is pressing his nose, smashing at the nose.

"What do they steal?" Robin cries.

Hannah yanks her hand.

"They're well-known thieves," says Moshe.

Stephanos kicks him. Moshe's pants tear. He falls and rolls on the dirt of the suk, into vegetables that have slipped from tilted boxes, into fresh donkey dung. He grabs for Tsiporah. Hannah is pulling her. Stephanos leans over Moshe, his two hands together, almost prayerfully. Moshe screams.

"What are you doing?" yells Robin.

"Karate, the Ultimate Fist."

Moshe lies there.

Tsiporah begins to flutter. Her arms agitate. Her legs feel scaly and scratchy. She twitters, twirls. Hannah lets go. Stephanos watches. Gradually she rises above them, above the courtyard, feeling the air under her, through her body, as she settles in a niche of the Kotel, the Western Wall, preening, cleaning, against the warm, soft stone.

# 15
# Trampling the Lion and the Dragon Underfoot

Tova is taping a song by her Arab lover. First he sings it in Arabic, then translates.

> I am the son of Hagar,
> not a wild man,
> my hand against no man's.
> Why is Isaac's hand lifted against me?
>
> I am the son of Hagar,
> the eldest of Ibrahim.

What aileth thee, Hagar?
What aileth thy son?

They sent us off with bread
and a bottle of water,
to wander afar,
I and my mother Hagar.

Who uses my bed?
Who peers from my window?
For this is my land
and my legacy.

I am his eldest son,
when I was thirteen
I gave him my foreskin
and he gave me his.

It happened before.
It happens again
to the sons of Hagar,
to the sons of Ibrahim.

"Ibrahim?" asks Deedee.

"Abraham," says Tova. "It's his southern accent."

Gloria and Hepzibah cry, "The song is a lie, a distortion!"

Tova says, "But it's the way he feels."

Hepzibah says, "If he feels like killing us, should we let him?"

Tova says, "He's not killing us. He's singing to us."

Hepzibah: "He'd like to kill us."

Mickey: "They're all alike. You see one, you've seen them all."

Voices rise.

Joan says, "Like women, you've seen one . . ."

Gloria interrupts, "It's our land. He can share it."

"He doesn't want to," says Tova.

Gloria asks, "Too bad for him, and why are you sleeping with him anyway?"

Tova: "I like circumcised men."

There are groans and boos.

Gerda and Antoinette try logic.

Antoinette says, "It is dangerous to use the power of speech to arouse."

Gerda reminds them, "Don't forget, Hitler came into Austria through the Youth Movement."

Tova asks, "What has Hitler to do with this?"

Gerda says, "First come the students, then the uniforms, then the songs, and, with the last salute, comes Hitler. First this young man, then his lament, then his comrades, then their guns, then the PLO."

Dahlia listens to the lover's song over and over.

"Well, Dahlia? What is your opinion?"

Dahlia says, "In my opinion, his voice is too nasal."

Simha remains silent.

Joan asks, "Doesn't this enterprise of ours have conflict and drama?"

"That it does," says Terry.

There is a din, an uproar. Gloria and Gerda against Tova and Joan.

Mickey accuses, "You're giving away the city."

Hepzibah says, "They would take the food from our mouths."

At last, hoarsely, Simha says, "And our babes from the womb."

There is silence. Then the changing of subject.

They remember Robin.

Simha speaks again. "Let us find a lost one. No one comes into this house and leaves unnoticed. There is no one without a mark, a print, a track, a trace."

How to follow tracks in the air? The women summon the wayward girls and go in a caravan to the Wall.

Which one is she?

"The Hasid said, 'She has her own little niche on the woman's side.'"

"The gray one with the beady eyes and the head cocked to one side?"

"They all look like that."

"When you've seen one pigeon . . ."

"No. Look! Look! The one with ruffled feathers, frizzy, light. It's looking at us."

"SHE."

"Hello, there! Hello, little Tsiporah! *Ma shlomech?* How's it going?"

Gerda: "Maybe you could study to be a carrier pigeon and go to the States."

Antoinette: "Tsiporah, birds are very important. The ancients divined by them."

Hepzibah: "Be careful, Tsiporah. There is a controversy over the weeds in the Wall. One side wants to pull them out so they don't undermine the structure. Another says it's God's will and the weeds must grow. Tsiporah, don't get involved in this controversy!"

Terry: "I will show the Ministry of Welfare the desperate measures our girls will take when the Home is threatened."

Dahlia, whistling: "Motek, how's it up there? Meet any nice . . . ? Seen any good . . . ? How's your nest? Roomy? With a view?"

Mickey: "Robin, you're in a real position of power. You could do favors for everyone. See all the notes crammed into the holes in the cracked mortar? Take them and ascend with them. Don't let the street cleaners sweep them up in the early morning. See, here's one—it's bad luck to read, Robin, but, for example, 'Let my son be safe on the border.' Very moving, no? Another, I can't read, in Russian. Ah, Rumanian—I can read—ooo ah! What she's asking? Not nice."

Hepzibah: "Mihal, the notes are only for His eyes."

Mickey: "He's doing *some* reading, I'll tell you."

Rina and Shula say nothing. They huddle together. They didn't much care for Robin. She didn't take to them either. Why do they have to like her now?

"Say something, girls."

"Hey, Tsiporah!"

A feather drops.

The girls confer and Rina speaks.

"We'll save this in memory of you, Tsiporah, in a nice box with ribbons and earrings."

Deedee: "Go everywhere, traveler, and come back to tell of it."

"That's expecting a bit much."

Dahlia whistles. "Robin."

The pigeon is restless in its niche.

"Tsiporah, small bird."

The pigeon ruffles its feathers, pecks at the mortar.

Dahlia lets out a long note. The praying men shake their fingers at her. The bird rises straight into the air to waltz over the women, chirping and crooning to Dahlia's tune.

They return to the house.

Joan and Tova are whispering together.

What? What?

"We think Robin's experience should be part of *The City Between Us*."

Antoinette: "That's exploitive! Scandalous!"

Tova: "Not at all. Everyone fights for our souls in this city."

Simha is grumbling, cross in warming weather. She is the fullest bodied of the women, the first to react to climate. Already, before summer, she begins to fan.

"She was the second victim," says Simha.

Mickey spits. "Don't talk. *Ha ayin ha ra*, the Evil Eye! What It sees, It makes worse. The Evil Eye—the stars there in the sky. Each star wishes you bad luck. Do you feel it? Don't you smell it? A faint, burned smell?"

Maybe.

The women huddle.

"Quick!" says Mickey. "Recite something with the word 'eye.'"

Simha says a line from Psalm 91: "'Only with thine *eyes* shalt thou behold ... There shall no evil befall ...'"

"It's not enough yet," says Mihal, "or more victims will be chosen. We must spit three times."

"Into something, please," says Simha, "or outdoors."

The women open the door and spit three times.

"Now," says Mihal, "draw a circle around yourselves to protect yourself."

"What about Robin?" asks Deedee.

"Robin!" says Mickey annoyed. "Let her go already."

Simha says the Prayer for the Traveler.

"Robin, we pray you on your journey. May you be led into the haven of your desire. May you be delivered from every enemy—hawk or swooping creature. May you be protected from ambush, boys throwing stones, eggs cracking. May you suffer few of the afflictions that trouble the world—conflicting air currents, hunger, lice."

She recites from the Psalm, of the angels that:

> "shall bear thee up in their hands,
> Lest thou dash thy foot against a stone.
> Thou shalt tread upon the lion and adder;
> The young lion and the dragon shalt thou
> trample under foot."

"Robin will do that?"

"A dragon?"

The wayward girls are impressed.

"Keep in touch, Robin."

Giant moths are whirring at the windows. Their eyes are black. Their legs slip on the panes. Their wings are like fans or fluted mushrooms.

"Ah hah!" says Mickey. "Demons, and we have kept them out!"

Something is happening in the little stone house to make the women uncomfortable, yet to attract them there. *The City Between Us* is being prepared. At any moment Joan's flashbulb goes off in the face, or her tape recorder catches one's slightest remarks.

The women begin to speak self-consciously, sonorously, reminiscently. They become essences of themselves, characters, legends.

The wayward girls come in, giggle and run out.

Who speaks into the tape? Everyone.

The police come by and speak of the dangers of the city. Arab merchants in the suk say, "Ah, yes, business has improved since 1967, but not our spirits. Who are we, neither from Israel, nor from Jordan?"

Warriors from both sides of the battlefield speak of their land. The Israelis speak of the War of Independence and the fierce battle raging at Latrun. They speak of the Six Day War, the gathering of the paratroopers on Nebi Samuel to converge upon the Old City. The Arab residents of the Old City speak of the Black Sudanese Arabs, the fiercest warriors, who defended the city in hand-to-hand combat.

The Israelis speak of taking the Hill of Ammunition near Ramat Eshkol, a promontory with hollowed-out tunnels and gun emplacements that overlooked the city.

The Arabs speak of the monument built to their fallen in battle.

Every area bordered on something. Each citizen moved over or was moved away from a boundary.

Tova finds two Jewish families who trace their lineage three and four hundred years in the city. The two households feud bitterly for honors.

Joan speaks to Arab women whose houses were blown up in the War of Attrition. Authorities said terrorists dwelled in those houses.

"My son a terrorist?" one mother asks. "Not possible."

"My daughter a bomb-thrower?" says another. "She was studying to be a nurse in Haifa."

Tova interviews an aristocrat returning to the ancient Jewish Quarter. The woman receives them, wearing an encrusted gown, seated on an embroidered chair. It was her father, the Jewish mukhtar, who raised the white flag to the Jordanians in 1948. When the Jewish community filed out, the synagogues were razed. The daughter presides in her home but mold attacks the walls and the curved archways are crumbling.

There is anger; there is pride. There is displacement; there is replacement.

From hours of conversations, from boxes of slides, the women have to cut down their presentation. They get it to an hour and forty-five minutes. But no theater will show *The City Between Us*, no matter how long or how abbreviated.

Terry, from Parliament, calls every theater, threatening, imploring. But no Israeli listens to another. Why should they?

Terry makes her maiden speech on the Knesset floor: Freedom of Speech, Press, Assembly and Theater. Most of the members are missing. One who watches her attentively, she finds out later, has removed his hearing aid. Others rustle the morning papers at their desks. When Terry concludes and steps down from the podium, her colleagues pinch her cheeks or behind as she goes down the aisle to her party seat.

"Maybe we should take the theater by force," Terry suggests.

"That's what I need," says Mickey. "Another demonstration, another knock on the head."

"We could gather in front of a theater," says Joan, "begin our play, attract attention and lead them either inside or elsewhere."

Tova is excited. "It happened! It did happen, just like

that. The nineteen thirties, an anticapitalist play, *The Cradle Will Rock*. The theater locked it out. So Orson Welles and Marc Blitzstein gathered the audience and walked them to another theater. The audience swelled from street to street. The play is a classic."

"Street theater," says Antoinette, "has had a long and respectable history—the miracle plays, mystery plays in the town square, the courtyard of the inn and the church."

"I should sing outdoors against the wind?" says Dahlia. "You're all crazy. You do it. Each note would come back and attack me."

"If we meet outdoors where will we project the slides?"

"If we meet outdoors how can we sell tickets?"

"If we meet outdoors, there's bound to be a riot. Every chakchak passing could bully his way in."

"We could hang disturbers publicly," says Deedee. "The British did that."

Shh. Think. Be responsible.

Terry has a plan, as usual.

She rises in the Knesset the next day and invites her fellow parliamentarians to an event: of political importance (disinterest); of artistic excellence (boredom); an event that might have dangerous consequences (Vered's former lover leans forward); an event in which the most beautiful and talented women of The Land will participate. Out of courtesy to a colleague, Parliament decides to attend.

Did you think it would be mere journalism? You have no faith in these women. Avishai Ayal will design portable sets light enough to lift and run with, if necessary. Ruth Ayal will choreograph. Mimes from the Tel Aviv School of Drama will act.

There is controversy. Do Arab actors always have to portray Arab characters? Jews, Jews?

"No," says Tova.

A young Arab actor says the words of the Jewish soldier who has reunited the city. A Jewish student is the bitter wounded Arab who has lost Ha Ēr Ha Attika, the Ancient City.

The cast and supporters assemble at the Khan blowing shofars, beating drums, whirring greigers, clanging sheep bells. The patrons of the Khan arrive for a piano recital. The audience gathers around the noisemakers, with the Knesset members viewing cautiously from a distance. The police become suspicious. The manager of the Khan and his scheduled pianist plead for the audience to enter the auditorium.

*The City Between Us* begins.

Tova's lover sings his song. Riot! Police. Clubs raised. Suspended as Dahlia sings, first, Nomi Shemer's "Jerusalem the Golden," then Joan and Tova's "Jerusalem the Torn." Dahlia's voice is Yemenite. She throws it to a far distance, to a mountaintop. She ululates. Bellies begin undulating, necks moving, arms stretching. The crowd sighs.

A messenger arrives from the municipality. He is polite, ordered by the mayor to use utmost tact, to give every chance for a peaceful solution.

"You are on private property."

"The city owns it."

"You are on city property."

"The people own it."

"You do not have permission to perform."

The police begin an encircling action.

Terry rises. "We will gather where our people have always gathered in time of strife and of rejoicing. Follow us!"

The crowd fills the narrow streets, down into the City of David, into the Walled City, a bottleneck at the gates, descending to the Western Wall. It is after evening prayers and the court is deserted but for the religious police, who rise at the sight of the hundreds. The pianist and manager of the Khan have shrugged and joined with the crowd.

Jerusalem lights up its historical sites. The court is a stage. Joan and Tova project slides on the Wall, faces of Jews and Arabs enlarged against this ancient remnant of the Temple.

Arabs attending the mosque in the courtyard above lean over the railing and watch. Students in the houses of study stream outdoors. Everything in the clear air is sharper in sound, stronger in feeling. The audience weeps, hisses, quarrels, shouts, interrupts, shoves the interrupters, applauds, boos.

The TV talk shows are filled with commentary on *The City Between Us*. University drama classes assign it. But they cannot continue performing at the Wall. After all, there are holidays, bar mitzvot, gatherings.

The Khan is leased, but *The City Between Us* is not as successful contained. The Land's most eminent archaeologist walks out of the theater shouting, his bald head glowing like a spot light. On this basis alone he runs at the next election for Prime Minister of the State. The National Religious Party and the right wing condemn it. Vered's former lover accuses Terry of appeasement.

"Before you know it," he shouts in the Parliament, "the young will smoke hash and the sands will blow once more over the streets of the city."

In the Human Interest column of the *Post*, a journalist writes:

During the performance at the Wall, pigeons disturbed our enjoyment. We shooed them off but one persisted, a curiously polite pigeon, hovering like a hummingbird, crooning and chirping in accompaniment with the singer.

# 16
# Habibi

An actress has her own words. A time precedes the present.
This is Tova's story. She does not realize it but she started
work on *The City Between Us* the day she arrived in
Jerusalem. That was 1972, after a war and before a war,
after the States and before The Women.

Tova is not as young as she looks. Curls make us look
younger. In the States, where she taught Public Speaking
in high school for three years, her hair was straight. So was
her life. She becomes younger and freakier as she gets into
her thirties.

People want to pinch her cheeks. Once two aunts, on a visit from the Soviet Union and long separated from the family, met Tova. She was fresh-faced and smiled widely. Each aunt grabbed a cheek and yanked. Tova's eyes crossed. People want to do that to her, if not so violently.

*Tova* means "good one," feminine. It is the Hebraization of her Yiddish name, *Gittle,* "good little one." How did a good little one come into the arms of the enemy? By avoiding them.

Who thought of Arabs? They wore veils and rode camels. They belly danced, rode across the desert on Arabian horses, brandishing swords, never against Jews. Sometimes Jews dwelt among them in great fame, like Maimonides, who lived in Egypt in the twelfth century as adviser and physician to the caliph. Baghdad, once an Arab city, was a seat of Jewish culture. At Halloween one became an Arab out of desperation if no other costume was ready in time.

Once, when little Gittle was a child, she made her parents laugh by calling the race "spare ribs."

Gittle grew up studying piano, tap, toe, acrobatics, Scottish and Hawaiian dancing and baton twirling. She won a blue ribbon in a Singer Sewing Machine contest. Only the acrobatics is still useful.

When Gittle left the States her father pinched each cheek softly. Her mother nibbled her neck. An aunt also came to the airport and told the story of Gittle in the stroller.

When Gittle was a baby her grandmother walked her to the park. Gittle was three with fat cheeks and fat tuchas. All the other little ones were running and falling and running in the playground. Gittle squirmed to get out of the stroller.

Her grandmother said, "You think we feed you so you should run it off?"

"Go, Gittle," whispers her father at the airport. "Run it off."

In her organized fashion Gittle signed up for Ulpan, intensive Hebrew classes, in Jerusalem.

The radio began, *"Shalom rav,* many hellos," and then the morning announcer quoted, " 'How goodly are thy tents, O Jacob.' "

Gittle changed her name in Hebrew class and she changed her voice. It used to be firm and definite and a slightly higher pitch. Now Tova's voice is husky, giggly and breathless.

In her Beginners Plus class are Jews from Switzerland, England, America and Argentina. There are two Christians, Clement, a monk from Italy, and Christina, a missionary from Finland. And there are two Arabs, Thomas and Jerome.


GITTLE/TOVA'S STORY:


Every morning I hear Thomas complain about Jerusalem. He complains about the line of Arab peddlers sitting along the walls of the Old City and the Israeli toughs mocking them. He complains about the unsolved murder of two Arab taxi drivers.

"The Jewish police are smart, very smart," says Thomas. "If they wanted to know a thing, in a minute they could find it out."

Thomas is full of statistics that I cannot find in the *Jerusalem Post.*

"Four hundred marriages a year," says Thomas, "between Arab and Jew."

Or, "The police give me trouble. They know which of us to ticket as a revenge." And, contradictorily, "Of course, sixty percent of the police are Arabs. They like the uniform. They like to direct traffic."

Thomas and Jerome are Arabs? Thomas's eyes are blue. His hair is light brown. Jerome has straight dark brown hair, carefully cut. He wears glasses. Where are glinting swords and prancing horses? Thomas seeks them also.

"The paratroopers are beasts," Thomas says one day when the army is visiting Beginners Plus to meet the newcomers. "They are murderers."

The army, a girl and boy soldier, question the Beginners Plus. They ask us the first-learned phrase in Hebrew: Where are you from?

Thomas keeps his hand in the air. He wants to tell the army he is from Bethlehem in the Occupied Territories.

"Shekit!" Shulamith, the teacher, silences him.

But Thomas can no more refrain from speech than he can from smoking under the Forbidden to Smoke sign.

What can Shulamith do about him? He is not a new-comer to The Land. He and Jerome speak Hebrew fluently. They are here to learn to read and write. If anyone hesitates over a word, Thomas calls it out. If the teacher asks a question, Thomas, out of order, answers.

"Go into a lower class," Shulamith tells him. "Start again."

"No, my teacher," says Thomas. "This is just right for me."

Their battles make the class uneasy. Shulamith has limited choice. She can make Thomas the butt of humor or leave him out. She has reason to attack. He is late to class, often absent, homework never turned in. Not so Jerome, whose head is turned down toward his desk, who dresses neatly, speaks softly and whispers witty remarks to blonde Rita of Suisse-Deutsch.

When Shulamith bawls out Thomas he grins. He always grins in class. I see that Thomas never frowns until the ten-minute class break each hour.

"Hey, Jerome!" he once called across the room, for Shulamith had separated them. Thomas called out some-thing in Arabic in a raunchy voice. Shulamith turned on him and tongue-lashed him in Arabic. Thomas laughed and congratulated her on her fluency.

She, Shulamith, looks more Arabic than he. She had, in fact, been born in Baghdad. Her skin is swarthy, her hair thick, straight, blue-black. She does not shave her legs or the nests of hair in her armpits.

It is warming in The Land and warm in the classroom. Out of the window I see that the children from the primary school across the street are taking home the flowers or vegetables they've grown. They decorate their hair for one holiday. They carry home green cabbages on another day.

It is warm in the classroom. The fan is not working. Thomas stands up, tall and thin. His body is slender and muscular. He hits the fan to make it turn. It does not. He works the switch. Shulamith, who has been writing at the blackboard, is startled.

She teaches the class a new verb, "to disturb."

"Thomas *mafrialee*—disturbs me." The lesson continues. What else disturbs us? We answer. The Old Clothes Man early in the morning. The grape vendors during afternoon rest time. The evening whistling of Israeli street boys.

Thomas's hand is up. Shulamith ignores him.

"Teacher," he says in English.

"No English."

"My *morah*," with exaggerated tenderness.

*"Ken*, Thomas? Yes?"

"The Israeli soldiers disturb me. The planes overhead disturb me—"

She cuts him off.

"Thomas disturbs me," says the teacher to the class. "Does Thomas disturb you?"

"Ken, Thomas mafrialee," shouts out his Bethlehem neighbor, Jerome.

We take a class break. Thomas is reading an Arabic newspaper. He looks older than Jerome. Jerome is going to a *makalet*, grocery, for beer.

*"Habibi,"* says Thomas, "my love, my friend, beer for me, too."

He will drink the beer in class and will throw the can into the wastebasket where it will clang, if there is other metal, or thud if there is none.

I am lonely in Jerusalem. I am also hungry in this city. Perhaps because of the Judean Hills, that mountain air, I always have such appetite. My grandmother would be happy. I have gained ten pounds since I came. My cheeks are tan in early spring, my skin is smooth, my hair clean and soft. I let it fluff. I don't blow-dry it anymore. I am getting younger. Now, with warmer weather, I wear few clothes. I have given up wearing bras. I even wore T-shirt blouses until a jitney driver flicked my nipples through the purple cotton T-shirt. Now I wear loose cotton blouses over the T-shirt.

The man behind me, that time in the jitney, was also touching my shoulders. The moon had come up, and a single, dazzling, Christmas-card star. A breeze blew across my shoulders while the man behind me rubbed his knuckles over my back and whispered to me. His words blew backward on the highway. When the jitney discharged its passengers at the last stop in Jerusalem, the driver held me back.

"What did that man say to you?"

I did not understand what that man said to me.

"He is an Arab," said the driver. "Do you like Arabs?"

*"Lama lō?"* I asked. "Why not?"

"And do you like Jews?" asked the driver.

*"Be-emet,* in truth I do."

The driver pulled out of his designated parking in front of his jitney company.

"Where do you live?" he asked.

I hesitated.

"It's nothing. I have yet time. I can drive you closer to home."

I told him generally near the railroad. He drove down the dark side streets.

"Where else?"

I did not tell him.

He parked. "Are you attached?"

I was not.

"I will tell you," said the driver, "I am attached. A wife, three children. But on a night with an Amerikanit, I am not so attached. Live today—tomorrow an Arab bomb, tomorrow a Russian pilot or a French plane."

He touched my leg, flicked my nipples.

*"Ata mafrialee,"* I told him. "You disturb me."

I opened the door. He did not follow. They do not follow in Jerusalem.

That night I lay in bed, on the hard Israeli sofa bed with the wooden platform under the hard foam mattress, and not only did my arms feel sunburned, but my breasts and belly. I dreamed of his touches, of the knuckles of the Arab passenger, of the wind blowing across my neck.

The next day at Ulpan I look hard at Thomas. I have the wastebasket next to me. He looks at me slowly and carefully. He has been laughing. He stops. My face feels sunburned. Thomas lowers his eyes.

At the end of the morning session Thomas says, "I have something to say, class. This Thursday is my birthday. You are all welcome to my birthday party in Bethlehem."

Shulamith is erasing the board vigorously. She does not respond.

"How will we get there, Thomas?" I ask.

"I will provide for you all, my class," says Thomas, "and for you, my teacher. You are to worry about nothing. Just to be here at the school parking lot at five."

"I have babies," says Shulamith. "I cannot attend your birthday."

"Oh my teacher should be at my birthday," says Thomas. "It cannot be a class party without the teacher."

Ariah, a lawyer from the States, and Dr. Freddy, from Argentina, ask Thomas what they can bring.

"All is provided," says Thomas. "When we invite, we provide."

"How old are you?" asks blonde Rita.

Thomas comes over to our side of the room and looks down at her cleavage.

"You'll find out."

I dislike them both, Rita and Thomas.


Thursday at five Thomas is waiting in front of the Ulpan. I see him walking back and forth smoking. Friends of his have brought cars, old small cars, but four or five of them to transport us to Bethlehem. His friends are shorter than he. Some have the traditional mustache. Thomas is the fairest, the tallest. Jerome is waiting in Bethlehem to greet us.

Shulamith and her husband arrive.

"Hello, oh my teacher," says Thomas, "and oh the husband of my teacher."

He is overjoyed. He puts out his cigarette and busies himself matchmaking the passengers in the various cars. He puts American lawyer Ariah with German Esther, Dr. Freddy from Buenos Aires with blonde Rita from Suisse-Deutsch.

Thomas dances in the parking lot of the Ulpan. He sings an Arabic song. His friends are in their cars, waiting at the driver's wheel.

"Habibi," they call, "Thomas habibi."

Thomas places Christina from Finland into a car with Clement, the Italian priest. Christina is tall, her skirt and blouse modest, her breasts full.

"Watch these two," says Thomas to their driver. "Don't let them do a honeymoon these ten kilometers between Jerusalem and Bethlehem."

His driver friend nods and laughs.

Alicia of Philadelphia and I, also of America, go in

Thomas's car. Alicia sits next to him while I ride in the back alone. Thomas gives the signal to the drivers and drives out of the lot. He drives fast across the railroad tracks near the Ulpan, down Emek Raphaim, Valley of the Monster, where the prophet Isaiah walked, past the Khan Theater, which was once a caravansary, along the walls of the Old City and down the road to Bethlehem. He is slowed up by a creaky Arab bus.

Thomas is driving too fast. He passes the bus and his friends also pass. He is speeding on the winding road. A friend of his has been hiding. When Thomas's car passes, his friend's car rushes at us from an intersection. We are almost sliced in two. I scream. Thomas goes the faster. Alicia keeps her head in her hand and cries. From the rear seat I watch Thomas in the mirror. His eyes meet mine. He smiles a slow smile. I do not hide my head in my arms.

It is dusk when we get to the stuccoed "Y" where Thomas has catered his birthday. The proprietor is there with his wife and children. They unlock the gate for us. A pool hall across the road is brightly lit and the players watch as our cars park in the "Y" lot.

"This way, my friends," says Thomas.

We are led into the garden behind the "Y."

Jerome is there with a portable phonograph and records of Greek music, of sambas for Dr. Freddy from Argentina, Italian music for Clement the monk, and Arabic music.

"Drink, my teacher, my class," orders Thomas. "Drink to me."

Opened bottles of wine are on the long tables. We fill paper cups and wait. Thomas's friends, who have driven us here, now stand shyly against one wall. We are across from them. Thomas puts on a samba and pairs us off, for each Arab a classmate. Dr. Freddy from Buenos Aires sambas with Jerome's sister. I dance with Shulamith's small husband, who speaks to me pleasantly in his limited English.

Esther from Germany remembers the class present to

Thomas. It is a two-volume Hebrew-Arabic dictionary, Shulamith's suggestion.

"I will memorize all the words right now," says Thomas, "the good words with the bad words. I will go to the head of the class."

The wife of the proprietor and his children carry out the food. We dip the Arabic bread into *hummos*, ground chickpeas, into the eggplant mixtures. We fork out the fresh salad. We drink all the wine.

Soon Clement bows and excuses himself. Will one of Thomas's friends consent to drive him back to the monastery? He has to keep hours. Some of the others are suddenly tired and also want to leave.

Thomas asks each one, *"Lama?* Why?" and pleads for them to remain.

"But it is my birthday! You insult me if you leave early on my birthday."

"Go home, everyone," laughs Jerome. "Leave the whiskey to me."

Thomas graciously accompanies those that must leave early to the parking lot. He unchains the heavy chain that extends across the lot so they can drive out. The pool players in the roadside tavern pause again to watch.

Suddenly the garden is crowded. We all have more partners than we can accommodate. Thomas shouts to the newcomers to leave. His friends advance on them. The new arrivals from across the road remain, grinning. Some have carried their beer cans across the road, others cue sticks.

"My friends," says Thomas, "the party has ended. If it cannot be perfect, it cannot be."

We are herded into the lot, placed into cars, returned to Jerusalem. I sit beside Thomas. He is white-faced and drives swiftly back over the land where David herded his sheep in the wilderness of Judah, where David became king of these olive and fig trees, the cities and the fields. Thomas does not look at me on the ride. When he leaves me at the Ulpan, a few blocks from my apartment, he says, "Tova, I will take you to a restaurant in East Jerusalem. I will take you to the cinema in Arabic. I will bring you to cousins near Haifa. I will take you wherever Jews don't go."

He does not look at me as he invites me.

"I will come for you Friday when the class dismisses early," says Thomas.

Thomas will not pick me up at my apartment, nor does he ask for my address. He is waiting for me after class, having skipped Beginners Plus that morning.

"We will be gone the weekend," he says.

I am chilled though it is in the heat of noon. My bare arms are goose-bumped. Thomas rubs my skin with the knuckles of his right hand.

"You will love Arabs," he promises.

We drive up to Haifa in less than two and a half hours.

"Are you enjoying the ride?" Thomas asks.

Yes, I am enjoying the ride.

"Why are you studying Hebrew?"

I think about telling him it's because I'm Jewish and then wonder if he'll be offended. I tell him it's because I'm Jewish.

"Why are *you* studying Hebrew?" I ask in turn.

"Because I'm Arab."

We giggle.

"I like the class," says Thomas. "Everyone there is my friend. Didn't they come to my birthday?"

"How old are you, Thomas?"

"I am thirty," says Thomas, "an old man. Time to have children." Abruptly: "And you? Do you have children?"

I have not had time to have children.

"Every living thing has descendants," says Thomas. We pass a donkey on the road. "Even the *homor*."

Then why hasn't he married if he's so anxious for descendants?

"I am restless," he says. "I cannot come home to a woman or to children."

"Nor can I," I say.

"It is not the same for a woman as for a man," he says angrily.

I tell him he is wrong.

"You are my guest," says Thomas, "so you must make yourself agreeable to me." He looks at me. "That is why you are not married and have no children. You are disagreeable to men."

Yes I am!

"I have heard that Jewish women are that way," he says.

Before Haifa Thomas turns off the road for Beach of the Carmel.

"Did you bring a bathing suit?" he asks.

"You didn't tell me we would swim," I say.

"You won't swim, Tova," says Thomas. "You will wade."

I wade in, hiking my skirt. I'm still warm in the hot sun. I submerge into the blue Mediterranean with its Haifa oil slick. The cotton skirt becomes waterlogged. I wade out, dragging my legs under the weight of clothing.

"You will meet my family and you will look ugly," says Thomas.

We get into the car. I climb over the front seat into the back. Thomas stops the car, skidding onto the shoulder of the road.

"Drive," I say, "I'm uncomfortable. I'll let my clothes dry, and they'll dry faster if they're not on me. Then I won't be ugly for your friends or your family."

I wrap Thomas's towel around me. I put clothes out of the window and let them flap, rolling up the back window to catch onto the hems.

"Bring the clothes into the car," says Thomas, "or I will not drive."

"You will be ashamed of me, then, before your family."

"That is true," says Thomas, "but I have a special license plate from the Occupied Territories. When the police see a girl's skirts hanging from my car they will think I am an Arab rapist."

"Then park somewhere secluded for an hour and my clothes will dry."

"But we have to be there at a certain time."

It is a dilemma. I am sorry I came and Thomas is even sorrier.

My clothes dry somewhat by the time we reach his cousins in the village north of Haifa.

They are awaiting us, smiling, his cousin Leila the social worker and Michael, who is studying at the University of Haifa to be a high school teacher.

"She does not want to have children," says Thomas of me. "Not even children like these?"

The little girl cousins have black eyes and dark hair. Their complexion is dusky. They wear matching, two-piece pink bathing suits and swim in a little grotto their father built for them.

"Yes," I tell the cousins. "I want to have children just like these."

"Ah!" say the cousins.

Thomas sprawls on a straw chair, his arm extended over the back of another and watches me throughout the meal and the tour of the vineyard, observing how I am with his nieces.

If I am with Thomas, he is not at ease. He is long with graceful hands, yet he lurches, his arms jerk. He gasps, he laughs uncontrollably. His foot locks on the gas pedal when he drives. He is handsome yet, with me, his smile is either strained or foolish. I cannot be there when Thomas is himself.

Our visit comes to an end.

"Did you like the day?" asks Thomas. "The ride? My cousins? The food?"

We drive into Haifa at dusk.

"I have cousins here, too," he says, "where we can spend the night."

"I don't want to."

"Spend the night?"

"No. Be with more cousins."

"You didn't care for my cousins?"

"Very much. I just don't care for more cousins."

"But you haven't met them."

"No more cousins."

He is silent. He is actually a fine driver. Now, in the last light of the day shining through the windshield, his face is expressionless and his eyes pale.

"If you do not want to stay at cousins," he says quietly, "I will drive you back to the parking lot of the Ulpan. I will take you to no hotel."

There's nothing for me to say.

"They check my identification and question me because I am Arab and you are not."

"All right."

"It would be unpleasant."

"I don't mind sleeping on the beach."

"No," he says, "it isn't perfect. If it's not perfect, I don't want it."

In class Sunday Thomas is tired and depressed. I never know, Lord, that's the terrible thing, I never know how he will be.

After class Thomas speaks angrily to me but what he says is loving.

"Do you want to be my girl?" he asks.

"No," I say.

He turns abruptly away from me and asks Rita and Esther.

"Of course," they each say, uncomfortably flippant.

Thomas knows none of us will be his girl, but he does not know why. He comes to Ulpan erratically after this.

My last morning attending Shulamith's class, Thomas shows up. Shulamith is crying. The doors of all the classrooms are opened and students are gathered in groups.

The principal is rushing back and forth from the main office. It is stuffy in the classroom and Thomas tries to fix the fan.

Shulamith turns sharply. "There is an assembly today in the bomb shelter."

Thomas groans. "I am sick of Jewish assemblies, my morah. I am tired of hearing about those holidays and singing those songs. Today let us have Arabic music and I will go."

Shulamith looks at him with her eyes so much darker than his, her face so much sallower, her lips bluer.

"What is it, my teacher. What have I done?"

She says something sharply in Arabic, and runs out of the room.

"What is it?" asks Esther from Germany.

The students are coming down from Advanced.

"It is the massacre," they say, "of our team at Munich."

Jerome and Thomas look at each other. Another girl from Advanced, Bessama, also from Bethlehem, joins them.

"It has nothing to do with you," says Dr. Freddy. "Join us."

"I'll be your girl," I tell Thomas.

"I don't want you," says Thomas. "You do everything at the wrong time."

The three Arab students get into Thomas's car and head for Bethlehem.


I do not return to class. Periodically I hear class news. Clement, the priest, has returned to Italy, and Christina to Finland. Esther of Germany has asked to be transferred from Shulamith's class.

I am at the Western Wall on Yom Kippur and meet Esther. She tells me that she saw Thomas just a few minutes ago.

"Where?"

"Where would a fool be?" cries Esther. "And what would a fool do?"

He is driving his car, on this day, the holy of holies, in Jerusalem, the pious city of The Land. His car, the only car in the city, is driving down main streets, down King George, King David, along Emek Raphaim, even to the empty Ulpan.

"He saw me," says Esther. "He slowed and shouted, 'Habiboti.' He told me where he had driven and then drove off, scattering the people who were walking down the middle of the street. He is a fool!"

There is shouting as a car careens around the corner. It is Thomas, throwing beer cans out of the window. Someone picks up a can and hurls it back at him and cracks his windshield. Thomas is laughing as he U-turns and drives with that jagged windshield out of Jerusalem to his hometown.

"What will happen to him?" I ask Esther.

"Something," says Esther. "Something will happen."


Thus it happened that I learned my Hebrew not in an Ulpan but in a kibbutz. I learned drama not from my M.A. in Speech Education but from The Land. And I learned Arabic, a little at a time, from my lovers. Thus I have prepared myself for living here.

# 17
# By the Street and by the Holy Path

The wayward girls have nightmares. They dream that furniture is flying out of the window, couches are flattening and sliding under doors. Faucets disconnect from sinks and washtubs, knobs fall from drawers and doors. Machines turn upon them viciously, the scaly hose of the tank vacuum cleaner stretches, hisses and coils to strike.

The girls are afraid of windows since the drapes were removed. Shula thinks old people are peering in and scolding her, grandparents in babushkas, aunts from Poland. Rina huddles from the stares of young voyeurs. She dreams that boys are held up in baskets to look into the top windows. She pulls the shade; they can see through it. The shade buckles; someone has crawled inside.

Both girls dream that the stone house is moving, sliding along the streets of the Old City. They are lying stiffly in bed. It is like the funeral corteges in the Old City; they are the dead, coffined in the house.

Robin has taught them a lesson. Flight brings not dishonor but ceremony and honor. Look at the fuss over her!

But where would they take flight? Home? Their homes are less receptive to them than the courts or the strange rooms where they prostitute themselves.

Rina's house is a God-fearing house. Every piece of furniture has the name of "G-d" on it: stools, handles, cabinets, oven doors. Her family came from Morocco with nothing but with every kind of amulet of bark, paper, cloth, glass, with gems, of ancient parchment.

There are amulets to be worn around the neck against the Evil Eye, amulets of coral and knots, amulets of acronyms. Rina never knew what the initials attached to a cord around her neck meant until a religious customer told her: "I have awaited your salvation, O Lord." She was so impressed with his scholarship that she gave him freebies.

Everything has writing on it. The eastern wall has a *mizrah*, a calligraphic decoration of prayers to the sun. The names of angels are scribbled everywhere, mnemonic terms, seventy angels compressed into one amulet. Angels understood Hebrew and helped, and archangels controlled the zodiac and that helped even more.

All of Rina's life was an attempt to outwit the Eye with colors, spitting, fingers, spells. How came it then that, surrounded by acronyms, amulets, zodiacs and the appropriate color, Rina was on the streets by thirteen?

That was the age at which her brothers were to be bar

mitzvahed. That was two years after Rina menstruated and stained everything the unlucky color of blood red. Her mother slapped both of Rina's cheeks after the first menses and when Rina cried, "Why did you do that?" her mother said, "As it was done to me."

No one hit the boys in the family. Slaps, pursuit, curses were for the girls. The girls grew to deserve it with their mean mouths, crying, shrieking, cursing back. Who could blame parents for beating them?

Rina used to dream of the World to Come. Her grandfather had told her what to expect: King David plays his lyre, Miriam dances. All of Israel, the past judges and rulers, seat themselves at an immense table to eat of the Leviathan.

In the World to Come there will be no slaps in the face, pulling of hair, screams of disgrace.

In the World to Come Rina will be less plump, will walk with grace.

In the World to Come Rina will speak English like the BBC, pronounce Hebrew like a singer and forget Arabic.

In the World to Come Rina will sit on her grandfather's knee while her father feeds her sponge cake dipped in brandy. The whole family will prepare for her bot mitzvah. The women will throw candy down upon her from the upper balcony. She will be wrapped in a full-length prayer shawl and sing the holy words from her birth section of the Torah and Haftorah. At the meal of the Leviathan, presents will be heaped upon the velvet seat of her chair.

Her mother will caress Rina's soft hair (not Moroccan stiff) and will say, "You are greater to me than seventy angels." Her sisters will put Rina's name on their amulets, for her name means "happiness." Her brothers will beg her to educate them.

In the World to Come Rina will sing in a voice like Miriam's. It is said in the Legends that when Miriam led her people out of Egypt, suckling babies let go of the nipple to sing, children on the knee sang, and babes yet unborn sang in the womb. Thus it will be when Rina sings her Haftorah.

On this earth there is only the sound of the slap, the honking horn from a customer, the blown whistle of the police, the judge's gavel.

In This World the mother slaps her for going on the street, but also reminds Rina that she cannot afford to feed her, and who will put food on the table, and what can Rina do to be useful? Money is accepted—with the evil, the averted eye—by her parents.

Shula from Poland has no amulets, Evil Eye, demons, crowded family or illiteracy. There are only two daughters in the household, but it is a displaced household. The father never earned here what he had in Poland, never gained the social status, never learned literary Hebrew. In Poland he was a journalist; here he is a *pekid*, a clerk, in the bank. There he had a literary circle. Here he has a lunch break with other pekidim. There his home was sunny and filled with books, magazines, furniture, laughter. Here he lives in a government high-rise. No neighbor knows another. Each has his castle inside the apartment and no one tends the hall that is outside of the castle. Shula's father stumbles over refuse on the stairway when he returns home from work. His wife weeps as soon as he enters. Another insult to her from a bureaucrat, a neighbor, the news vendor, the grocer.

Daughters are the ultimate insult to a family. If a man cannot duplicate himself, it means that he is dominated by the image of his wife. A mother-in-law is another insult. His wife's old mother is given a visa out of Poland. All of their savings go to buying her out. She becomes an older, weepier, more nagging wife.

In one way the mothers of Shula and Rina are alike. Each slapped her daughter in the face in honor of tradition when the girl began to menstruate. It is supposedly so that the girls will have rosy cheeks. But it is because, from now on, she can sin and her sin can swell, a growth, an abscess on the family name.

You must slap your daughter so that she will remember to keep locked the secrets of her belly, discreet the words of her mouth, downcast the longing in her eyes.


Where will Rina and Shula hide as each room is being dismantled? If they run from one room to the next, the movers will enter, lift out the rug, the couch or bed, carry away the chairs, rip out their hiding place in the closet.

They cannot hide across the street in the little stone house. Simha is disconsolate and silent. Terry is now not merely in charge of Wayward Girls, but of a party, the Independents, and has to think how to vote on war and peace, safety and disarmament. Each issue affects a tribe, village, nation. She does not seem to notice what is happening in her own constituency.

There are no places to receive prodigal daughters, the way the yeshivot welcome the prodigal sons. The sons are entreated to return to the fold. The girls are unfolded.

Where to turn?

They love Antoinette, who reads them bedtime stories and brings them little presents each night of Hanukah. But maybe she would rat on them and tell the other women. They cannot ask Robin at the Wall for help. They had never liked each other. Why should she help them now? They are tempted by the beautiful women, Deedee, Gloria, Dahlia. They talk and fantasize. They will travel with Deedee, dye their hair red like Gloria and be trained for the stage by Dahlia. But these women are poor, and the girls would soon be out on the streets to feed them. They are responsible girls, after all. They think of the smart woman, Gerda, the scientist, but she doesn't seem to notice them. Tova lives with Arabs, which shocks the conservative girls. Mickey, the divorcing woman, they understand—her shrieks, curses, complaints, superstitions. They don't need more of that.

Vered is always talking about her clients whom she has placed in agricultural schools or in kibbutzim. Rina and Shula, from the big cities, shudder. No outdoor cafés, no promenading the avenues, no window-shopping, but working in the fields, eating communally. Unthinkable.

Hepzibah returns from shopping in the merkaz to find the girls inside her gate. She brings them in, gives them washcloths and towels to cleanse themselves from their journey, makes a salad, serves fresh rolls, margarina, jam, cake. The girls eat quickly and furtively.

Rahel comes in, Hepzibah's daughter. She is instantly jealous. They are more needful than she. They will soon want her clothes, her books, to study at her desk, to sleep in her bed, take her mother.

Rina and Shula do not know what to talk about with Rahel. They are polite girls, though.

"Nice house, Hepzibah."

"Haifa is a very nice city."

"Your daughter is very pretty, looks just like you."

Rahel runs from the room. She looks just like her father, those liars.

The next morning, Hepzibah asks the girls if they would like to attend classes with Rahel. Rahel gives Hepzibah black looks. The girls thank both Rahel and Hepzibah politely but think it would not be a good idea. It would be burdensome to Rahel and her teacher. The girls improve slightly in Rahel's esteem.

When Hepzibah cleans, the girls rush in to help. Squeegeeing down the floor? Wetting each leaf of the plants? Putting drawers in order? Cooking?

They are, indeed, Jewish Future Homemakers.

Rahel returns from class. Hepzibah cannot refrain from praising them. Rahel dislikes them again.

They meet the father. He smokes in their faces. They have met men like him before, in their homes, in the courts, in the bedrooms. They tremble. It is not going to work out at Hepzibah's. He has already been insulting Shula for her immodest bosom, Rina for showing her legs, both the girls for wild hair and makeup. He works his way down to their painted toenails, like some abomination, a scaly polished creature that creeps into unholy places.

Hepzibah is smiling and serving dinner. She tells her husband how helpful the girls were in the preparation. Immediately he worries. Did they use the proper utensils? Do they know anything at all?

"Rest tonight," he says. "Tomorrow we start you on a new life: school, job, Torah training, proper hygiene, proper dress."

That night the girls whisper to each other of departure plans, but Hepzibah is also awake, planning. Shula has something of the artist about her, and Rina a strong sense of order. They cannot be in a household or in the rural country, and the city is no good for them.

The following morning, Hepzibah asks the girls to accompany her on a surprise adventure. They are leery. But they trust her for she is gentle with everything. No chair is pushed roughly into place, no shade yanked, no door slammed. Her voice is smooth, her face, even for her age, unlined, her eyes childish in their candor.

They spiral down Mount Carmel to the bus station. Kibbutzim line the bus route. The girls shudder. Hepzibah will sell them to the kibbutzim. They'll be apple pickers and fall from the highest branches and break their backs. They pass some towns and factories. Hepzibah is humming, looking out of the window. They relax and even doze until the bus lurches and stops. Hepzibah has rung the buzzer. "Ein Hod," says the driver and also mentions the name of the religious community up the hill.

Which will she take them to? She'll sell them to the religious community as dishwashers. They tramp up the hill. Hepzibah sticks out her index finger to a passing van, filled with yarmulked men. They knew it! They're going to the religious moshav!

At a fork in the road Hepzibah taps the driver. They

descend and keep tramping up the mountain. Hepzibah is winded and stops to recover. She compliments the girls on their hardiness.

In the artist's village of Ein Hod is a café. Hepzibah leaves the girls there. They eat from a great buffet of hard-boiled eggs, sardines, fish salad, "cottage," grated red cabbage, Swiss, fresh rolls, butter, milk and, always, oranges.

They order Cokes. It is extra. They worry. Rina eyes the proprietor and lifts her brow. He understands. She licks her lip with her tongue, her brow with spittle. He rushes Cokes to them.

Hepzibah returns to bawl out the proprietor for serving this unhealthy, sugary drink to the children. He is open-mouthed.

"I have an idea," says Hepzibah to Shula. "This village has a school for artists. I told them about you and they want to see your portfolio. I told them you'd give them a portfolio after a year of study, and now they are willing to let you take classes if you clean the student dorms in exchange."

Shula is looking at the view of the Carmel range. It is green and hazy in the warm weather.

"Which is the cave where the old man was found?" Shula asks.

"The old man? The Carmel man?"

One of the oldest human specimens was found in the caves.

Hepzibah waits.

"I can see the Mediterranean," says Shula.

Then Shula bursts into tears.

"You don't want it?"

"I want it. I didn't know I could ever have what I wanted."

So it is arranged. They will return to Haifa for Shula's clothes. Tomorrow she starts. And on Sabbaths she goes to Hepzibah.

The girls weep. Though often quarrelsome, competitive, of different backgrounds, accents, traditions, they are family. They don't curse one another or slap, scratch, insult. Who will ever love them as they love each other?

"What of *me?*" asks Rina.

"I will surprise you also."

Hepzibah phones Terry at the Knesset in Jerusalem.

"They are here," she says.

"Wait," says Terry in that underwater, crackly voice of the Israeli telephone user, "I've been wanting to phone and tell you my idea."

"I, also," says Hepzibah, "but you, of course, must speak first."

The girls listen. Terry has forgotten them, Terry the Betrayer, never mind the parades they marched in, the pamphlets they passed out—

Hepzibah hangs up the phone. This time her eyes are not so calm.

The women in the North gather. Hepzibah is there, Rina, Shula in from Ein Hod, Vered from Tel Aviv, Mickey is with them and Terry has jitneyed up from Jerusalem.

"Tell it again," says Rina. "How you made it happen."

While the Jerusalem Home for Jewish Wayward Girls was being dismantled, Terry was gathering statistics on sex discrimination: the difference in money spent on boy delinquents and girl delinquents, the data on the army that teaches boy soldiers to read and rejects girls for illiteracy. Terry has statistics on the number of girls prostituting and of recorded abortions of girls under fifteen. She is releasing this information to the local press and the Jewish Telegraph Agency. Everyone will know how Jewish daughters are treated. She has compiled more: case histories of beatings, child molesting, sexual abuse. No one wants to hear more. It's a shame before the goyim.

Let them dismantle Wayward House. She has bigger plans. Girls Town of Haifa.

Will the girls ruin a good neighborhood?

Not at all. The house will be located in a religious neighborhood and will be supervised by a *tsaddika*, a saint, Hepzibah.

The Ministry of Religion is somewhat interested.

Funds will pour in from all over the world, says Terry. Maybe they'll make a movie: *Girls Town*. Once they made such a film in America—*Boys Town*, with Mickey Rooney and Pat O'Brien. It still plays on the kibbutz circuit.

The Ministry of Religion is more interested.

The Ministry of Absorption will help, under the prodding of Vered.

Rina is to be the assistant of Girls Town. She is a good organizer.

"A whore taking care of whores?" frowns the Ministry of Religion.

"Is there no reclamation of the soul?" asks Terry. "Is there not a prodigal daughter?"

"So we'll give it a try," agree the Ministries of Religion and Absorption, and the Haifa municipality.

Hepzibah's husband is the stumbling block. He does not want his wife making more money than he. The Haifa municipality is happy about that. He does not want his wife working after Rahel returns from school. The Ministry of Absorption is glad to save money on her working hours. He wants her home early so she can prepare Shabbat. The Ministry of Religion is content with that.

Hepzibah herself speaks up when her husband suggests that he help supervise.

"They think that women should take care of women. It is according to *Halakah*, the righteous way."


An old Arab house is rented and the girls help with renovations. Rina wants the apertures painted blue and the doors blue. She wants amulets on the walls and psalms about the sun on the eastern wall. So it is done.

Shula comes from Ein Hod with a mazuzah for the door lintels. It is made of hammered brass and is affixed on the front door with a woman's prayer.

Terry says: "O God of Women, Thou hast made us holy by Thy commandments and commanded us to affix the mazuzah. This designates a righteous house of women."

The girls from Jerusalem Wayward have moved in, as well as new members from development towns, from poor communities or from recent immigrant families having absorption problems, the Russians and the Americans in particular.

On every window ledge are flowers. The tables are laden. Almond trees are in bloom and the air is unbearably sweet.

Vered recites the fifteenth Psalm of David, but in the voice of Vered:

"O, my Shehena, who shall live in your tent? Who shall dwell in the Carmel? She that is upright and proud, that worketh righteousness and speaks truth ... speaks no ill with her tongue, does no evil to her sister.... She that doeth thus shall never be moved from this dwelling."

Rina, with outstretched hand, greets everyone at the front door. "It is a pleasure, indeed."

Hepzibah stands behind her smiling.

The parents of Rina and Shula arrive.

Rina's mother grabs the arm of visitors:

"That's my daughter, Rina. She gets it from me. I have a natural talent."

Shula's parents come by briefly. They are so shy they never visited Shula's teachers during Parents' Day. They leave now so suddenly that Shula has no opportunity to introduce them around. Nor do they know that the mazuzah is their daughter's craftsmanship.

Rahel is jealously pouting. She would live in Girls Town. Her father scarcely wants her to visit.

"It is dangerous," he says.

Is it dangerous for Rahel to learn of the streets? No, the streets have moved indoors.

Hepzibah is smiling. She knows the way of the streets and the way of Halakah. She writes a parable and sends it to her class at Writer's House.

## THE STREET PERSON AND THE HOUSE PERSON

A street person sees a lantern in the window. She knocks, first on the window and then on the door. A house person answers.

The house person is wearing a nightgown that ties around the neck and the cuffs. It is warm and sprinkled with flowers.

The street person is wearing a slight garment that squeezes her breasts and hips together. She speaks very politely.

"May I seek shelter here?"

The house person nods.

The street person, once inside, feels uncomfortable and takes very little space, wrists one above the other, knees pressed together, ankles touching.

The house person is a regal hostess.

"Where have you been?"

"On the streets."

"Drink some hot broth and tell me about it."

The street person sips the broth, burning her lips slightly.

The house person sits in an armchair and waits.

"I stand on edges," says the street person, "on corners, alleyways, doorways. I stand within the circle of light but allow shadow on my face. I am selected by the passing caravan, not because of my eyes, my hair but how convenient I am to the road."

The long-haired hostess leans forward.

"Sometimes we go behind a bush. I get grass stains on my clothes and my underwear."

The hostess listens, scarcely breathing.

"My legs are scissors, pliers, they have a pivoted jaw that holds all girth. I ply my trade."

"How does it feel?"

"I am often chilled. All the apertures of my body are open. It is drafty. Once I tried to paint blue around each opening, eye shadow around the eyes, circles under each ear and nostril, blue around the three magic rings of my pelvis. But the color wore off. Now I close my eyes. I do not want to know who has found out my address."

"Does it hurt?"

"Yes. Or it is numb. Sometimes, if there is heavy traffic, I lie on the grass, an accident victim."

"Do they love you?" The flowers on her robe snuggle under the hostess's breasts, cling to her wrists, gather in her lap.

"They cannot," says the street person. "For they are all blind men. Their apertures are closed and I am their Evil Eye. I know it is a man because of the white cane that taps its way into me."

"Are you unhappy?"

"My body is. I always have a vaginal infection. My bra is tight to push me up and leaves red grooves on my back. My breasts have no feeling. They are loaves of bread. My hair is always pulled. The buttons of my clothes are ripped if the client is in a hurry. My shoes throw me forward so that my back aches. I have black and blue marks on my knees. I bleed rectally from the strain. My urine burns me. And worse—worse—"

"What?"

"I cannot concentrate on anything, a line, a song all the way through, even a joke. I am impatient. I always expect disaster—the police will drag me in, touching me all the way; the lawyers will insult me, the judge will not look at me. My clients forgot me before they know me."

"Was it better when you were a child?"

"The same."

"Do you dream?"

"No. It is my only time without a partner. I exclude, I forbid anyone to come through the apertures of my dreams."

She is weary and a little sleepy.

"Are you hungry?"

"I am never sure."

The hostess tiptoes out on soft slippers to bring cheese with caraway seeds, biscuits, tea.

The street person awakens.

"How is it to be a house person?"

"I open all windows. I beg people to enter but no one comprehends my language. My door blows open and slams in the wind. I wait for an intruder, a prowler. Someone will howl outside my window.

"I lie on my bed and dream of my bridegroom. He has different faces and is of varying sizes, but he always comes into the room dressed in white. He removes his white satin yarmulke. He removes his prayer shawl. He has been praying for me."

"Oh, how lovely," says the street person.

"He is my pillow. He blankets me. He transports me. We are a boat, he the oarsman. We are an auto, he the driver. I am the mare, he the rider."

The house person's voice is fast and high. Her cheeks redden.

"Oh, the excitement of your life," says the street person.

"I wear nothing tight that will prevent the wind from touching, the bath waters from buoying me, the air from encircling me. I wear no undergarments, only long skirts and loose blouses. I wear my hair so that no pins will dig into me if I have to lie down quickly. I wear perfume, lightly, in case I'm found by a dream. I put on a blue ribbon at night for good luck so that when the windows and doors are open, the angels will find me. A minyan of angels will crowd upon me. I will know it is they by the tickling of their feathers. Sometimes something unholy enters by mistake. I know that it is he, the Evil One, by the scrape of his scales against my chest. All animals come here from the woods: the noses of deer nudge me. I hear scampering feet in my bed, birds' wings under it."

The street person has ceased eating.

"Oh, my morah," she says. "May I come here and learn from you?"


H. sends this to her old writing teacher. He enters it in the annual contest and H. wins first prize. There is a formal presentation which she does not attend. Third Prize accepts in her name.

The women from the North sing a round with the visitors. It is from Isaiah, and they make it fit their voices:

> Here it is so sweet, so pleasant.
> Let us sit, sisters, together.

A late visitor comes into the house. She is carrying a pigeon.

"*Feh!* You'll get lice!" says a guest.

The young visitor says, "It was climbing up and down the steps."

"It probably was sprayed along with the trees and has brain damage. Why else would a pigeon climb up and down steps? Look how slow it is, what a stupid pigeon!"

They put it outside. The pigeon perches near the door. The young visitor claps her hands loudly. It soars gracefully and flies south to Jerusalem.

# 18
# Gehenna

How came Deedee to the group? Through villainy. Villains are not strangers who dwell across the border. They may live in our midst. That which we call sensual, they name despicable.

## THE VILLAIN SPEAKS

When I was thirteen I learned that there is magic in the grain of wood and in the shape of the letter of the word. As

I would read, letters stretched until they spaced themselves off the page.

At that time I also began to smoke cigarettes. I noticed then that the burn marks on my study table, where the cigarettes had been placed too close to the table's edge, would move. The brown spots clustered, rolled like grapes, jerked, lumbered.

All of life is in the grain, the seed; all of time in the second. One does not have to look at the horizon for meaning.

From thirteen on, my glasses became thicker as I peered closer. I moved to the minute examination of objects other than the study table. And I learned that there is evil everywhere, even in the nutshell. For it is there, as King Solomon said, that "the delights of the sons of men are male and female demons."

One must read Ecclesiastes closely for this interpretation. It is evident from the text that he, the King, lay besotted by wine and had paraded before him both male and female slaves. He would witness their copulation and the issue from their delight, born in his house. Often he was in attendance, standing hidden by curtains or at the open womb, amazed. Sometimes he would have the woman afterward, although she lay barely conscious, weak, still spilling forth filth from the cavity.

In Ecclesiastes the words erupt: "body," "sin," "folly." King Solomon is in his garden or his parks, or he is planting fruit trees. In the orchard the fig tree spurts juice, the ripened fruits smash to the earth. Solomon tramples the figs as he walks past the bearing trees, past the slaves with child, reviewing his pregnant flocks. His hands are everywhere, feeling the ewe, if the time is upon her, touching the fat belly of the slave or the fig.

There is a lesson in this. One must keep close track of the past, expose the sins of our forefathers, prevent their recurrence in our contemporaries.

If Solomon is given to madness and folly, to pain and

vexation, then how do we keep ourselves from lusting or from biting our nails, chewing our knuckles? We must judge the judges. Further, we must examine those who have hitherto escaped detection.

My mother is beneath my feet. She is scrubbing the concrete tile floor. The rugs have been beaten and are hanging out on the balcony. I hear the thud, thud of the whisk every day.

My father died after my sister was born. I hardly remember the Kaddish for him. My mother and I slept in this large room, next to the kitchen, with the stove on at night to keep us warm in the damp winter night. Almost until I was bar mitzvahed, my mother and I shared the mattress in one corner of the room. Now she sleeps with my sister. In the day the mattresses are leaned up against the wall.

"What can a widow do?" asked my mother as she fitted my tzitzit after a bath, squeezed my knees, patted my hand. Against me she never raised a voice, much less a hand. But against my sister, that is another matter.

"Bethsheva!" she would scream. "Your underwear! Who taught you how to wipe? You take the garbage of your body and give me the garment to wash."

"I am going out," I tell my mother.

"Without food? Like a beggar into the world?"

I kiss her hand, wet and smelling of disinfectant.

Often I go to the Wall. I am not as directed as some whom I call Wall Watchers. They must see the Kotel, the Wall, in the cool light of morning or late at night. They cannot sleep. They dress hurriedly, go, without socks, at a pace almost running to the Wall.

It has been stuffy and still in our rooms. My mother poured water on the floor and let it evaporate before we slept, but there was not sleep that night. The tiny flies bit without noise or forewarning, like sins entering the body. The body rejected the poison infused. There was swelling, lumps, itching, as the soul does when gluttony or lechery enters, with snouts like pigs, the tongues of serpents, the naked skin of worms.

I am at the Kotel, not a breeze blowing, but desert dust in the air. My clothes are covered with the dust, on my black hat, black silk coat, black leather shoes. Like a ghost I enter through the Dung Gate and walk the streets of the suk, with the boarded-up stalls. Behind each dark covering press the rugs striped purple, orange, yellow; on their hangers swing dresses.

American hippies are sitting in the courtyard. One woman is among them, lying, despite the wind that has arisen, with bare legs. Her light hair spreads on the dirty stone. I think she is dead and go closer. Her chest has rapid rises and falls, like a bird's or a frightened young animal's. As my shadow falls on her, she opens her eyes.

She awakens smiling into my eyes.

I hurry to the Wall and pray. It is said that a man leaves his father and his mother and cleaves unto his wife and they become one flesh. But, between them, edging, wiggling, is Lilith, the seductress, the serpent. I pray that she not rise once again.

The woman is dozing and moving a bit to keep warm. Her arms are bare, uncovered by the garments of maidenly modesty that Bethsheva wears. Her legs are bare and have the imprint of the courtyard stones on them. As I walk backward, facing the Wall always, praying a different prayer at each step, I stumble over her.

She opens her eyes, utters not a word but holds her hand up, warding me off. The wind rises and my coat flaps, my hat blows off, for she, that spirit of Gehenna, is already at my outer clothing.

There are invaders in the Temple site. These are unnatural creatures from pagan lands with great heads of hair, mustaches, round or square glasses, their homes like a hump on their backs. There are the black ones, black as the excavated earth in the Golan and dark as deep within the center of the globe. There are yellow ones with cameras like snouts, like trunks from their bodies. There are the Christians spying, blond Vikings who come here speaking tongues from the Tower of Babel.

I go home quickly as the doves upon the Wall coo and the Wall weeps wet dew.

When I return my mother has information. Bethsheva's friend will come by to tell me. Her friend appears. He is from a different yeshiva than I. His hat brim is slight. His beard is not luxurious like mine, nor does he wear the caftan, the full, long, silk coat. He appears like a crow with his beakèd nose, black small hat, black suit.

I do not like him. He is too fastidious. He smokes but uses a holder. I think Bethsheva will never marry him, sew away on her dowry though she may. His little finger is up when he drinks tea or coffee, even when he talks, even when he picks his horny bill.

"The police want me for something," he says.

"I always knew you were a *ganov*," I tell him.

"Not a thief," he says. "On the contrary, rather than taking, I replaced. I replaced the meaning of Shabbat."

I settle in my chair. I am tired from having no sleep the hot night before.

"This will be a long weekend of a story," I tell him.

"It is a story that fits into a small place," he replies, "into a phone booth, in fact."

I sit up. I understand.

"Which Shabbat?" I ask.

"The week past, the Shabbat before."

"How do the police know about you?"

"From the sinner."

"How could he tell them?"

"He is alive."

"How many were you?"

"The first-year students and the last-year students. The rest were apathetic."

"Have a cigarette," I offer.

He takes out the holder. I don't mind waiting. As the sages would say, "Joy consists of three parts: the anticipation, the participation, the recapitulation."

He and his friends are the vanguard for the gates of our community and the gates of our faith. They are shepherds and watchdogs, soldiers, warriors against trespassers.

*Lēl Shabbat*, the eve of Sabbath, as they strolled ready to pluck sin, like a mote, from the eye, they came upon the evil. Knapsack outside the phone booth, person inside trying, with difficulty, to make a phone call. He actually opened the booth door to them! He actually asked them how to use the phone. He was startled, not yet ready, when they pulled him from the booth. It was too sudden. There were too many upon him, when all those black suits, small hats, horny bills pecked at him, scratched at his eyes, pulled at his fingernails. They left him as he had been born, naked upon the earth.

"What can he tell the police?" I ask. "That you all had glasses, the same hats and suits? Why should they be looking for you especially?"

Bethsheva's friend is disappointed.

"Maybe I did a little something extra," he says, "to remind him that one does not phone on Shabbat."

"What little extra, my friend?" I ask.

Is he thinking? Lying? You can't tell.

"A kick here, a twist there," he says finally.

"Go to sleep, fool," I say. "The police won't be looking for you."

The days go as my life has gone. I am as the seven eyes of the Lord that range throughout the earth, sent to patrol the earth. It is my responsibility as a Jerusalemite to purge the city. If I am not alert, the horns of other nations will blow once again to scatter Judah, Israel and Jerusalem.

In the evening, the air smelling of jasmine, I go to the Kotel. There is the scent of spices in burlap sacks, penetrating through the closed stalls.

I see Bethsheva's friend threatening an American who would photograph him. He comes to me.

"I have some information," he says. "If you stay there could be something."

I wait longer than I am prepared to do, for I have not yet supped. Pigeons are restless, flying in the air, settling into crevices. Greenery grows out of cracks in the Wall. Above, on the long ramp up to the Gate of the Mughrabins, the Arabs silently watch.

On the square I see the Americans. The girl is barelegged, shameless.

Just then a Special drives up. The taxi is stopped by the police at the barricade and the group of black suits stiffens. Bethsheva's friend almost dances to me.

"It is he whom we await. He is on the way to make a journey and is coming to the Wall before he goes to Lod."

He dances back. A figure climbs out. It is a man on whom I see no horns, nor the signs of dissolution, but Satan is a beautician, a surgeon.

People greet him, "Doktor, a good voyage."

The Doktor approaches the Wall. The group from the yeshiva comes closer to him. No one can quite see what is happening, for the group marches off and no one is standing at the Wall.

The Special awaits, meter running, at first unconcerned, then it begins to honk. The women guards run to shush the driver's horn.

The American girl is sitting on the ledge behind the courtyard stones, eating a roll and yellow cheese. She uncaps a bottle of black olives. The woman in uniform approaches to tell her it is not appropriate to eat there. I watch her but listen for the yeshiva. The girl is chewing on the olive. The woman guard grabs the bottle and the girl spits the pit in the guard's face.

The yeshiva boys are walking off quickly, the taxi driver is leaning on his horn. The voyager is not at the Wall. The police search in Wilson's Arch, to the left of the Wall. I follow. There, with a burlap sack over his head, the sack reddening like the setting sun over the high wall, his arms and legs bent inward, lies the voyager.

I return home to await Bethsheva's friend. I think it unwise to go to his house. It is safer for me should he attend me here. He does, knocking the soft Israeli knock. I am the only one still awake. I go outdoors with him; I do not want to be in his company for too long.

"This time you are right," I say to him. "The police will search for you."

"What can he tell the police?" Bethsheva's friend quotes to me. "That we all had glasses, the same hats and suits?"

"They will find out the name of the yeshiva. You were there too long awaiting him. Surely classmates of yours have recognized you."

"They would all agree with me," he says. "It had to be done."

"I don't question that," I say. " 'Let the eyes be open,' as Solomon has said."

"Did you recognize him?"

"The doctor from Hadassah," I say.

"That one."

"A histologist."

"Yes. You know what he does?"

"He desecrates bodies. He performs autopsies and buries our dead without their brains or vital parts, so that they enter paradise and cannot think, cannot see to look upon the heavenly sphere."

"That is his sin," says the assailant.

"Then, indeed, he deserves to leave this world in the same condition," I say.

Bathsheva's friend kisses me on both cheeks and flees.

The next day, there in my quarters, I see her passing. She and her hairy group, those spiders, who probably crawl all over her hairless body. They are sightseeing. I pass close to her and she raises her eyes and looks into mine. She is puzzled. Somewhere, in a dream, she has seen me.

She is wearing American jeans but a dress on top to be proper. I linger to count her trespasses. She stands in the light of noon. Every eye of her body is clear, the two blue eyes of her head, the eyes of her breasts, the eye of her belly.

I follow them a bit, going that way for a lesson with my rabbi. We are reading and commenting upon the Book of Job. We have been patient too long with the trespassers, we of this religious quarter. I read that a girl reported to the police with slash marks on her arms from walking bare-armed through my area. I have read that the Torah of a hippie kibbutz has been stolen and found desecrated.

Bethsheva is wringing her hands. Her friend has been apprehended by the police, as have many of his classmates.

I comfort her. We have never before been close, but, at this moment, we are a family. I tell her he was sent to patrol the earth. We hold hands, although I have almost never touched her before. I quote, *al peh*, by mouth and heart, the following:

"I lifted my eyes and saw ... four chariots came out from between two mountains of bronze.... When the steeds came out they were impatient to get off and patrol the earth. And he said, 'Go, patrol the earth.' So they patrolled the earth."

I explain to Bethsheva that her friend is such a patrolling angel.

We speak quietly of the actions open to us. It is decided that we will go collecting in order to hire a good defense lawyer.

Bethsheva says, "I think I love him. I have never thought so before this, but I see I have been sewing and waiting for him, and now I await the day of his release."

Since he has been pressing her to marry him for some years, we know this will be.

It is a busy time, trying to raise funds for the arraigned.

We are at the Wall collecting when I see the blonde girl there. She sees my sister with her collection box and throws something in, giving me that surprised look that she had when once she awakened and I was hovering near her.

She tells my sister, "I give money because of him." She indicates me. "He's been in my life before this."

My hands shake. I step further back, away from the Wall, in order to smoke. The blonde girl follows me.

"Where do I know you from?" she asks. "Did I dream about you?"

I do not answer her although I understand her speech.

"I am Deedee. Do you know me?"

Again I am silent.

"Am I wrong?" she asks. "Could I have mistaken you for someone else?"

I am no one else. I shake my head.

She sighs.

"Good," she smiles. "I knew something special had passed between us."

Without a word we leave the Old City. We walk along the Homa, the outside wall of the Walled City. She is not speaking. Her strides are American, her hands swing. I find that I, although taller, take more mincing steps.

An Arab boy is chasing his goats away from the road to the Jaffa Gate. The goats nibble farther up the hill. The girl Deedee laughs. On the other side of the road as we approach the ancient valley of Hinnom a goat is on his hind legs, nibbling the thin leaves of the olive tree. He stands there thoughtfully, one paw leaned against the twisted trunk. There is something of a man about him, a Greek mythological character, as he meditates and eats, and as his beard ruffles in the bit of a breeze.

"I am tired," says Deedee. "I want to rest."

I do not want to stop but she has already seated herself

at the southern end of the valley. The trees are leaning; the great white rock of the Judean Hills is corroded in this ancient place. Some junk has been thrown here, a can of *bēra*, packages of cigarettes. I fumble in my pocket for another smoke.

"Want some water?" She offers me her canteen.

I will not drink from the same mouthpiece. She realizes this.

"I have another way," she says and tilts the bottle to make an arch of water for me.

I smile even though the water splashes as I rinse out my mouth with it.

The grasses are growing long from the rock crevices. Around us there is new building but the valley is little disturbed. I can see the old City of David, the houses built down the slope of the hill, sand-colored, houses built on top of generations of houses.

"David the King lives," I tell her.

"You're being cryptic."

"Think of what I have said."

She understands. We are not merely now for time is a continuum. We are also in the days of the Valley of Raphaim, and the time when corn was gathered and vineyards produced grapes. We are in the time of Manesseh, the descendant of David.

"Do you know of Manesseh?"

She does not.

"He 'caused his children to pass through the fire in the valley of the son of Hinnom.' "

"Fire sacrifice?"

I nod. I am enjoying myself.

"Do you know where we are?"

"The foot of Mount Zion," she says, "where trials were held."

I flush as I speak of it. It is warm in the valley. I tell her that Jeremiah cursed this place and said it will be called,

"The valley of slaughter for they shall bury ... till there be no place. And the carcasses of the people shall be meat for the fowls of the heaven and for the beasts of the earth, and none shall frighten them away."

I have succeeded. She is frightened.

"Maybe we should go then," says Deedee. "I have rested."

But I am suddenly tired.

"Are you hungry?" she asks. "We might as well eat if we're sitting at the table."

The table top is a flat rock.

She has more of the canned olives. I accept a few, not from her hand, but from the glass jar. She has cheese wrapped in cheesecloth and I take a small knife from my pocket to cut a piece. She has some hard-looking bread or crackers which I refuse.

The last rays of the sun fall on her. She is a quiet woman, not coy or moving too rapidly. She allows the sun to pass down her forehead, over her eyebrows, shutting her eyes against it, on the tip of her nose, onto the upper lip. It becomes orange at that spot, as if on fire. I am startled. I touch it with a fingertip. She, too, is surprised at my touch. I withdraw my hand.

The sun has caught a button on her shirt, a pearl button, and becomes a rainbow in that tiny space. The miracle of the King's creations. Within a button is the prism, within the drop of water all life. She is warm. Sweat is on her forehead, slides along her cheek like a tear.

Then she falls asleep, her mouth open, breathing noisily. I lean over the tip of the nose, the button, the upper lip, the sweat of the brow. I lean over the buttons of the body. My hands tremble. Again that finger, of its own will, touches her teat, the warm udder of the woman, and I feel what must be an ancient spring, what will be a well of warm, sweetish milk. I touch it repeatedly, gently, touches like feathertips. She opens her eyes.

She pulls me down. I would not have gone of my own volition. She, a power beyond my reckoning, pulls me by my vest. The sun is warm. I look around. The shepherd boy is taking his sheep back to his village. She unbuttons my jacket. She undoes the cuffs of my shirt.

"What is this?" she asks.

"It's my tzitzit."

"That must be removed."

I am will-less.

After she sleeps, I am awake and shuddering. I am someone else in this Gehenna. I put on my tzitzit, dress, run up the rocky path, stumbling from the rocks and because my shoes are not tied. I look back, from the walk directly above her. I can see her. Her jeans are off. Those bare legs are roughened in the chill. They are still somewhat spread. She is the Temptress. She is lying there in wait. She is the mate of the goat.

I pick up a loose rock and hurl it at her. My aim is good. I hit her forehead. She only grunts. I hurl another, yet another. I will bury her in a pile of stone, as whores of all time were treated.

But I am interrupted. The Arab cab drivers are watching.

"Hallo! Hallo!" they call.

I flee. What can they say if a policeman asks? That I wore a caftan and a wide-brimmed black hat? Will the policeman believe them? I go, quite energetically, home.

# 19
# Ceremonies of Revenge

Above Deedee's head is a three-bladed fan.

"This fan is the gift of the Lerman family."

On each blade is a member, "Ronald," "Judy," "Shirley." When the fan whirrs the Lermans disappear and Deedee's nausea returns.

She weeps.

Jesus said, "When they persecute you in this city, flee to another."

She has been persecuted but she's too ill to flee to

another. She is dying. All the signs are there, double vision, numb fingers and toes, bloody pillow and sheets, blood through the nostrils, ears, rectum and pouring from under her fingernails.

And she wants to die.

Her last letter home was returned three months later: "Moved. No forwarding address."

She is unclaimed by home or land.

She grew up in disagreeable poverty. That is, her parents disagreed and her father split, her sisters and brothers quarreled, her mother whined. Poverty makes for obedience, in a way. Along with the ADC, one accepts used clothing and the opinions of others. For instance, when the high school assigned Deedee to a commercial curriculum, and the nuns warned her against striving beyond her financial or intellectual means, Deedee heeded them obediently. Much later, when she tried college, she found, of course, that they were right. If she had never read a book, how could she read a semester's worth? If she had never taken time for herself, how could she suddenly demand study time in her house?

She had helped to support her family for years but began holding back on her salary, enough to arrange for a cheap student flight to Ireland.

In Ireland she found her ancestry, many graves, proud history. Her family was legendary, not just mired in poverty.

Someone offered her passage to Crete to keep him company. She lived there four months, in the caves, spending no money, eating lightly, making friends.

In these months Deedee has become youthful, learning what she had never learned in her home: family, laughter, tenderness, excitement, guiltlessness, irresponsibility, passion.

Her hair has grown long and wild. Her clothing is minimal, cave clothing, shorts and shawls and a pair of jeans.

She, who never raised voice or hand in class, can now shout and sing. She has discovered that she is tall, for she had always stooped. In Ireland she learned to walk erectly in honor of her ancestry. In the caves she learned Yoga. She has learned to fit anywhere, city, townlet, village, cave. Anywhere, but the hospital, but this land.

Her friends shared their money with her when they booked passage to Israel. Now she has lost them.

Jesus warned his disciples they would go forth "as sheep in the midst of wolves." She must warn her friends.

Jesus gave them power against unclean spirits. She needed it. Where was it?—Against that freak, that ancient stone-thrower, probably living in Hell all these years, practicing his aim, waiting carefully for his target.

Maybe they, the outsiders, are all targets among the Jews. The Jews deny reality, the reality of Christ and of His rising. They go right ahead with Passover as if the ending were a happy one, with no sequel—*Gone With the Wind* without the Civil War.

The anger is bleeding out of her. She breathes bubbles of it. The world is red through her eyes. If she dies here they will put her in a pauper's grave, bought with the blood of her Lord.

She calls upon the only family she knows, "Mother Mary, my sweet Jesus."

Women are speaking. Probably in Hebrew. She'll go to heaven and only Hebrew will be spoken there. She'll have to sit for thousands of years, the dummy in the classroom.

Now German, spoken by a tall, skinny lady, shaking her finger, looking into Deedee's eyes, arguing with the nurse. Another language, soft, not Italian, not Spanish. She knows no such tongue. And a Slavic speech. She is not in heaven. It is purgatory, the Tower of Babel. Maybe they give you a passport to the land where they speak your tongue. But what if you're bilingual?

She is restless, turns abruptly and rips an intravenous needle out of her arm.

Nurses are there struggling with her. One young woman visitor rises from a chair and holds up her arm.

"Enough!" she says in a musical voice. "Enough torturing of her."

A short-haired, small woman is filling out forms, rushing in and out of the room. Young girls are peering at her from the doorway.

"What do you mean you can't release her because the Sabbath is coming and you're not allowed to sign. It is a greater sin to keep her. You are breaking the commandment against covetousness. You desire this girl's spirit and you cannot have her."

Deedee is back in the convent school. Soon they'll give her Holy Communion.

"You may not call anyone on her behalf," says Gerda. "You cannot let some man come in here and discourage her from living."

There is a fist fight. A nurse and a cleaning lady against a voluptuous, dark-haired woman.

A pail of water is overturned.

"You spilled that water across my feet on purpose," shouts Mickey, "you nursing whore, you cleaning witch."

Deedee begins to smile.

Who are these strangers? Are they fighting over her body? Will they divide her garments amongst them? Who gets her hospital gown? Who her striped robe? Who her bedpan?

She tries to speak. No one pays attention.

Jesus had said to the Jews, "Why do ye not understand my speech? even because ye cannot hear my word."

Suddenly everything is changed. She is wrapped in linens. The bed is rolled down the corridor. An ambulance awaits. Another fight. Too many women trying to crowd into the ambulance. Argumentation. Deedee faints.

"Fair is fair," says the ambulance driver. "Let her choose. If she chooses, it's settled and we go. Unless she's dead already."

Deedee revives.

She looks at these faces as if through a fish-eye lens, large noses, pointy foreheads. Demons. They swim in and out of view. One face seems steady. It does not become an amusement-park mirror but remains open-eyed, interested and calm. There is a scarf on the woman's head. Her nature is neat. Deedee finds herself extending her hand to the woman. The hand that holds hers is strong and dry.

"This one goes. Everyone else walks."

Deedee dozes and the ambulance drives over the cobbled streets. The driver, gruff, hairy, wiry-headed, thick-lipped, picks her up like a flower, a bouquet. He carries the stalks and stems of her, ducking to get through a doorway, into a tiny stone house. He deposits her on the bed. It is another cave. Deedee is home with cave women. It is her first entrance into the little stone house in Jerusalem.

The room whispers, corners shush, sheets slide sibilantly, doors groan, windows scrape. It is full of things, insects rubbing their wings, angels tittering. Only the woman in the scarf sits in silence. Her eyes light up the dusk.

"It's taking a terrible chance," says Gerda. "Massive hemorrhaging. I don't want to accept the responsibility for that."

A young woman with a British accent leans over her. The British hovering over the Irish!

"Will yourself to stop the flow of blood," says Joan from Manchester.

Another.

"Are you an American? I, also," says Tova. "You're home."

Home?

"With women," says Terry. "You're safe."

Safe?

"From men," says Mickey bitterly, "the damned stone-throwers. Every look a dart, every action a war."

Deedee is fumbling around her neck.

"Do you want something?"

She nods. Should she tell them? Will they crucify her if she does?

The calm woman leans forward.

"A necklace?"

No.

"A locket, pictures of home?"

No.

"An amulet."

Sort of—

"Ah, not a Mogen Dovid. More like a cross."

Yes.

"Do you have her things from the hospital?" Hepzibah asks Terry.

Terry shakes her head. "No, the Sabbath was coming. They were rushing away. I'll go back for them Sunday."

"Make her one," says Hepzibah.

"Actually," says Antoinette, "Joan of Arc was given two sticks tied together."

The others do not like this analogy.

"Wait," says Gloria, the convert. "I kept mine, just in case...."

In her pouch, along with telephone tokens and liras is a cross.

That Gloria, hedging her bets, a bigamist.

"In your hand or around your neck?" asks Hepzibah.

Deedee begins to cry.

"Maybe she doesn't like it," say the wayward girls. "Maybe she wants one of her own."

"Sleep," says Hepzibah, *"Eheye tov."* It will be good, the phrase of The Land, which there is little enough reason to believe.

Dahlia hums one of her melodies, wiping Deedee's perspiring forehead, kissing her dry lips. Although there are only surd sounds, Deedee thinks she hears words:

Jesus says, "God is not the god of the dead but of the living."

Does Dahlia say, "Among us you are dwelling; in our midst you are healing"?

There is a great busyness, a new mission, cause, purpose, enterprise, political issue, drama. Although one would not know it from Deedee. As she lies conscious and unconscious the earth does not quake, the rocks are not rent, the graves remain closed and no saints arise.

But the women in the house are obsessed.

Several times a day they gentle Deedee, changing the bloody sheets from under and over her, wrapping her in the softest old linen, taking turns sponging her, wetting her feverish legs, her dry, numb feet.

She awakens to shadows over the bed: branches crossed, reproductions of crucifixions, a macrame cross that Tova knotted, a woolen cross that Mihal knitted. Joan of Manchester finds an old sword from a stage set, so Deedee can swear on the hilt of a sword.

Mihal sees her looking upward at the walls.

"What's the difference?" says Mickey. "As long as it casts out devils. It got Dracula, you know. He ran from the cross."

Deedee can't laugh, her head hurts so. But she thinks she hears laughter.

The end of the second day she bleeds less and stays awake for longer periods. The wayward girls visit to give her lessons:

*"Oz, Oznī-ēm,"* ear, ears—they touch theirs, hers shyly. *"Aff,"* they touch noses; *"peh,"* the mouth. They close their teeth to show that in Hebrew one also has teeth.

Deedee is grateful. She had thought she was losing parts of herself. They count with her, repeating over and over patiently: *yad*, one hand, *yad-ī-ēm*, two hands; *regel*, one foot, *reglī-ēm*, two feet; one head, one body. Deedee is present and accounted for.

The girls explain, with difficulty, that the pairs of the body are female and the single members male: arms that embrace, female; eyes that see, ears, knees, legs, feet are the paired female. The head, on top, male, the liver, nose, mouth, chest, male.

"No," whispers Deedee.

They give her water.

"My head is female, my nose is female, my mouth is female, my heart is female."


The women gather daily to look at her. Simha has rolled out blankets for herself and her pregnant belly. Simha groans as she lifts her weight. She throws water under each of the pendulous breasts. She washes her face, then she turns and smiles radiantly at Deedee.

At last Deedee could ask, "How did you know about me?"

"The radio," says Terry. "The press. Stupid reporting. No investigative journalists. 'YOUNG WHORE ANGERS THE SENSIBILITIES OF THE GUARDIANS OF THE GATES.' You were a traveler, no one to inquire after you, no one to protect you."

Deedee skims consciousness again. The man's face is before her—pale skin, intense eyes.

Deedee screams.

The women are silent, sullen, enraged, worried, upset.

Simha cannot contain herself. Nor Mihal, the divorcing woman.

They whisper and agree. Each murmurs to the other, Simha and Mihal to Terry.

Terry: "Of course."

Terry to Tova.

Tova to Gloria.

Gloria: "Hot dog!"

Gloria to the wayward girls.

Shula bursts into tears. Rina applauds.

The wayward girls to Dahlia.

Dahlia: "That's it, exactly."

Hepzibah, Gerda and Antoinette are the Worrying

Women. Hepzibah worries about legality, Gerda about its getting out of hand, Antoinette about communication with the public.

The women listen politely and gravely to these experts in their midst. They are well counseled.

The women agree to keep it disciplined. They cannot, however, control the press coverage. And, Terry reminds the Three Wise Women, Hepzibah, Gerda, and Antoinette, there is nothing they do that is legal. There are no laws yet for these women. Are they, therefore, lawless? No. They have a strict biblical sense of the law. Hepzibah can protest against the wayward girls participating, Terry says, but no one knows better about law and lawlessness than they.

REVENGE RITES

*Weapons:* The Evil Eye, the Purified Stone, Blood, Sounds Which Shatter the Air, the Weapons of Home.

Rina prepares the Evil Eye. She paints it on the palm of her hand to shine into the face of the enemy. She paints it on dishes to throw, on the insides of cups to smash, on wooden shingles to hurl. She has Shula help her. Although an eye is the easiest of all things to paint, Shula is more artistic than she. Each of Shula's painted eyes is more malevolent than the last.

The stone is purified by boiling in agitated, roiling water. Carefully selected stones are placed in the pot in Simha's house and on the stove at Wayward. One hears them knock against each other for hours.

Blood is gathered from the trough of the ritual slaughterer. Other bloods are added: that draining from Deedee's wounds, that blood caught in a menstrual cup by Joan.

The women practice sounds: snarls, howls, grunts, snorts, squeaks, neighs, brays, cawing, quacking, cackling—

barnyard sounds, as well as wailing, shouting, shrieking, whining, whinnying, whistling—discord and pandemonium.

*Equipment:* The women carry the musical instruments of the kitchen: pots and lids, iron pans and metal ladles, wooden spoons and kegs.

The women prepare the ingredients for curses.

(1)  a name
     compared to another name
     to erase the first name.

(2)  a moan
     that echoes
     when hands cover ears.

(3)  a memory
     nailed to the heart
     with hammer blows.

(4)  a burial stone
     erected
     without name or date.

(5)  a word
     so genital
     it rapes.

(6)  a word
     that plucks at eyes
     and pierces ears.

(7)  a whisper
     so insidious
     that dogs and villains quake.

(8)  a future
     so bleak
     you hide in the past.

(9)   a promise
        your biography
        to be writ by the enemy.

(10)   erasure
        of ancestry
        and progeny.

The women are prepared.

"Deedee," says Terry, "describe what you can."

By the third day Deedee is drinking broth, nibbling biscuits, spooning in carrots mashed with butter.

The praises heaped on Deedee—her courage, her recuperative powers, her beauty, and now—what a good eater!

This is Deedee's land. This is Deedee's home. She will learn the anthem. She will name the relationships: mother/sister/aunt/lover/cousin/other/younger/smaller.

She will name them as parts of her own female body.

She will also prepare herself for the university.

"Maybe I also was guilty," says Deedee.

Mickey snorts.

"You're worse than Jewish," says Tova.

"Maybe I seduced him," says Deedee.

"That's what all victims say," says Joan.

"Maybe I offended his religion," says Deedee.

"That's what all fanatics say," says Gloria.

"Maybe I said something I didn't mean to," says Deedee.

"That's what all deaf people claim," says Dahlia.

"Maybe . . ."

"No," says Terry. "Describe."

Women are not used to this.

If Deedee was wounded, it was because she went on the target range. If Deedee was stoned, it was because she walked in the place where once they practiced stoning. If the villain fled, it was because he felt shame.

The bleeding starts again. Hepzibah begs the women to quit.

"A stone for a stone," says Terry.

They have a little to go on—description of garments, maybe a sister, a locale at the Western Wall, another in the quarter of the Hundred Gates. A man, like all others there, black beard, earlocks. They quiz her on the shape of the hat. Different yeshivot have different hats. And the coat. Was he alone? With friends?

There has been a series of incidents, beatings, a scientist on the critical list, but now this, somehow the same, somehow different, the stoning of a woman in the Valley of Hinnom.

"I will help," says Hepzibah suddenly. She rises. "Await my return."

Hours later, perspiring, red-faced, scarf and wiglet askew, panting for breath and dreadfully thirsty, Hepzibah returns.

Deedee is propped on pillows. She keeps her head thrown back so the nosebleed will cease. She closes her eyes frequently to rest them, although pain darts through her head when she is not distracted.

She watches the concern for the runner, the teller of the tale, the bringer of facts. Hepzibah holds onto her sheitel while the women dab her face with cool water, wipe her neck, put drops of rubbing alcohol on her arms and swollen ankles.

They ask nothing. They wait.

Hepzibah consents to a bit of brandy.

Then, panting, "I will lead you to him."

"Who will attend Deedee?"

"Alone," whispers Deedee. "Let me be alone."

"Should Simha come in her condition?"

"Should the girls go in their innocence?"

Should any of them go?

"Should we disguise ourselves?"

"Are we ashamed?"

"Is it dangerous?"

"Then let us disguise ourselves."

They find Purim masks, stretch stockings, paint, large sunglasses, wigs, hats, scarves, kefiahs. They take cabs.

FURIES DESCEND ON RELIGIOUS QUARTER, reports the press. "Women descend, dressed in masquerade, on the lower-class neighborhood of Mea Shearim, shouting curses outside the door of one of the inhabitants."

The mother comes out. The women begin smashing windows. The sister comes out. The women hurl the objects they carry.

"This is a preconceived and premeditated attack," says *HaAretz*.

Two women fight with the mother and sister while others push through into the two-room apartment and drag out the son, a Talmudic scholar, who makes a bare living tutoring.

"According to his neighbors, he has led the most righteous and exemplary of lives," says the religious press.

Curses are shouted, too bloodcurdling to be reprinted in a family press, although *HaOlam HaZe*, a left-wing scandal sheet, prints them. One mere child gives him the Evil Eye and spits three times at him over her left shoulder. Cups are smashed against the house. Cauldrons of blood are poured over him.

He is stood up like the victim of a firing squad. The women have stones in their pockets. He cries out for his mother and his sister.

"Stone me instead of him," his mother piteously begs.

His sister hides in the house.

The women slam lids against pots, ladles against metal pans, wooden spoons against kegs. They are a barnyard of disgusting sounds. Then begins a sustained long moan. The victim and his mother stand there bravely. Neighbors call the authorities, who are slow in coming.

The stones are piled. Each of the furies arms herself.

Suddenly a cab screeches its brakes. A bandaged young woman descends.

"My family," she cries to the women. "My friends. Let she who is without sin cast the first stone."

"Don't do this," says a small, short-haired woman.

"It cannot be otherwise," says the wounded person.

The police arrive.

"Officers," says the young woman, "I wish to charge this man with malicious attack with intent to commit murder."

The mother of the accused says, "It's her word against his—a woman's against a scholar's; a foreigner against a native, a goya against a Jew."

The young man begins to weep.

"Forgive me," he says to the newcomer. "I would have hidden my sin under a grave of stones."

He is led away while the mother protests, "He is overwrought, studying too much, praying without cessation."

Hepzibah is calm and smiling, unlike the other women who are puzzled, angry or feel foolish.

"It's as it should be," says Hepzibah.

Deedee is now sharing the bed with Simha and Terry. Soon Deedee will be given part-time work helping Terry and the wayward girls. Soon she will learn the new tongue so that she can attend the university.

They drink until they forget their curses. They drink until they set down their weapons without rattling them. They drink until the wounded and the healthy fall asleep.

Deedee thinks of those who follow Christ:

"In my name shall they cast out devils; they shall speak with new tongues; they shall take up serpents; and if they drink any deadly thing, it shall not hurt them."

As they all doze off Gloria says, "Deedee has risen."

"Deedee has risen indeed," answers Hepzibah.

# 20
# Joan on Merōn

These women are all, were all travelers before settling down in each other's friendships. Even in The Land they traveled, Mickey from her village to the city, Simha from disinterest to piety, Hepzibah from surety to a spiritual pornography. The wayward girls have come in off the street. Vered traveled from responsibility to irresponsibility, back to responsibility. Dahlia has traveled on every high note into desert, mountain, village and city, into the summer-burned brown of Jerusalem to the green of the Galilee.

They traveled from abroad into The Land. Gerda, the scientist, came from the camps in Germany. Antoinette brought Shakespeare to Jerusalem. Terry traveled from family to community, Gloria from California to The Land, dancing from one pair of arms to another along the way.

Deedee has climbed out of the cave and blinks in the blinding light of golden Jerusalem. Tova has gone from straight-haired to curly, from good girl to freaky. Robin has flown from the earth into the air.

Joan has clambered down the Mount of Merōn. That is how she met the women.

She is sitting in the café in the merkaz, her face dirt-streaked. Sometimes she tries to focus her camera on the people of Haifa. Sometimes she just puts down her head on the table and cries.

The young waiter wipes and wipes the table around her. He does not know what to say. He thinks he is wiping her tears.

Two women watch her, an older and a younger, one with covered head and one with luxuriant long dark-brown hair, one with modest dress, one with bulging breasts and swinging hips.

Joan spills her Nescafé, salts her bland ground chickpeas with her tears.

When a *pushtak*, tough character, hovers over her saying, "Listen, I know how to make you smile," Mihal says, "This is it!" Both women rise.

Hepzibah asks Joan if they may join her.

What?

"We have a neighboring table. Would you mind?"

"I'd mind, and mind your own bloody business."

"You talk tough," says Mihal, "but look at yourself. Come, tell, what is it? A death in the war, a broken heart, a cheating by someone, a stealing of money, bad marks in a course, a curse from a parent, an insult from a child? What else could it be? Don't be ashamed."

"I have visions," says Joan. "They're out to get me."

Mihal lifts a brow at Hepzibah. This *could* be something else, a hospital something else.

"Where are they out to get you?" Mihal asks.

"The holiday," says Joan.

"Ah," the women say, "of course."


JOAN'S HOLIDAY

Joan begins her tale with her arrival in The Land. She is in the bathhouse in Jerusalem, in the Quarter of the Hundred Gates.

The women are cleansing themselves for the coming holiday, Lag B'Omer, and for the trip up the mountain.

The women plunge from cold pool to hot bath. They lie on steaming stone benches. They carry pails of water into the steam room to throw at their faces as they climb, step by step, up into the rising heat. Afterward they lie naked on the roof or in the lounge, on Persian rugs, eating cheese-filled *borākes*.

"What do you do on the mountain?" Joan asks.

She is the cultural reporter for the *Manchester Guardian*.

"We sing," they say. "We dance."

They rise naked on the roof. Clouds float by. A low plane buzzes. They gyrate their bellies.

"We make love."

An older woman tells Joan, "We go there to learn."

"To learn what?"

"The lesson of the mountain."


"If she had only asked us," say Hepzibah and Mihal.

"I have had another lesson in my life," says Joan. "My

father told me, 'Watch out for the blackball.' "

Joan's father was a respected merchant in Manchester, inheriting his father's business. In his middle years he applied for membership to the local social club. To his shock and to the shame of his sponsor, he was blackballed.

"Who did it?" Joan's father asked.

But there was a gentleman's agreement not to tell.

"Joan," said her father, "in this town there is a hidden enemy. In every town in England there is the waiting blackball for the Jew."

Joan became his emissary into the world to prevent that blackball. And what of Joan's studies at the London School of Drama? Never mind. To inherit a father's dreams makes you eldest son. To further his ambitions makes you heir to the throne.

So it was that Joan, before she met the women of Jerusalem, followed the precepts of her father and of her teachers.


"Who were your teachers?" asks Hepzibah.

"The rabbi who trained me," says Joan, "and who tried to kill me."

Mickey's eyes widen. "Tell! Tell!"


Joan's father insisted on rigorous training for her bot mitzvah when she was twelve going on thirteen.

The rabbi came and sat as far away from the child as he could and still read Haftorah with her and still hear her. She was audible but invisible, for no religious man looks upon a woman. He never touched her or met her eyes, but sat protected in sweater and vest, jackets, with several pairs of socks on his feet. He was the layered traveler ready to leave any land that ejected him.

He always came late to her lessons as if he had an

appointment until that moment and he would arrive panting. Once inside, his chest would quiet; he would sigh and let his breath expire slowly.

But when he sang, a young voice full of love and passion came from that shriveled mouth. A dybbuk would sing through him who, perhaps in life, had been a deaf mute and now had a tongue to wag and vocal cords with which to praise the Holy One.

As she grew older Joan would ask herself if she were dreaming as a child or did the rabbi really tell such tales that made her cry, laugh or squirm in her sleep all night.

He would close his eyes and that high bar mitzvah boy's voice would issue from his mouth.

He told her stories of women, uncleansed women who tried to fool their husbands that three days had elapsed since their ritual cleaning, for from their organs sprang diseases, from them came the odor of pus, the staining of garments. He spoke thus on the days when Joan menstruated. Since he never looked upon her, since they never uttered one personal word, how did he know?

He would expatiate, wandering from the subject of unclean women to that of unclean foods: things without scales in the ocean, without hooves upon the land, without feathers upon the winged, things that tried to force their way onto the plate, into the stomach.

One speaks to girls in a tone that one does not use with boys. An excitation, revulsion or strange ecstasy would seize the child Joan.

One day the rabbi, moving to the most distant chair of the study table, decided to prepare Joan for encountering angels.

"You will know them by their terrible countenance," he said.

"What are their names?"

"They will tell you no name."

"Should I ask them?"

"No. If one such were to appear unto you, you ask nothing."

"How will I know if it's an angel?"

"By sight and odor. If you wait, unmoving, you will see a flame, and upon that flame will ascend an angel. In the air will be a scorched smell as of feathers burning."

"Will it have a sound?"

"The sound of flapping."

"Will anything else happen?"

"A slight wind will stir the flame. There will be a sudden chill upon the air."

"But, Rabbi, I'll be so afraid!"

The rabbi then, for the first time, did look upon her. He fixed her with that eye, with that terrible countenance, and she was afraid of nervousness ever after.

She, a child of Manchester, was filled with his ruminations of the travels he had made, travels he would make, and of travels the soul should never undertake.

"Where should the soul not travel, Rabbi?"

"It will know when it gets there."

"How do I avoid evil, Rabbi?"

"By doing all the six hundred thirteen *mitzvot*, commands, and more."

"What more? What else should I do?"

The rabbi looked upon her directly for the second time.

"There will be no way for you."


Hepzibah and Mihal inhale sharply.

"A prediction predicts itself," says Hepzibah softly.

"I think I am meeting that rabbi over and over. It is as if in The Land I recognize people I have never met or a place unfamiliar."

"It is anticipation," says Hepzibah.

"After the day at the bathhouse," says Joan, "I had a bad dream. On the train going to Jerusalem there had been a rabbi in the only empty seat. I sat next to him."

"You should have stood," says Hepzibah.

"I leaned my pack against the seat and half-dozed. I awoke with a start to find him staring at my reflection in the windowpane."

"Bad luck!" cries Mihal.

"His beard had a yellow stain, like a trickle of tobacco or of rust in a white basin. I thought he called my name.

" 'Did you call me?'

"His eyes in the pane closed.

"Then I met a news vendor. He tapped on the sidewalk with his cane for me to buy his paper. I looked upon him, that bundled, bearded man, and I thought the man from the train had followed me."

"Could be," says Mihal.

"The night before the festival I dreamt of these old men fixing me with their terrible glances, and suddenly their eyes glowed red like embers, and the whole dream turned red: red of fez, red earrings, red pants in which a fat dancer does the shimmy. And there is a ticket taker whose eye has a streak of red like a spoiled egg. His red sweater is snagged, his teeth uneven."

"You are dreaming of Merōn," says Mickey.

"You are being warned not to go," says Hepzibah.

"Women do not know how to sense danger," says Mihal. "It's why we're so foolish."

It storms all night before departure. Joan waits at the bus terminal where the storm has knocked boxes around the station, lifted papers, puddled the ground. The sun comes up crookedly.

"Ah hah, what did I tell you," says Mickey. "A crooked sun, you limp through the day. A pale sun, you regret you're born. A bright sun, the world's begun."

Joan waits obediently in line, putting her gear in place periodically to photograph the Sephardic Jews preparing for the trip up the mountain. Suddenly the line is overrun.

Both Hepzibah and Mickey burst into laughter.

"We knew it!"

Passengers who were not in line force open the back door of the bus and cram into all of the seats.

"That's how it goes!" says Mickey.

The ticket taker heedlessly continues to punch the tickets of those in line for whom there are now no seats. When it is departure time and all the seats are filled, the ticket taker shrugs and tells those in line that there is no room left. They will have to await the next scheduled bus and he will collect money from the seated passengers.

"I would not allow this," says Joan. "I'm a person. He can't treat me this way."

Laughter from the women. "That's what it is to ride a bus in The Land."

"So I use my pack to block the doorway and prevent departure."

Whistles from Mickey.

"Then the ticket taker looks upon me. The blood spot in his eyes seems to spread. He lifts a shoe from his position on the bus steps and kicks me in the chest."

"Tsk! Tsk!" says Hepzibah.

"Behind me the crowd is ready to stampede as I fall. It is my dream of warning, only it is worse. I will feel the bottoms of their shoes as I felt the driver's, all those shoes: the women's house slippers with wooden heels, those clogs the young people wear, the army boots of the soldiers, the dark leather lace-up shoes of the older men, the slip-on black leather of the Hasidim. All of those hooves will be placed upon me!"

Joan weeps.

"It is a bad holiday," says Hepzibah. "It has become thus."

"They put another bus on," says Joan, "and we go up the mountain."

They ride to the green Galilee, the shimmering Kinneret, past castles and parked trailers, picnickers near Tiberius, past Roman arches.

"I sit and hate," says Joan.

Maybe it is at that moment of the working of bile in the mouth, of the reworkings of the mind that evil finds its subject. Evil is a changeling, the rabbi had warned Joan, and can appear anywhere. Evil always looks for its victim.

But the bus climbs into rarefied air, higher even than Jerusalem. Legend says that the air of the city of Safed is so pure that when one dies, one steps immediately into the Garden of Eden. Mount Merōn, a small distance off, is higher yet.

Joan begins to forget, for passengers are singing, the women behind cupped hands ululating. A drunk leaves his seat to dance in the aisle. The driver takes the dangerous curves one-handedly.

"From there on," says Joan, "I cannot tell what is evil from what is not, for it all turns out the same, the good and the evil."

Once on the mountain Joan begins a fruitless search for a place to stow her gear.

"In the caves," says an old man.

"Where are the caves?"

He leads her on goat legs, a satyr, looking back at her, nimble, chewing on things along the way, bits of green from branches, food in stalls, chunks of meat on spits. He leads her to a cave. She peers in. Old men are defecating.

Joan turns away.

A young man, bearded, wild-haired, is watching her.

"Where can I spend the night?" she asks.

He laughs, "Don't make announcements or you will

have offers. You can sleep anywhere that you find dry ground."

But the ground is muddy from the rain of the night before. Joan wanders into the tomb of Merōn, housing Reb Ben Yohai and his son.

The young man is there. "You can't sleep here," he laughs. "This is the Torah room. The Torah sleeps here."

Where the law sleeps, woman cannot.

Nothing is as Joan expected. The old parchments of the Torahs are in cases decorated with lions of Judah. But they are primitively cut and sewn. The lions of Judah become puppies of Judah, with flat manes and panting tongues.

The women in the room make obeisance to the Torah and decorate it with their silk kerchiefs. They sing to the Torah. It is their baby, their beloved.

"Idolatrous!" Joan tells the young man.

"What isn't?" he asks.

He turns out to be the social worker in charge of this group of Moroccans and Kurds; they have bused up from Jerusalem.

In the room of the coffins there is more idolatry. Cripples swing in on crutches, leave their crutches and crawl out. A man in black suit and sunglasses throws his sunglasses at the coffins. Under the dark glasses, shaded by his black hat, the man has holes instead of eyes.

In the next room, an old woman with a mattress rests against the flaking blue wall. She draws in her knees to make room for Joan. The woman's space is in a drafty doorway but Joan decides to share it, temporarily at least. She sits against her pack, unties her sleeping bag and uses it for a cushion. Joan is weary and her throat raw. She wishes to photograph the old woman, who forbids it with one gesture.

"Are you married?" the woman grabs Joan's left hand.

"I am not."

"Ah," the woman is so sorry. She puts a veil over her face. "Pity, pity."

"Are you?" Joan asks.

"No," the woman is not. "Pity, pity."

"Let us move," says Joan. "It's too chilly here."

"No," says the woman. "Wherever I set down my mattress I must spend the night."

"Just away from the draft," says Joan.

"No," says the woman. "It is bad to move too often. A mattress gets restless and crawls out from under you."


"She was telling you something," says Mickey.


There is excitement in the court. The Torah is passing. Men near the Torah kiss it. The old woman lifts Joan's hand and kisses the hand.

"Women do it this way," she explains. "They are always upstairs or separated from the Torah so they must kiss each other and kiss at the Torah. Now kiss at the Torah."

Joan laughs.

The woman insists. "Kiss at."

Joan is staring.

"Do it or it will be bad luck."

Joan kisses at the Torah and once again averts bad luck.

The court empties. Joan moves her gear inside the court and finds a broken box to sit on. It is next to a barber's open case. He is set up to cut hair, but no one has come to him.

"It is a holiday with no one shorn," he tells her sadly. "Do you want a haircut? Good luck to have a haircut on this festival."

No, her hair is English long, fine Manchester hair.

He begins to weep. One eye weeps, the other drily watches her.

"Do you want your hair cut?" he asks again.

She is shorn, a lamb at shearing time. Her hair is on her shirt, windbreaker, mountain climbing boots. People who gather silently to watch are her mirrors. She regrets her appearance in their eyes.

"I wondered about your hair," says Mihal. "So chopped. Never mind. My beautician will even it out and, slow-by-slow, it will grow."

Everyone leaves the court for the roof. The Hasidim are dancing on the dome above the tombs of the ancient cabbalists. Olive oil is poured into stone basins and set afire. Notes, supplications, candles are hurled in. Women dip handkerchiefs into the burning oil.

Joan wants to photograph. The soldiers restrain her and bawl her out for trying to capture the souls of the dancers and then using them for her own evil purposes.

"How many are here?" Joan asks the soldiers.

They tell her, laughing, "Not one, not two, not ten, not many." For Hasidim may not be counted. It is bad luck.

Suddenly Joan glimpses someone familiar. An old rabbi whose hands shoot up into the air, white against the black night, the center of the circle, like the flames against the sky.

When the rabbi dances, the circle dances. When the rabbi stops, the circle suspends. Joan has stepped too close to the circle. It stops. The rabbi looks upon her and shakes both hands at her. No link will allow itself to be broken by a woman. The rabbi is familiar, both in his averted eyes and direct gaze.

The young social worker approaches her.

"They will call you a whore if you go too close," he says. "Have you a place yet for the night?"

No.

"Then come with me."

She goes. He takes her hand, his warm, his eyes level and relaxed.

"It is a long walk," he warns. "You may not be able to come back for the dancing."

That's all right.

"You will be isolated with me."

That might be all right.

He settles her on the bus in which his clients came, the Moroccans and the Kurds. He is busy looking after them but will soon join her.

"Cover your head while I'm gone," he whispers.

"Why?"

"Just sleep."

She buries her face into her muddy pack. She has almost no footage of film, has done no interviews, has captured no event for the *Guardian*, cultural or otherwise.

She lies still. There is Yiddish in the air, a sentence.

"The seeker in turn is sought."

Joan lies chilled. She does not move until the young man shakes her to make room for him.

"Were you whispering to me?" she asks.

"I will now."

"How is Jerusalem?"

"Good, very good. How is England, London?"

"England, Manchester is good, very good."

"Have you gone to Canada, that is owned by England?"

"Yes, I have gone to Canada that is not owned by England."

"Have you gone to Montreal?" He is very excited.

"To the Exposition for my newspaper. Yes. I have been to Montreal."

"I have always wanted to go to Montreal."

"Montreal is good, very good."

"And it has snow?"

"Not during the Exposition, but it has snow."

"Not like Israel."

"No. You would have to buy a fur coat."

He laughs and touches her hair.

"Why do you wear your hair so short?"

"It's my religion."

"Are you religious? Was it short like that when I first met you?"

"This isn't really my hair. It's my *sheitel*. Under this wig I have a great flowing blonde mane."

"In truth?"

"Not really. Nothing is really."

"Montreal isn't real? It isn't really nice? It doesn't have snow?"

"In truth, Montreal has great amounts of snow. Why do you want to go to Montreal anyway?"

"Leonard Cohen is from Montreal."

"The singer?"

"Yes. You know Leonard Cohen?"

"I know Leonard Cohen."

"In truth?"

"In truth I know the songs of Leonard Cohen."

His voice is louder. People on the bus become restless in their sleep. He lowers his voice.

"I like Leonard Cohen. 'Suzanne' is about Montreal. I saw Leonard Cohen in Jerusalem, where there was a riot. Leonard Cohen wouldn't sing. He saw the big audience and said, 'This is worse than my bar mitzvah.' He wouldn't perform. And we begged him. 'Please, Leonard.' Then he said, 'I will sing if all the Canadians here go home.' Nobody left. 'Please, Leonard Cohen,' we said, 'we love you.' So he sang and talked about Montreal. Now he loves us. He would do anything for us. Didn't he sing for our soldiers during the Yom Kippur war? I owe it to Leonard Cohen to visit Montreal."

She kisses him. "You're wonderful. Go to Montreal and get a fur coat and sing songs."

*This* she will write up for the *Guardian*.

"I can't sing," he says.

She is shocked, "I thought all you Israelis could sing, dance, had natural rhythm."

He does not understand. It must be his faulty English.

"No," says Joan, "it's my faulty mouth."

He kisses her faulty mouth. He kisses her faulty hair, her faultless neck, her faultless fingertips, his hand on her windbreaker.

"Take this off," he whispers.

"Not if we're going to Montreal," says Joan.

"Tonight on Merōn."

She takes off her windbreaker. They turn in toward each other. His hands are on her shirt, unbuttoning, stroking the breasts. He is shocked that her breasts are so close to the shirt. She starts to explain about not having room in her knapsack for extra underwear. She is unbuttoning his shirt, rubbing his stomach.

"You have no brassiere," he tells her.

"Neither have you."

They giggle. A woman cries out. She calls upon the names of her mother, her father, grandmother and grandfather.

They are upon each other. Joan makes soft whimpers until a flashlight is shone upon them. Her body is revealed, her shirt pulled aside, her breasts nakedly hanging.

An old Kurd stands in the aisle. His flashlight is a single glaring eye.

"It will not do," he says.

The young social worker presses his pant legs together, does not yet zip up. Joan is still illuminated.

"Who is this whore," asks the Kurd, "for whom you disgrace the bus and desecrate the holiday?"

"My friend," corrects the social worker, "havera, female friend."

"Your wife is your havera," says the Kurd, "your havera from Montreal."

The young man looks out of the window, while Joan rebuttons her shirt, puts on her windbreaker.

She rises to leave. He is silent.

The Kurd descends after her, hurling her pack out of the bus, hissing at her. She turns to regard him one last time. The Kurd is faintly smiling and looks familiar.

Around Joan are the bonfires of Lag B'Omer. The last of the meat has been roasted. Children are sleeping. An old Moroccan is snoring and his two wives keep his body warm with theirs. Joan treads her way past the area of the buses. It is too dark to walk back to Safed.

First Joan cries, then curses, then, finally, she, the pilgrim, laughs. Experiences are dancing by: the ticket taker, the dancing drunk on the bus, the gray-coated barber, the woman on a mattress.

She is tired of walking and finds an abandoned fire still burning slightly. Joan builds it up. The ground is not too muddy now. She can rest and feed the fire until dawn when she will jitney down to Haifa, whatever the cost, and leave by the first boat from Haifa port. Her shoes are muddied, her hair shorn, her pack torn.

The fire burns down. Wearily Joan gathers crate wood and blown paper to build it up.

She cannot get warm and thinks of her family in Manchester. She cannot warm herself enough and thinks of that bit of sex on the bus. She crawls closer to the flame and is warmed through. She sleeps sweetly—until she dreams.

This is the dream of Joan.

"The best student," says a voice in Yiddish. "She was ever my best pupil."

There is a scent like burning, a sound of the beating of arms. She beats at herself wild-eyed. The flames stare back at her. They are the eyes of the Hasid, flickering yellow in the center. They are the eyes of the dancing rabbi on the roof of the tomb, of the rabbi in the train windowpane, of the Kurd cursing her. The eyes in the flame beckon Joan to dance.

She thinks she is screaming but maybe she is singing.

The Hasid is singing in a boy's sweet tenor:

> "To the teacher belongs the pupil,
> to the seeker the temple."

His hand closes over her. There will be no more breaking of circles. He takes her for his bride. Her body dances on the flame. Her hand leaps with his. He whirls her to the purest air of all, so pure that one need not pause at Purgatory before entering Paradise.

This is the lesson of the mountain. That the child-bride, the woman-to-be is prepared, is lured into marrying her doom, into journeying toward it. The doom accompanies her on trains and buses, takes her ticket, excludes her from the circle, seduces her into the innermost fire. It consumes her soul.

No woman can survive such a journey.

Dawn. Joan hysterically jitneys to Haifa. She is both chilled and burned, reasonable and babbling.

Her film, she later discovers, does not come out. It is as if none of it had occurred. Now only the mountain is behind her, blurred.

Hepzibah and Mihal have heard her out.

"This holiday," says Hepzibah, "commemorates the lifting of a siege. We will have to lift the siege of this holiday. Come with us."

They rise.

The waiter whistles. "Who pays the lady's coffee?" he calls after them. "One minute she cries, the next she leaves."

# 21
# Holy Body Day

Joan is taken to the bathhouse to cleanse herself of memory and to begin preparation for the new holiday.

What do you need for a holiday? A date, a legend, a blessing and a meal.

"A counterholiday," proclaims Terry.

To the shyness of the world, where everything is lidded—eyes, cooking pots, windows and shades—there in the bathhouse nakedness prevails.

Bellies undulate, breasts point and flop, ankles are sunk into flesh or bracket the legs. Thighs shake or saunter, knees dimple or are bony.

Everything stares: eyes, navels, nipples, opened mouths. Joan, also, stares through her camera lens.

When they return from the bath, they say a blessing, a prayer on first gazing upon forests of hair, scales of nails, desert sands of smooth bodies. It is a reworking of the *Shhehianu* prayer: "Blessed art thou, O Mother of the Universe, from whose body we descend, who has kept us alive, preserved us and brought us to this time, this season."

Joan is feeling flushed and photographs and tape-records to distance herself. She films Terry sitting with crossed legs and bent hand. Terry's dark hair is sprouting white wisdom hairs. Joan pans dozing Tova, who whistles and wheezes and makes birdcalls to the flocks in her dreams. She Extreme Close-Ups on Gerda's eyes, those eyes like time pills, thoughts popping out periodically. Mickey is sullen. She will have to return to Haifa. Her dark eyes seem to shine through the closed lids.

Rina pushes Shula aside to get into the film, to be respected by camera and listened to by recorder.

"On Lag B'Omer," says Rina, "my mother goes to the tomb and prays for a son."

"But she has a son," says Shula.

"There are never enough sons," says Rina.

"What does she do there?" asks Joan.

"My mother tries to throw herself across the tomb, but now there are guards stationed to prevent the women from doing this."

"Which tomb?"

"Where you were, Yohai's on Merŏn or David's in the Tower of Jerusalem."

"What does she expect to happen?"

"Yohai and David will rise from the tomb."

"To impregnate her?"

"Yes, of course. And with sons. Everyone says it works."

"Does she say anything, call their names, pray?"

"I've followed her," says Rina. "I also want to know what to do. She lies on the stone and says, 'The seed is greater than the womb, the sperm stronger than the tomb.'"

Joan shivers. How is it, she wonders, that the ancient muscle entombed, that worm is still actively pursuing and wiggling through casket and stone? The chill of the holiday, of the tomb, the burn of the dreams will never leave her.

Simha is watching Joan.

"How shall we count this holiday?" asks Simha.

Women are in the habit of counting days. Because these women have spent so much time together, their menstruation is approximately the same time. They count thus: "One week after the onset of menses.... One week and a day after the onset of menses.... This is the twenty-first day after the onset of menses."

Simha says, "This date is Holy Body Day."

The women pray that they be restored to their own Temple, that they no longer be captive, for there is no God of women, there has been no reaping of the sheaves in the land of women and no bringing in of tribute of dry measure.

What is the offering on this first Holy Body Day?

> Fine flour mingled with oil
> The juice of fruits
> The green ears of corn dried by the fire,
> frankincense thereon.

They speak of the legends of their bodies.

"My body," says Gerda, "can walk miles. My feet never get bunions, calluses or plantar warts. My thighs do not rub. My hips are narrow from walking and mountain climbing. My hands are not afraid of stings, pressings of the pencil, of holding test tubes delicately, of being burned or cut. My wrists are steady. I hardly perspire. My eyes have twenty-twenty vision. I can peer through a microscope equally well with either eye. My ears can hear a neighbor's child turn over in the middle of the night. I am almost never ill. When I am, I cure myself. I command my body, and it is a battalion of obedient soldiers. I go on the March to Jerusalem, and I alone could still circle the city another three times. I climb Masada up and back down and do it again. I have climbed Mount Sinai without losing breath, four hours each way. I came down hungry and ready to cook a meal for a crowd."

"What can't your body do, I wonder?" asks Gloria sarcastically.

A long silence.

"It doesn't know how to say, 'I'm sorry. I apologize. Did I hurt you?'" says Gerda. "It doesn't know how to feel what other people are feeling. Since the camps I have been careful not to know too much about my surroundings."

Gerda's head, with its 20-20 vision, perfect, cavityless teeth, clear nasal passages, turns abruptly away. She is crying.

The women kiss away her tears. She is more perfect than ever.

Joan speaks.

"In Manchester I was always afraid of the hidden blackballer, of someone not hearing me or not seeing me, so I developed long arms of equipment, with eyes that extend into far-seeing lenses and magic ears that hear and record everything. Every whisper is on my machine. Every shout. I photograph all the inhabitants of my life. Nothing will be forgotten. No one will slide from me."

The women speak of lovers.

"Why do you have Arab lovers?" Mihal asks Tova disapprovingly.

"They're sensitive," says Tova.

"Haha!" says Mihal, "like the PLO."

Rina speaks up. "I want a man."

"Oh," says Mihal, "look who's talking!"

"I never had a man," says Rina, "only customers. Sometimes I think I want an old man who will give me the key to all the rooms in his house, to his cupboard and treasure chest and safe, who will rock me in his rocking chair, cover me with his heavy robe, call me 'little girl,' feed me tidbits from the table. He says words no one ever spoke into my ear. He sings. For an old man, you know, he can still carry a tune! He tells me bedtime stories, such stories that I sleep dreamlessly, never moaning, never stirring, in his arms all night."

And you, Shula?

"I cannot go shopping for more sizes of men," says Shula. "They are smooth and silly or prickly and rough. They roughen my face. They bruise my thighs. I will sleep alone."

Shula does not know that she will take voyages with smooth-faced men, rides with prickly men.

Vered is hesitant. "I sometimes think of loving someone like me, soft, with parts not alien. I would rest my head on her belly. It would gurgle, rise and fall, move until it glided me to sea."

Since it is a holy day, one is free of sin. One begins customs.

Mihal says, "I want a new ceremony. Let it be added under the bridal *huppah*, under the canopy, that the man says, 'I will never hurt you. I will never punish you. If I shout at you, may my tongue be struck dumb. If I strike at you, may my arms become numb. I will not smash the glass underfoot for fear slivers will enter your heart.' "

Applause.

"Talking is for weekdays," says Dahlia. "Singing is for holy days."

"No songs have been written for this holiday."
"We'll write one."
"I can't carry a tune."
"We'll carry it with you."

*The Women's Song of Songs*
Look upon us.
The sun has kissed us.
Our mouths are raspberries,
small sweet strawberries.
Our eyes are the black sky in storm
over the Mediterranean.
Our thighs are pillars of the Temple.
Our hair is red as David's,
gold as the skirt of the desert,
black as the Sudanese.

We daughters of Jerusalem
have scent like the clementines in their season.
Our fruits are both tart and sweet,
the lemon, the apricot.
We are the seeds of the pomegranate.

In the evening we wait,
we daughters of Jerusalem.
We smell of nana and cinnamon.
We smell like the gardens of the king.
Between our thighs is the grotto of Ein Gedi.
The ascent of our breasts is like unto
the hills of Judea.
Seek us and ye shall find us,
lovers of
the daughters of Jerusalem.

Our juices are fresh,
like Ein Feshca, the mouth of the Jordan.
Our flesh is smooth,

like the sand of Nuweiba.
Our eyes are blue, the waters of Eilat.
Drink the salt of us,
ye voyagers.
Rest from your weary travels
with the daughters of Jerusalem.

My love, my body is a crane's,
a stork flying to Egypt,
the rich soil of the Galeel,
my belly is Mount Hermon.
Come, ye sportsmen,
on the slopes of the bellies
of the daughters of Jerusalem.

They cannot find us.
Oh watchman, let them enter.
Unlattice the windows.
Open the gates.
Come, our beloveds,
to the daughters of Jerusalem.

Joan is dozing, sweet from the bathhouse, warm with
the women. She is no longer plagued by Merōn and will
unpack in The Land.

A holiday concludes with a meal. So must Holy Body
Day. Dahlia prepares a fish dinner, Saint Peter's fish from
the Kinneret, the Sea of Galilee. Dahlia stuffs the fish with
the succulent fruits of The Land, with its savory spices. The
women sit and eat. They think it is the World to Come with
the meal of the Leviathan, for their plates never empty.

# 22
# Maiden to München

There they are on shore, dots, waving dots. The women from the North are there, Hepzibah, her daughter Rahel, and Mickey. Terry's come up from Parliament. The mayor of Haifa is there. And Rina. Rina waits on shore from the time Shula boards until three hours later when Shula embarks. Rina waits, waves, leans, straightens out to wave again.

Sea gulls shriek at the boat. One pigeon soars and dips almost to the deck.

Shula has ensured the safety of her journey by reciting the Pilgrims' Prayer at the Western Wall.

"Our feet are standing at thy gates, Jerusalem."

This time Shula's parents accompany her, proud of their daughter, the scholarship winner.

"May peace be in her walls, tranquillity in her towers."

The recitation of the Pilgrims' Prayer is one means of propitiating the evil forces. A second is by rolling up a paper note to the Father of Us and pressing it into the crack between the stones as Shula's ēma does. Yet a third way is her father's. He gives Shula a five-lira note to be delivered into the hands of the first person she encounters when she lands. If she has a mission, she is not an endangered traveler en route, but a messenger entitled to special protection by all of the gods.

Her parents had, at first, been fearful.

"What do you want to go to Germany for?" they asked Shula. "It's still a cemetery."

When Shula was years younger coffins came rolling from that cemetery of a country. It was late afternoon before the High Holy Days, windy at the airport of Lod, the flag lashing, hair flying across eyes. The army chaplain, a portly cantor wearing sunglasses under his army cap, sang, *"Rahamim, pity, pity,"* for the Olympic team murdered at Munich. *"El moley rahamim,* O God, full of pity."

Since that time the German government has enlarged the stipends given for Israeli exchange students and has included travel funds to study at the Munich Art Academy.

The women have sent Shula on her way.

Simha said the prayer for traveling:

"Our Lady bless you and keep you, shine her face upon you, be gracious to you, turn her face unto you and grant you peace."

Each did for Shula what she did best:

Mickey fixed Shula's hair. Shula was Dahlia's guest at a concert. Gerda gave Shula a Hebrew-German dictionary.

Hepzibah gave her a *Mogen Dovid*, a Star of David, blessed by a great scholar. Deedee, the traveler, gave her an atlas. Rina gave her an amulet to safeguard her. She was given such a pack of presents that she secretly had to store some at Girls Town.

The night of the sailing Shula's head hangs inside the toilet bowl. She counts the tiles on the floor of her booth. She gives thanks and praises for clean bathrooms and for her own stall. By morning she has memorized data: tile broken, size of paper rack, markings on the wall.

At 7 A.M. the boat docks in Cyprus at Famagusta. Shula is the first passenger off the gangplank, and to the pharmacy. It is there that she gives up her father's five-lira note, too soon, too soon.

Shula sleeps all day and into the night on deck. She is undisturbed by a nosing dog, guitar players or a truck that has been hauled on board and rolls and strains at its fastenings.

For the first time Shula is on a vacation. She is not on the streets or in the classroom. She is on deck.

She kicks off her jeans, unbuttons her blouse and presses her clothes to the bottom of the sleeping bag that Simha and Terry gave her. The rain begins, heavily. Another figure is searching for clothing, a young, light-haired man who has boarded at Cyprus. Shula rises, a walking sleeping bag. The young man is in underwear, gathering his pants and shirt while Shula takes webbed steps down the hatch to the reclining airplane seats below deck.

She is settling when she sees white underwear climbing down the stairs, bare feet, the fellow clutching his sleeping bag and dog. Water beats on the stairway and against the portholes. Reluctantly, she lifts her feet from the extra chair next to her and makes room. He curls toward his dog.

In the morning Shula, the young man and the dog are

ferried to shore at Rhodes, as the S.S. *Athena* continues to Venice. They separate on shore. Shula is frightened. She was always frightened, even as a wayward girl, on strange street corners waiting, on the curve of a road waiting. Here she is, again, waiting.

The young man passes her as she wanders into a marina. He tries a greeting in Polish. The dog is interested. They meet again in Old Town where Shula has ordered Nescafé. The Pole is at the next table, his dog lying under it, barely visible. He rises, bows to her and approaches. Shula knows home-Polish. She invites him to join her, tremblingly. She has never done it quite this way before, not offering anything, not selling. The dog dozes under the empty table.

They walk to a park near the Turkish-built double walls that guard the harbor of Rhodes. It drizzles slightly. From her knapsack Shula pulls out food her mother has prepared: tightly sealed jars of pickled eggplant slices, turkey balls, canned preserves, raisin-sweetened rolls. The Pole eats her offerings.

As the rain falls lightly the Pole opens his windbreaker to her. His sweater is soft and of good wool. He is not a poor man.

When her head is inside his jacket, the dog whines until he is included. The dog licks Shula's face while she knocks her head against the Pole's chest to be let out.

This is Shula's first childhood. This is her first playing.

She has a prepared list from her teachers at Ein Hod. She must see the ruins of Rhodes before departure. She is subdued—three broken Greek columns against a sunset sky, no building, nothing for the columns to support. There is just the silhouette of broken columns.

"The remainder is more important than the original," Jerszy, the Pole, tells her.

They return slowly to the café on the pier where the ticket taker will come and her boat for Crete docks.

Shula's heart is broken, she who has vowed to look at no man.

"We will sail together," says Jerszy.

Shula laughs. Her laugh sounds accented, Polish.

The night on board is a nightmare of noise. The dog barks and knocks over woven baskets when he sniffs out sausages. Shula and Jerszy lie on the upper deck, spreading themselves on adjacent benches. Shula is anxious. She knows the end of every dream, of all sleep. Instead, they remain separated and chilled. They can discern, even on the blackish sea, the dark shadows of the mountainous Greek isles.

They land in Crete about 10 A.M., transferring their luggage to the bus for Iraklion. He holds her hand during the scenic two-hour ride while she sleeps, her head outside of his jacket this time. She awakes to find that she is holding not only his hand but the dog's paw.

The *maskira*, secretary, at Ein Hod, has given Shula the address of an inexpensive pension.

The Pole conducts business with the landlady in German.

"How many rooms?" she asks.

Jerszy turns to Shula; Shula blushes. He tells the proprietress one room. She charges him extra, for this is not merely double occupancy but there is the dog. As the owner leads them to the room, she is true to her word, there are three single beds. She closes the door behind her. Shula and Jerszy giggle and cover their mouths.

The dog, left in the hall, whines to be let in. He leaps upon the bed, licking them both, then licking Shula regularly, rhythmically in her sweaty places.

Jerszy gently pushes the dog aside.

"My turn," he says.

It is Shula's first night of lovemaking, the first night in her life of tender whispering. There should be a special name-giving prayer, *Sh-hehianu*—that we were brought to this bed in tenderness for the first time.

It has been a long time since Shula was a wayward girl.

She is now, in fact, the follower of instructions, the serious student. She has been told by her teachers at Ein Hod that she must visit the museum in Iraklion and take notes for all of the student artists unable to pay the travel taxes.

The art work, protected in cases, is from the nearby Palace of Knossos. There is an ivory acrobat, four thousand years old, still bull-leaping, even with his missing leg, missing arm, lost parts of his head. They see fresco fragments of the bull dance.

Jerszy comments. Shula is entranced.

"In this culture," he says, "the pieces are the whole. The three columns on Rhodes are the temple, these shards at the Palace are the great pots; a nose of a dolphin is a fish mural."

Shula asks Jerszy what she could be reduced to and still be restored, still be recognizable. They play. He turns her around, looks at this and that, pinches wrist and behind, touches her, catalogues her. His hand on her face, he decides.

"To an eyebrow," he says. "I would know that winged brow anywhere."

In Athens, two days later, she sees three toes and the thong of a sandal that is Apollo. She sees fingers lifting a fragment of cup that is Athena.

She has, however, taken chill on the passage from Iraklion to Piraeus and arrives in Athens with a sore throat. Despite the Akropolis, visible from their window, dark at sunset, clear in the morning, she stays in bed. The dog is restless, Jerszy calm. He reads books he has taken with him from his motherland. He looks steadily at the temple. He washes socks and underwear, his and Shula's. She is embarrassed. He tells her that nothing embarrasses lovers.

When she is well enough to visit the Parthenon, she is disappointed. It is crawling with people, tours from Denmark, Germany, France, Japan. Jerszy hurries to greet a tour from Poland. He writes down addresses, exchanges information while Shula photographs in expensive color film. She must send back slides to her teachers and the art history class at Ein Hod.

That night, when they eat moussaka in the Plaka, Jerszy tells Shula that he wants to go to Spain. He has only a short time left of his thirty days' vacation. The Poles at the Parthenon are also going to Spain. Would Shula care to go with him?

He looks worried. Shula wonders whether he worries that she will not go or that she will go, she an Israeli joining a group whose government is officially anti-Israel.

When is the group leaving?

Tomorrow.

Shula feels like spitting. There seems to be vomit in her throat. Or tears. Or sobs. She says that her throat hurts and she must return to the hotel.

Of course. He is courtly.

She sleeps. When she awakens, he is gone. Her clothes have been washed and hung on the balcony. Near her bed he has emptied his pocket of stamps from Polska, reproductions of masterpieces for Shula, his artist friend.

Shula spits and enrages. She is fifteen again. She is nothing. She gave it to him free. If she charged, she could stay abroad longer.

She is exhausted, sitting on the bed, looking at those foolishly romantic stamps. Jerszy has been her romance and she will have others. The world is full of lovers who speak her tongue or other tongues. Shula is growing up. She wipes her face and looks seriously at her gift.

What is happening to art in Poland? Nothing for the last fifty years has happened, at least to stamps: hunter in fur cap with bushy beard, holding his musket; a half-draped classical figure running across the landscape, her breasts as solid as the platter she carries; a red-haired girl in a blue frock, holding roses; a woman against a cloud-spread sky rides a galloping white horse.

Look! Jerszy has left her his address in the town of Lodz and an invitation to visit not only his homeland but his home.

Shula rises, sore throat, never mind, sore heart, pay no mind.

She has a destination and a purpose, and safe passage is assured.

The train to Germany is made up in Athens. She has arrived ahead of time, but it is already crowded when she boards. Everyone and their packages have pushed past her. She looks longingly into compartments of young people but they are jammed with students, knapsacks and sleeping bags. The compartments hold six, but there are eight students in some of them.

Shula looks into a compartment, only three men. They stare at her when she enters. As she tries to sling her camera and packages up on the rack, the chubby oldest, with thick eyebrows and matching mustache, helps her. The youngest, curly-haired blond, like the statues of the kourus, lifts her suitcase onto the rack for her. The other, thinner faced, sharper dressed, helps push her knapsack under her seat. As the train pulls out of the station the three gentlemen are already busily opening their parcels.

The pudgy man offers her chunks of bread, a greasy, spicy piece of salami, yellow cheese. The younger has crisp green pears, large apples and a plastic container of meatballs. He pushes them toward her and brings out a fresh plastic fork for her. The thinnest one has a bunch of crunchy, seedy grapes, light green and reddish blue in color. He also has wine that he passes around. In a few minutes, after eating heavily, they retie the food parcels.

Greek inspectors board every few hours, at Lianokladion

at 10 P.M., at Larissa at 12:30 A.M. The train is crawling. The inspectors make the men untie all the food parcels. The train will never get to Yugoslavia, will never reach Germany.

Shula is used to waiting, to being passive. It is only recently that she has been active. She returns to that waiting-room time of childhood, *Koupat-holèm*, socialized medical clinic, at the police, for trial, in the temporary homes. Now is a time of transit. She makes her body sleepy; she makes herself wait, and she ignores all danger signs.

Her compartment mates talk, grunt, sleep, all three of the men with their hands at their crotches. Shula has trouble sleeping. The white shirt of the pudgy one shines at night. She discovers the next morning that it is really light blue. His shoes are off and his woolen blue socks have the odor of soft cheese. They have to pass through Thessaloniki and Idomeni before they get to Yugoslavia, early in the morning. With fewer searches by guards and with the lush scenery, the compartment mates become more cheerful, chummier.

They take pleasure in teaching her German food words, for they will be in Austria the next morning: *"Weingarten,* vineyard"—observed from the train window—*"Fisch," "Suppe," "Taube"*—the last with flapping arms, for pigeon.

Shula laughs. She knows a Mr. Taube, a Mr. Pigeon, at Ein Hod. There is a *Weingarten,* Mr. Vineyard, who owns the newspaper stall near her parents' high-rise. And there is *Hecht,* a pike, and she knows a young pike who works in the bank. She will go down the street next year when she returns and greet those meals of people: "Shalom" to the pigeon, the pike, the grape.

She learns that poached eggs are *verlorene eier*—lost eggs. She repeats like a good girl. They applaud her. The youngest embraces her for fine mimicry.

Their beards are growing through Yugoslavia. Shula begins drawing, secure in her family of the compartment, looking at the pleasant autumn in Yugoslavia, and feeling no hint of bristles.

Shula dreams of The Land. There are presents to buy. She has purchased blouses and Cretan bags for the women already, but can she keep them unworn, unused this whole year? She thinks of Rina, who is somewhat officious these days, Rahel, who is somewhat calmer these days, and Hepzibah, the mother of them all.

She fingers Hepzibah's Mogen Dovid. The compartment mates have already asked her about it and exchanged glances when she told them.

She thinks of Jerszy. There was no insult in that relationship. There was the choice to be together and the time to separate. She will buy him a present—ask her friends to send beautiful Israeli stamps to her—and will visit him in Lodz.

Her spirits have improved. In her sketch pad she draws peasants with oxen and carts, coveys of geese, flower gardens around small houses, women in Turkish pants. She draws streams swollen from the rain, muddy, rushing rivers, green everywhere. Night falls as they come into Belgrade at 6:42 P.M.

From the next compartment comes singing. She peers in longingly at the young Americans and two long-haired German university students. The Germans see her Star of David and greet her. They have been at a kibbutz in Israel.

The train gets into Zagreb at 10 P.M., into Ljubljana at 12:30 A.M. Shula wants to cry. Stupid girl, rushing through Europe. The ride to München is becoming stupid as well as endless.

Shula discovers that the thinnest of the trio in her compartment is smuggling in whiskey and spreading his luggage around the train to hide the contraband. The other two look for empty places in other compartments to stretch out more fully. The smuggler is left with her in the compartment. He ceremoniously opens a bottle and offers her a drink.

She shakes her head, but he holds her head, then her mouth and tries to pour. The schnapps spills on her two-hundred-lira pantsuit, one-quarter of her father's monthly salary. She screams at him, and he shouts back angry Greek words. To her relief, the bushy-browed compartment mate returns.

They speak of his three babies in Crete whom he seldom sees, for he works in München. It makes him very sad. He shakes his fat face and she thinks his babies must look like him.

"*Schlaf,*" he orders her to sleep now.

They have passed Jesenice and then Rosenbach at 2:53 A.M. She begins to relax. He is opposite her, his hand under his belt buckle, either dozing or looking at his own reflection in the dark glass. When her head flops over, she finds he is sitting next to her. The long seat across the way is empty, and the compartment drapes are drawn shut. He is moving sleepily. She is alert but confused. An arm lands on her heavily, rests there until she lifts it off. His eyes are closed, his mouth pursed, not for kisses, but snores. An eye opens at her, unrecognizingly, shuts. Again, in a few minutes, that heavy arm and a fat leg. She struggles as they both slide down on the seat. He is awake and quick. He pulls at her pants. She catches hold of the seat separator and clanks it down on his head. He rises and leaves immediately without his shoes. His blue socks have stiffened until they are like leather soles.

Shula is watchful now. The furtive part of her nature returns—years of watching out for violence. She decides once more to enter the compartment of the Americans and German students, but one is lying across the sliding door and she cannot get in.

She goes back to her compartment. The youngest is there with his classical smile and his kourus-curly hair. He takes out his tape recorder and checks it over. It had been roughly handled by the Greek guards. The conductor enters, wearing the brighter uniform of Yugoslavia. He is

apologetic about disturbing the couple and leaves. The boy
puts music on softly and asks her to listen. He holds the
tape recorder against her ear and she hears a love song, he
tells her. He sits next to her, holding the machine. His arm
holds it against her ear, the other curves back to his body.
One arm begins to encircle her. Shula waits a moment. His
beard scratches, his body is dirty from traveling, but he is
the youngest and handsomest of them, and he has been the
most proper, unlike Pudgy Daddy or Sullen Smuggler.

But quickly he tangles Shula's legs in his light green
sports pants, takes off the pink and black tweed jacket,
keeps his tie on and begins tangling her slacks in her legs.
She yells. He holds Shula's mouth with one hand, and the
other turns that examined tape recorder loud.

"Tickee tickee too," sings the lady love.

Shula yells, *"Lŏ, lŏ,"* in Hebrew, but no one hears.

The drapes are drawn against the light in the corridor.
She can see the gray-white of his teeth. She can see, soon,
the gray-whites of the eyes of the others.

At 7:30 A.M., Salzburg. Her compartment mates move
their luggage to a roomier, emptier compartment. They
look around them at Austria, the green uniforms, the
feathers in the Tyrolean caps of the older men bicycling by,
the frost from early autumn, bedding hanging out of
windows, houses of stucco with wooden balconies and red
dangling flowers, a chimney smoking, the smoke in a still,
thin line. Another chimney in a valley with vines growing
around the smoke stack.

They arrive at München at 10:25 A.M. The men rapidly
walk away, the smuggler struggling with the bottles that
weight his suitcase. The Cretan gentleman, holding the
leather case with handles that had held the food he shared,
is also gone. The curly-haired blond boy has leapt lightly
from the train steps into the arms of his father, who is also
employed in Germany. Boarding passengers see Shula
sleeping, or parts of her visible around her sleeping bag, a

bare foot, her head turned to the high leather upholstery, her hand open. Near her, the clasp broken, lies her Mogen Dovid.

Incoming passengers try to rouse her and turn her head toward them. From every orifice her seat mates had drunk her, biting the flesh of the nose, opening her mouth, eating the tongue, the ears. Her face is leprous, sections missing from their hunger. She was the communal lunch, the licked bones. Of the whole her curled fingers, her foot, and loose hair remain. In the lands of the Minotaur, the lion and the crooked cross there is never enough of sacrifice.

# 23

# The Excommunication

"She is the third victim," says Simha.

Simha has become maudlin this year and Mickey is more superstitious than ever. Mickey goes out at night with Day-Glo paint to mark the Evil Eye on rocks that will stare back at the great Evil Eye in the sky. At dark, near the Jewish Quarter, these painted eyes are watchful.

What will save these daughters of Jerusalem? And do they have to be saved over and over: Vered from public humiliation, Mickey from the wrath of the rabbis, Deedee from stoning, Joan from the shadow of the mountain, Simha from those who would rip out the issue of her womb? Is there no protection, no way to make a walled city around their lives?

Vered is concerned about Rina. Rina weeps without cessation. Vered has sent her to a psychologist.

"Rina says she should have gone along with Shula," says Vered. "Shula was too naïve. She—Rina—knew the streets better."

The women sigh.

"Rahel and Rina have nightmares," says Vered. "Even though the coffin was closed, they know. They dream of separated parts wailing for their owner. They dream of vultures, hawks, birds of prey. Rahel claims to hear hyenas laughing in the Carmel mountains."

Shula's parents, who have only acknowledged their daughter recently, claim her totally now. They ignore their younger daughter, enlarge the photographs of Shula from the press, wear black and frequent Girls Town. Each day they wait on chairs outside of Hepzibah's office. When she escorts them in, they clutch her hands and ask, "Why?"

Under Terry's prodding the municipality of Haifa and the Israeli Parliament ask for an investigation. The German consul shrugs. Shula's past is against her—a wayward girl, waylaid by anonymous foreign laborers. The German government is sorry, but can take no responsibility for the action. A *mädchen* should not travel alone. Overtly or covertly, she must have led them on.

Gerda immediately drafts a letter in German asking for reparations from the German government for the bereaved family.

Terry rises in the Knesset.

"Must women stay within approved borders? Are mountains forbidden, trains dangerous? Is this world unsafe for women? If so, then declare a curfew and keep the men indoors."

Vered's ex-lover makes one retort, half-rising from his seat.

"If you go looking for danger, you find danger."

Hepzibah declares a week of *shivah*, of sitting, at Girls Town. Mirrors are covered, pillows removed from couches and all the girls are in slippered feet. When ten girls over thirteen years of age gather, there is a minyan. They don prayer shawls, adjust their yarmulkes and pray for Shula's soul.

Deedee goes back to the spot in the Valley of Hinnom where she was attacked. The rocks still bear a rusty bloodstain.

Gloria pickets the Knesset, naming by name Vered's ex-lover. He alerts the press and goes out to encounter Gloria, who has been frisked carefully by Security. She stands there with her flaming hair, flashing eyes, taller by two heads than he. She stands there screaming in her nasal American accent, *"Hazar,* hog."

Vered's ex-lover begins to laugh.

"First of all, young lady," he says, "I am not a hog. I am kosher meat, male kosher meat, circumcised male kosher meat."

The reporters applaud, although they cannot put that into the press.

Then he is kindly. "Come inside. I can see that you are upset. Let us speak and I will tell you my side of it, for I really had nothing to do with it. You look like a sensible young woman. You can judge for yourself. Who knows? Maybe I can even convert you."

Antoinette is shocked. "It's *Richard the Third!* Treachery! It's Richard of Gloucester courting Anne, after killing her husband. 'Your beauty was the cause.... Your beauty, that did haunt me in my sleep....' Oh, Gloria, what foul deed didst perform?"

Once again, Gloria, the convert, is converted. Is it on the floor of the Parliamentarian's office? Is it from the reasonable accent of his words, the warm glow in his eyes, the full redness of his lips?

Before Gloria settles in this warm spot, she has to try other kitty litter boxes.

She goes to visit Tova and spends the night talking with Tova's Arab lover. She listens to his poems attentively, praises the passions and the metaphors. He begins to write a poem to Gloria. Tova falls asleep in the other room. Whenever she awakens she hears the murmur of their voices. In the morning, Gloria is gone, the poem completed and the lover weeping.

Gloria goes to Haifa. She visits the beach and then takes the bus up the Carmel to the cafés. There she meets Mihal's divorcing husband. Gloria finds him, contrary to description, a husky, jolly fellow. They laugh together over Mickey's histrionics.

Gloria goes across the Galilee, along the winding road. She is terribly bus-sick and relieved when the bus finally stops not far from the kibbutz. Gloria contacts Simha's kibbutznik. He awakens in the sweltering afternoon to greet her. Gloria offers to register at the guesthouse of the kibbutz. After a while the kibbutznik tells Gloria, "No need to register at the guesthouse. I am given my own room."

Gloria returns to Jerusalem, her suitcase full of souvenirs from the Arab, the divorcing husband and the kibbutznik.

At the Jerusalem Bus Terminal she spies Shlomo Sassoon. He has been on a selling trip with his fabrics and is carrying the sampler case.

"Shlomo!" calls Gloria.

He walks ahead of her.

She whistles gaily. She is the most beautiful woman in the terminal. All the soldiers say "Ooh ah!" when she passes.

The peddler walks on vigorously.

"Hello! Hello!" she calls, and runs after him.

She hears a strange sound. From the suitcase comes a hissing. Saliva edges the clasps. Over his shoulder Shlomo makes "horns" at her and spits three times.


In the house of women all is accepted, all is forgiven, except for the breaker of commandments.


Some weeks later, after a prolonged absence, Gloria is summoned to the women. She is nervous about attending, decides not to, is persuaded to by her curious lover.

"What can they do to you?" he asks. "I'll alert the police in the Old City. I myself will be at an Arab café not far off. It intrigues me to hear what they have planned."

The house is so dark Gloria thinks no one is there. It is so shadowy she thinks the walls are painted black, until the shadows begin to sway. Gloria screams. Eyes glow like cats' eyes in the dark. Illumination. The sharp shadow of candlelight held under the chin. The candles are deep black.

"What has she done, O Mother God?" asks the widest of the shadows.

"She has smashed and broken and trodden upon," says the chorus.

"How do you know this, our Mother, our God, and God of our foremothers?"

"We heard the smashing of the glass, the cracking of the stone, the breaking of hearts," says the chorus.

"What was writ upon the stone?"

"Honor thy friends for thou art the accumulation of them."

"Did she bring them to dishonor?"

"Yes. She is guilty."

No one can Gloria recognize. The voices are spoken into

clay pitchers, into large glass vessels. They echo. No one is a friend.

"Thou shalt not break up the family."

"Did she?"

"She tried to break up the family of women. Yes. She is guilty."

"Listen, you guys," says Gloria. "This is crazy. This is medieval."

"Thou shalt not kill feeling."

"Did she do that?"

"Yes, she is guilty."

"Thou shalt not tempt the weakened in spirit, the foolish or the lonely."

"Did she break that law?"

"Yes. She is guilty."

"She broke other laws. Stealing—"

"Aw, you guys," says Gloria, "what the fuck did I steal?"

"Attention, time, affection, memory."

"Did she do that?"

"Yes. She is guilty."

"Thou shalt not bear false witness against thy woman friend."

"Did she do that?"

"Yes," says a voice. Mickey's? "She is guilty."

"Thou shalt not covet that which is precious and hard won by another."

"Did she do that?"

"Yes. She is guilty."

"Thou shalt not covet that which is discarded by a friend, that which has humiliated a friend, for in the coveting, thou also would humiliate the friend."

Vered?

"Did she do that?"

"Yes. She is guilty."

The voices echo. Gloria's eyes close and she trembles. It

must be an early storm. Lightning goes through the stone house. She hears thunder claps.

"The last commandment. Thou shalt not replace a trusted woman friend with a new male face."

"Did she do that?"

"Yes. She did that. She did that. She did that."

The chorus, "She is guilty."

"OK," says Gloria. "Fuck you guys. Sit here in the dark and play spook and see if it makes you feel any better. See if it brings back Shula. See if it brings back Hava."

There is the strange sound of hissing again in the house. A teakettle?

"And see if I care," says Gloria.

A candle is blown out. The figure is in darkness.

"We divorce you from us," says the voice.

Another candle is blown.

"We separate you from us."

A third. That corner of the room is in darkness.

"You are cut off from all rites—"

"Privileges—"

"Fellowship."

"You are put out of this community."

Half of the room is in darkness. One shadow advances on Gloria. Gloria screams.

"We excommunicate you from us."

"You are not a person we have known."

"You are not an experience that has touched us."

"You are a feather in the air."

"You are as dust."

"You are omitted from all future conversation."

"You are erased from all past memory."

"You are obliterated from all reference."

"Your name is eliminated, annihilated."

The room is deadly still. No sense of presence.

Gloria feels as if a pillowcase were over her head, a gloved hand across her mouth.

She screams again and again. The door flies open. It is Vered's ex-lover. It is the police of the Old City. They stumble. They light torches, matches.

The room is empty, save for Gloria.

She looks around. There is nothing she recognizes. Even the address is unfamiliar.

# 24
# The Tents of Sara

As Gloria departs from the life of the women, Shula refuses to leave.

In the North, Hepzibah awaits her for Shabbat dinner. Rina leaves the bottom dresser drawer empty for Shula's visit. In Jerusalem, Terry dreams about her. Once she dreamed they made love. Once Terry awoke with her pillow damp.

She thought, "Shula is angry with me and is spitting again."

Simha eats nothing. Her fleshy body is gaunt.

"Every food that is of flesh I cannot eat," says Simha. "Even cheese is smooth and fleshy."

In the village of Ein Hod, Shula has entered legend along with the suicide of one of the village's lively young founders. The students of her classes speak among themselves. In her memory they vow never to venture forth across the border of art or life.

Dahlia writes a lamenting melody. She plays it for a friend who has a recording connection.

"What is it called?"

" 'Shula.' "

"Put words to it."

"It has one."

"One is not enough."

Joan and Tova begin work on their next play, *Crossing the Border*. It will deal with the girdling, tightening and frightening of the citizens on this small land.

Slowly, singly and together, the women decide to cross borders.

None of this is apparent. They scout The Land, climb towers, study, do stretching exercises, squat. They intend a large deed.

Something about The Land makes this possible. In the Judean Hills one walks on stilts. Prophets come to this city to preach, or people, after a sojourn in this city, decide they *are* prophets.

In the North prophets live in caves. Elijah lived in a cave at the base of Mount Carmel. A street, not far from Girls Town, is named for him, Street of the Prophet. It would be unthinkable to shirk such ancestry and responsibility.

In the meantime, the inhabitants of Girls Town watch the sun from numerous parks in Haifa, from the view of the harbor or from a bench on Beautiful View Street. There is a little pool in which a stone deer has buried its face, drinking. The girls catch the sun in the afternoon on their balcony. It is still warm at four. The sun sets over the Mediterranean, an orange beach ball plopping into the sea. From the university, on top of the Carmel, the head of the sun rolls down the mountain.

The daughters of Jerusalem eat the biblical foods of The Land: the grape, honey, fig, date, pomegranate, almond. The Valley of Hinnom has been planted over with nut and fruit trees and with fruit of the vines.

The women go to a nearby Arab village to buy salty white, granular goat cheese. They go to Super Sols for the pickle tray of green tomatoes, red peppers, small egg-plants. They prepare eggplant in a hundred ways. Hepzibah holds eggplant on a long fork over the gas flame of her burner and chars it. She mashes the pulp with olive oil and adds fresh parsley. Simha puts eggplant into her blender and it becomes a dip with Arabic bread.

Friends come by with good and bad news.

Shlomo Sassoon comes by, his shoulders sagging, his sample case empty. His wife has died. She missed Kashmir. Perhaps in the World to Come she will again have servants, palatial quarters and a tongue she comprehends.

In the North and in Jerusalem birds are busy. In Haifa a phosphorescent blue-feathered bird, often mistaken for a hummingbird, eats the blossoms of the flowering almond. In Jerusalem bulbuls eat red berries.

Disaster first exhausts, then bestirs the women.

Their stone house in the Old City will be destroyed. A high-rise apartment for male yeshiva students will take its place, the annex being across the street in the former Home for Jewish Wayward Girls.

The stone house is a reminder of more modest times. Now the city is engaged in a massive rebuilding. In the Old City buildings are being dedicated; ministers of state, rabbis, educators, architects are moving in. Still there remains that street of promiscuous Simha and outspoken Terry. The street has been too full of trouble-prone maidens, their periods coming at ten, their breasts developed at eleven, their vaginas infected at twelve. Who needs this in the city of the World to Come? The inhabitants have committed the sin of poverty in a time of relative prosperity.

The women seem, perversely, undisturbed, their patience untried. They greet one another; they enter, they leave, they meet, they part while the street around them is being torn up. They observe plain days. They observe holidays.

The city is busy with overlapping holidays. The Day of Remembrance of the War Dead ends with the Day of Independence.

The morning of the Day of Remembrance all the cemeteries of the city have visitors, including the Mount of Olives. Joan is there to photograph, Simha to visit Hava. Simha has secrets for Hava and seasons to tell her about, news reports and light gossip, nothing too distressing for a baby.

At the ceremony on the Mount of Olives is a young city official in tweed jacket. He calls upon the mourners for the dead of the many wars.

*"Banot,"* he calls.

Two girl soldiers, daughters, weeping, carry garlands of orange roses.

*"Bonim,"* he calls.

Two young boys, sons, in bar-mitzvah-style jackets, carry daffodils.

*"Almanot."*

Women in black, the widows, carry white flowers.

It is the blooming time in The Land. Blue and golden flowers, orange, purple, white. All of the flowers are represented.

*"Ēmahot!"*

The mothers carry a garland of forget-me-nots from the mountains of the Golan Heights.

*"Avot."*

The fathers are the slowest to approach. They each carry one carnation and seem to have trouble placing them properly with the other flowers.

"*Kvotsot!*"

Clubs, groups, kibbutzim carry the trembling heads of flowers.

A distance off, one mother mourns one daughter.

Somewhere on the outskirts of the city is the family of women. They have scouted The Land. They have trodden in the paths of the Matriarchs' Way. They have gone through the Cheesemakers' Valley on the south, Mount Zion on the west, the Valley of Kidron on the east. They traversed the old road to Jerusalem past the Trappist Monastery at Latrun, past Emmaus, Abu Ghosh, places where battled the Philistines, the Canaanites, the Maccabees, the Romans, the Christians, the Moslems, and now will battle the women.

> We have come into the valley.
> Let this valley be tilled,
> for the clang of the sword is silenced,
> the mouth of the battle cry is stopped.
> Ashes are in the city.
> Families have fled the city.
> Their people are encamped.
> The city was laid to waste.
> We shall rebuild
> speedily, speedily
> the city.

The women have squatted in a deserted Arab village that has fallen to ruins awaiting real estate speculation.

All day, with the other mourners, the women mourn their bruised, stoned, humiliated, arrested, molested, murdered. Abruptly, evening, the Day of Remembrance ends and the Day of Independence begins. People wipe their tears. Children dance in the street. The flag is jerked from half- to full-mast. Parks are decorated and piles of wood are gathered in fields for the *Kumsitz*, come and sit and roast potatoes. It is the birthday party for the State.

Fireworks explode: pink into red umbrella spokes, descending greens and oranges, blinding whites. An American tourist looks upward and exclaims, "There! And I hope the Arabs saw that!"

In the women's commune fireworks explode. From the city it looks like new stars, planets, constellations have landed on the outskirts. The women raise their flag: WAYWARD WOMEN. The commune will be *Havurat Shula*, the friends of Shula.

The women, long accustomed to birth stools and to squatting, stay on their territory and beat off marauders. Other squatters had tried before. Their names are painted on doors that are now unhinged and banging. The city gave those squatters no services and they eventually departed.

The government sends emissaries. The women refuse them. Other women's groups are sent, Hadassah, Pioneer Women, Zionist Organization and B'nai B'rith women, Christian Daughters, all begging them to return to the fold.

The women cannot. There is no fold. They must enfold their own, date their calendar.

They are modest women, even without arms covered, skirts below the knee, hair shorn. For they have modest needs, a fire, some warmth, a land of their own, leaders of their choosing, borders of their crossing.

It is a women's government in exile. Terry is Prime Minister, Simha and Hepzibah are Ministers of Rites. Dahlia is the Singer Laureate; Joan is the Minister of Contemporary Culture; Antoinette, Minister of Classical Culture; Gerda, Minister of Science; Vered, Minister of Concern. Terry asks Deedee if she wants to be Minister of War. Deedee is tempted. No, she decides. She is made

Minister of External Affairs to keep them from being parochial. Tova is the Minister of Arab Affairs.

There is much the women must concern themselves with, subsidy, crops, finances, holidays. If this is a political kibbutz, should it raise candidates?

A settlement begins with ceremony. Even in a pioneering country traditions are deeply rooted. The olive trees gnarl around the commune, hundreds of years old; the pitted stones are millennia old.

It is the Time for Sending Forth.

The women assemble and, with them, those men who have befriended them.

Terry is Parliamentarian. In her hand is a gavel.

"We must separate," says Terry to Mihal. "We send you forth with our blessings."

Mihal is dressed in her long skirt. Her hair is shiny, her eyes not sullen but looking at distances and unknown terrain.

"I go forth," says Mickey, "the daughter of your blessing."

"We send you forth with love."

"I go forth," says Mickey, "armored with your love."

"We send you forth," says Terry, "to see for all of us."

"I am your eyes."

"To hear for the Hevra."

"I am your ears. I will listen attentively to other tongues."

"We send you forth," says Terry, "to study what we must know."

"I go forth," says Mickey, "in order to return."

The Wayward Women are sending Mihal to London. She will finish her undergraduate work there and return for law school. She will become an expert on the laws governing women.

The rabbinate has given her permission to leave Haifa, and has given her husband permission to her furniture, car and apartment.

Vered rises.

"I send you forth," says Vered to her brother, "my brother, my past."

He is going to London for more surgery. He is going to London for extended study. He is going to London to forget the incinerated world from inside of his tank. He is going to London to lay to rest his battalion.

"I go forth, my sister," says Vered's brother.

"I send you forth with half of our inheritance," says Vered. "With memories of Poland, memories of shared speech, memories of our mother, memories of the agricultural school, memories of frightened nights, memories of too many deaths, memories of healed love."

"I carry on the inheritance, my sister," says Vered's brother. "I will return to The Land to plant the seed of new memories."

Vered's brother and Mihal will accompany each other. She will hold carefully his wounded hand, he her bruised heart. The government and the Jewish War Veterans will pay his expenses. Mihal's family will help to pay hers.


There is to be a wedding. Shlomo Sassoon, recognized as an Orthodox rabbi, is allowed by the State to perform it. He will deliver the sermon. Terry will deliver the "herman."

It is to be the wedding of Simha and her kibbutznik. They have already celebrated and mourned together. That is the proper preparation for marriage.

Simha goes to the bathhouse to ritually cleanse herself. The kibbutz packs a car with the wedding party, honey cake and almonds, pine nuts, flowers and a cage of chickens for the women to get started on.

Simha will divide her time, like Persephone, between the kibbutz and the Havurat Shula. Every winter she goes away from the women to the Galilee and sleeps in the arms of her kibbutznik; in the circle of the hora she dances, near the bonfire she warms herself. Every spring and summer she returns to the women, to walk among the Judean Hills, to plant the land that borders the city.

They must properly celebrate the wedding:

There is a riding on donkeys and a walking around the village of the women.

The wedding party blows the shofar, clangs cowbells, carries torches.

There is the dressing of the bride in finery. Shlomo's remnants wrap around Simha and cling to her the more in the wind. Rina and the members of Girls Town come with costume jewelry. Hepzibah arrives with her late father's prayer shawl. The kibbutznik is an atheist and refuses it. Hepzibah places the tallith around the shoulders of the bride.

They are led to the huppah by diverse routes.

The wedding party walks around the house with their instruments, harmonicas, Jews' harps and a guitar brought by Tova's Arab lover.

The bride drips with beads and necklaces. She is like a Bedouin in the desert, a Yemenite crossing the border. She is ready.

Shlomo Sassoon says:

" 'He who has no wife abides without good.' Thus it is written in the Talmud. 'Serve the Lord with joy.' " Shlomo smiles, for "with joy" is *"b'Simha,"* the name of the bride.

They drink wine, consecrated to one another, in the name of their foremothers and forefathers.

"Soon may there be heard in the cities of Judah and in the streets of Jerusalem the voice of joy and gladness, the voice of the bridegroom, and the voice of the bride."

Shlomo has brought two glasses, wrapped in white damask napkins.

Simha smashes one, the kibbutznik the other. They have lived through the destruction of their temple. They will speedily rebuild it.

Terry's "herman" is addressed to *her*, Simha.

"May the house not be a cage. May the love not be a trap. May routine not be your undoing."

Terry says to Simha, "Repeat. I promise, I promise, I promise to live."

Terry says to the bridegroom: "Repeat. I promise, I promise, I promise to love."

The kibbutznik, in rare shirt, even a tie, even a yarmulke, promises.

Terry says, "I now pronounce you life and love."

She reverses this.

"Simha, say, 'I promise, I promise, I promise to love.' "

Simha does so.

"Bridegroom say, 'I promise, I promise, I promise to live.' "

The bridegroom will love and live. He has loved Simha since first he saw her. He will love her in the North during the winter and in the South during her absence.

"I promise," says the bridegroom.

"I now declare you love and life," says Terry.

In every book there are pilgrimages, returns, weddings and births. In this there are also announcements.

Shlomo Sassoon and Antoinette announce their engagement.

When did they do it? Where? How did it happen?

Shlomo has willed strength into Antoinette. His ears reddened and the flow of his life's energies poured into her. Her cheeks are not merely English pink and white, humid weather complexion. She is now inflamed. She reads books to completion. She sits through films. She bakes at the seashore, readying her body for all weather, for the invasion of armies of desires.

Mazel tov!

At the wedding Antoinette will wear a sari. The bridesmaids will be adorned in strings of pearls. The huppah will be made of remnants of silk and velvet.

Mazel tov! Mazel tov!

There is a ceremony for Terry who has birthed a political party and a commune. She is a mother married to her contingent. She takes an oath of office and vows to represent them for better or worse, richer or poorer, in the eyes of women and of the state.

Vered has become head of her Office of Immigration. She is filled with new plans for the *olim*, arrivals to The Land. For the Russian musicians there will be orchestras everywhere, in each large city, in each development town, in restaurants, at every kibbutz. Each planeload of musicians will be rushed into a musician's chair.

The young daughters of the newcomers will go to Girls Town in Haifa or to Havurat Shula. There the women will prepare them to become daughters of Jerusalem. During this announcement, a pigeon overhead drops a feather.

Vered stands at Terry's right hand. Vered is left-handed. Together they are ambidextrous, mothers of The Land, lovers in this deserted Arab village.

Dahlia has made a record, *Lament*. Each woman in the commune orders several albums. Also some outside of the commune. Dahlia will make a little money. She will still have to grab for jobs, and she worries about her throat and about aging. But her throat will warble in the city and in the desert. Her skin, with regular visits to the bathhouse, will be lineless for years. Her government will send her abroad to represent The Land.


Night. The women bed down. There is no heat and it is chilly. The candles burn to stubs and the bonfires to embers.

What will happen to them, this caravan of women that encircles the outskirts of the city, that peoples the desert?

How goodly are thy tents, thy reclaimed ruins, O Sara, O our mothers of the desert.

# The Daughters of Jerusalem

Joan Anker, Englewood, New Jersey, printmaker
Donna Katzen Altshuler, New York City, community worker
Prof. Jacqueline Berk, Drew University, Madison, New Jersey,
    educator-writer
Anne Bernayse, Cambridge, Massachusetts, novelist
Prof. Nadean Bishop, Eastern Michigan University, administrator
Marjorie Bitker, *Milwaukee Journal*, journalist
Prof. Jane Bonin, University of Southwestern Louisiana,
    educator-critic
Sari Broner, Detroit
Nahama Broner, Bennington, Vermont
Dr. Phyllis Chesler, New York City, psychologist-visionary
Prof. Ruth Cohn-Barter, University of Haifa, painter
Gladys Dahlberg, Michigan, librarian
Prof. Cathy Davidson, Michigan State University, scholar
Genora Dollinger, Los Angeles, UAW organizer
Dr. Susan Garrett, New Centre, Massachusetts, corporate officer
Meta Goldin, New York City, educator
Annie Gottlieb, New York City, writer
Ebba Kossick Hanse, Deer Isle, Maine, weaver
Harriette Hartigan, Detroit, photographer
Phoebe Helman, New York City, sculptor
Mildred Jeffrey, Detroit, union and feminist organizer
Faye Kicknosway, Detroit, poet
Dorothy Knox, New York City, family counselor
Barbara Levin, Detroit, attorney
Charlotte Hoffer MacDonald, Racine, Wisconsin, social worker
    (deceased)
Barbara Stein Mallow, New Jersey, cellist
Beatrice Weckstein Masserman, Oak Park, Michigan, homemaker
Helen Merrill, New York City, agent
Ann Mikolowsky, Granite City, Michigan, artist
Anita Plous, Southfield, Michigan, student of Akkadian
Hannah Por, Haifa, organization woman
Prof. Francine Ringold, University of Tulsa, poet-editor
Michele Russell, Detroit, activist-writer
Mary Gale Roberts, Detroit, composer-actor
Florence Schumacher, Southfield, Michigan, journalist
Prof. Alice Shalvi, Hebrew University, Jerusalem, administrator
Prof. Kathryn Kish Sklar, UCLA, historian

June Snow, Detroit, scientist
Gloria Steinem, New York City, editor-activist
Charlotte Stewart, University of Tulsa, editor-mystic
Tova Tsoran, Haifa, educator
Jane Weiss, Cleveland/Deer Isle, Maine, gallery dealer
Prof. Linda Wagner, Michigan State University, distinguished
    scholar
Shebar Windstone, San Francisco, broadcaster
Marian Wood, New York City, editor-battler


*Leaders of the Caravan in This and All of My Journeys*
Marcia Freedman, Haifa, politician-writer
Dr. Julie Jensen, University of Notre Dame, Indiana,
    playwright-director
Virginia Kelley, New York City, psychologist
Ruth Kroll, Detroit, organization professional
Leah Napolin, Sea Cliff, New York, playwright


*Tender Men Who Befriended the Daughters of Jerusalem*
*The Broners:* Robert, Adam and Jeremy
Irving Berg, Detroit, sculptor
Morris Brose, Detroit, sculptor
Prof. Robert Hazzard, Wayne State University, Detroit, theater
    director
Dr. Jay Masserman, Fountain Valley, California, physician
Paul Masserman, Oak Park, Michigan, journalist
Prof. Roger Ortmayer, Union Graduate School, Yellow Springs,
    Ohio, writer
Irving Pokempner, Detroit, independent scholar
Jack Sonenberg, New York City, sculptor
Dr. I. Bernard Weinstein, New York City, scientist

## ABOUT THE AUTHOR

ESTHER MASSERMAN BRONER is a feminist writer whose works are filled with "an enormous love for women" and a strong feeling for Jewish themes and traditions. She was born on July 8, 1930, in Detroit, Michigan. Her father was a newspaperman and a Jewish historian; her mother had acted in the Yiddish theater in Poland. Esther received her B.A. from Wayne State University in 1950; her M.A. in 1962. She began teaching creative writing there in 1962, later becoming writer-in-residence and an associate professor of English. She received her Ph.D. from Union Graduate School in 1978. A frequent visitor to Israel, she has taught at Haifa University, Hebrew University, and lectured at Bar-Ilan University. She is married to Robert Broner, a nationally known print-maker who teaches art at Wayne State. They have four children.

E.M. Broner began writing in the 1950s when she and her husband lived in New York City. Her essays, reviews, short fiction, and drama have appeared in such publications as *Commentary*, *Seneca Review*, and *North American Review*. Her first book, *Summer Is a Foreign Land* (1966), is a verse drama. An early feminist work, the title piece of *Journal/Nocturnal and Seven Stories* (1968), decries the passivity of women. Her novel, *Her Mothers* (1975), was acclaimed as the year's "best new book" by the *Boston Globe* and was called "a beautiful book, written by a wise woman" by Erica Jong. In 1977, *Ms.* magazine published her "A Woman's Passover Haggadah" (with Naomi Nimrod). And in *A Weave of Women* (1978), a novel set in Jerusalem, she rewrites patriarchal religious traditions and creates new feminist rituals in a book that celebrates women and womanhood.